CAUGHT

THE MISSING: BOOK 5

CAUGHT

Margaret Peterson

HADDIX

SCHOLASTIC INC.

No part of this publication may be reproduced, stored in a retrieval
system, or transmitted in any form or by any means, electronic, mechanical,
photocopying, recording, or otherwise, without written permission of the publisher.
For information regarding permission, write to Simon & Schuster Books for Young Readers,
an imprint of Simon & Schuster Children's Publishing Division,
1230 Avenue of the Americas, New York, NY 10020.

ISBN 978-0-545-49076-4

Copyright © 2012 by Margaret Peterson Haddix.
All rights reserved. Published by Scholastic Inc.,
557 Broadway, New York, NY 10012,
by arrangement with Simon & Schuster Books for Young Readers,
an imprint of Simon & Schuster Children's Publishing Division.
SCHOLASTIC and associated logos are trademarks
and/or registered trademarks of Scholastic Inc.

12 11 10 9 8 7 6 5 4 3 2 1   12 13 14 15 16 17/0

Printed in the U.S.A.

This edition first printing, September 2012

Book design by Hilary Zarycky based on a design by Drew Willis

The text for this book is set in Weiss.

For Tori and Andrew

ONE

Jonah Skidmore was in science class when time stopped.

It was mid-November, so Jonah had already had three full months of seventh-grade science with Mr. Stanley. He almost could have believed that time stopped every day in Mr. Stanley's class—or at least slowed down so much that every millisecond crawled by at a turtle's pace. Mr. Stanley was an old man with gray hair and gray skin and gray clothes, and he always explained even the simplest concept about five times more than he needed to.

"Gravity," he'd say, each syllable coming out slowly and distinctly. "Do you all remember what gravity is? It's a vital idea to grasp. It's important. You have to know about it. It holds us on the ground. It keeps us in place. It prevents us from flying off into the atmosphere. It . . ."

Jonah could never force himself to listen to more than

two or three seconds of Mr. Stanley's explanations at a time. He spent most of science class staring at the clock on the wall.

It didn't help that science was his last class before lunch.

On this particular day—a Tuesday—Jonah was peering at the clock's red digital numerals with even more desperation than usual.

Eleven forty-three, Jonah thought, his stomach growling. *Eleven forty-three. Eleven forty-three. Oh, come on. Shouldn't it be eleven forty-four already? Shouldn't this class be over? How long can a single minute last?*

Jonah shook his head in despair, shifting his gaze just enough that he caught a glimpse of Mr. Stanley.

Mr. Stanley was frozen.

His mouth was open, stopped mid-word. He had his right arm lifted toward the board, hovering motionlessly over an unfinished line: "Forces in natu—" The floppy sleeve of his ratty-looking cardigan had frozen mid-flap on his unmoving arm.

But what looked the weirdest was that Mr. Stanley must have just dropped his dry-erase marker, and it *wasn't* plummeting toward the floor. It, too, was frozen—in midair, about two feet below Mr. Stanley's wrinkled hand, about two feet above the scuffed linoleum floor.

Jonah automatically glanced around, waiting for some

other kid to call out, "Whoa, Mr. Stanley! How'd you do that? What's the trick? What were you just saying about gravity?"

Everybody else must have stopped watching and listening to him too, Jonah thought.

Then he saw what the other kids were doing. Or— what they weren't doing.

They were all frozen too.

Dylan Anderson was stuck mid-yawn, his jaw locked open. Blossom Gomez, one of the prettiest girls in the school, must have been stricken in the middle of tossing her hair over her shoulder, because she had a cloud of long strands frozen above and around one side of her head. CC Vorlov, the texting queen of Harris Middle School, had her thumbs frozen over her cell phone, hidden under her desk.

Jonah had never seen CC's thumbs *not* moving. Her stopping texting was every bit as strange as the gravity-defying marker at the front of the room.

Experimentally, Jonah lifted his arm from his desk, then put it back down.

He could still move. *He* wasn't frozen like everyone else. He sighed.

"Okay, JB," he said out loud. "What's going on now?"

In the past couple of weeks Jonah had gotten used to weird things happening with time. He'd learned that his seemingly ordinary life was a sham: He was actually a famous missing child of history, stolen by kidnappers intent on carrying him off to be adopted in the future. When time agents had tried to stop this crime, the kidnappers had crash-landed, leaving Jonah and thirty-five other babies to grow up out of place, in the late twentieth and early twenty-first centuries. Over the past few weeks Jonah and his younger sister, Katherine, had traveled back to the fifteenth, sixteenth, and seventeenth centuries to help restore time and rescue missing kids.

Their plans had gotten messed up again and again, and they'd been on the verge of disaster more than once. But with the help of a time agent named JB, they'd always mostly managed to work things out.

"JB?" Jonah said again.

Nobody answered. Nothing moved. Jonah noticed that outside the window, even the flag on the flagpole had frozen mid-flutter.

"I mean it, JB," Jonah said, trying to sound stern. This was hard, since Jonah was thirteen, and he could never be quite sure anymore if his voice was going to come out sounding bass or—and this was really embarrassing—soprano. This time his voice was pretty much in an alto range, which wasn't much better. He cleared his throat.

"I thought you were done messing around with time

for a while," Jonah tried again, almost growling.

Jonah's stomach churned, but now it wasn't because of hunger. Things had gotten very dicey on Jonah and Katherine's last trip through time, to the sixteen hundreds. A former employee of JB's who called himself Second Chance had forced time to split. After that, JB had told Jonah that it was too dangerous to schedule any more trips to the past for a while.

But the twenty-first century was supposed to stay safe, Jonah thought. *Wasn't it?*

Jonah tried not to think about what he'd overheard JB saying the last time they'd talked. Jonah had been on his way to play soccer, and JB had called out, *Have fun.* Then, when he thought Jonah was out of earshot, JB had muttered, *While you still can.*

Jonah's stomach moved past "churn" to "extreme spin cycle." He decided he might need to stay as motionless as the rest of the class just to keep from vomiting.

Just then the classroom door banged open.

"Oh, no! You're frozen too?" a girl's voice wailed.

It was Katherine.

For a split second Jonah considered being a truly cruel older brother and pretending that he really was unable to move. A month ago he would have counted that as a great prank.

But a month ago he'd thought he was just an ordinary (if slightly goofy) kid. He'd never had to save anyone's life. He'd never known that all of time could depend on his actions.

Responsibility really ruined pranks.

He turned to face Katherine and the door.

"No, I'm not frozen," he said. Amazingly, his voice neither trembled nor squeaked. "I was just sitting here . . . thinking. Trying to figure out what's going on."

A month ago Katherine probably would have taken that as a cue to tease him with a jibe like, *You? Think? No way! Not possible!*

Now she just tucked a strand of her blond hair behind one ear and said, "Okay. What'd you come up with?"

Katherine was not quite twelve. She still thought it was cool to wear T-shirts with words like AWESOME outlined in glitter on the front. She was a sixth grader—barely a step up from being a baby herself. Where did she get off, sounding so calm?

"I'm still working on it," Jonah said faintly.

"Right," Katherine said, in a tone that was every bit as insulting as if she really had said, *You? Think? No way!* She tapped her fingers against the door. "I don't think JB did this."

Jonah wondered if he should admit that he'd already

tried calling out to JB. But Katherine was still talking.

"I yelled for him as soon as this happened, and he didn't answer," Katherine said.

Jonah tried not to think about who might have stopped time if it wasn't JB. The possibilities jumped into his mind anyway: Second? The original kidnappers, Gary and Hodge? Some other enemy they didn't even know about yet.

Jonah was almost glad that Katherine was still blathering on. It was almost enough to distract him.

"So then I decided that, instead of trying to figure out why time stopped, I should figure out why *I* could still move," she said. "I thought maybe it was because I'd traveled through time before, so other time travelers would be immune too. So I went to the office and looked up which class you were in, to find you."

Sheesh, Jonah thought. *If Katherine had time to walk from the sixth-grade wing to the office to the seventh-grade wing . . . just how long did I spend staring at the clock still thinking everything was normal?*

Automatically, he glanced at the clock once more. But of course it was still frozen at 11:43.

"You came looking for me first? Before Chip?" Jonah asked, a mocking twist to his words.

Chip was Jonah's friend and Katherine's boyfriend.

He was also another missing child from history. But unlike Jonah, Chip had already resolved his past. Jonah and Katherine had helped to rescue him—and another boy, Alex—on their first trip through time.

Now Katherine was biting her lip.

"The office sign-out log says Chip went home sick at ten thirty," she said.

"*Was* he sick?" Jonah asked. "Or—" Chip's original identity had been that of a medieval English king. Chip had spent two years in that role. He was having a few problems readapting to life as a normal American teen.

Katherine's face went a little pale, and Jonah shifted gears.

"Let's call him," Jonah said.

He reached over to the space beneath CC Vorlov's desk and wrenched the cell phone from her grasp. A half-written text message glowed from the screen:

Meet u in—

Jonah began punching keys, but nothing on the screen changed. He tossed the phone down on CC's desk in disgust.

"Duh," he said. "The phone's frozen too."

This also cut off the possibility that they could call Andrea, the girl Jonah liked. Not that she liked him the same way.

Though she might someday, after she figures out how to deal with the results of her own time travels, he reminded himself. *Or maybe . . .*

Katherine tugged impatiently on Jonah's arm. Clearly, she wasn't going to let him just sit around thinking.

"Come on. Let's walk to Chip's house," Katherine said, pulling harder. "We'll make sure he's okay, and then all three of us can figure out what's going on."

Jonah frowned. He couldn't suggest walking to Andrea's as well, because she lived a lot farther away.

Anyhow, he could think of a few problems with Katherine's idea.

"Do you really think we should leave school?" he asked.

Katherine rolled her eyes.

"What—are you afraid time will unfreeze all of a sudden, and you'll get caught playing hooky?" she asked.

Well, yes, that was pretty much what Jonah was afraid of. It was terrible that he'd managed to survive all sorts of life-threatening situations in three different centuries and yet still had to worry about following school rules.

"Coward," Katherine taunted him.

"Boy crazy," Jonah mocked her.

But, to prove that he wasn't actually a coward, Jonah stood up and dashed out the classroom door ahead of his sister.

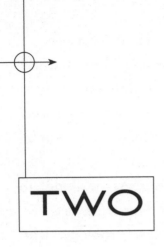

TWO

The stopped time seemed even freakier outside. A trio of Canadian geese coming in to land on the pond in front of the school were just suspended in midair. Some woman— was that Rusty Donavan's mom?—had evidently been driving over the speed bumps in the school turnaround a little too fast, and her entire minivan was frozen an inch or two off the ground.

"I don't like this," Katherine muttered as they walked down the sidewalk.

"We've seen time stop before," Jonah said, with more bravado than he actually felt.

"Yeah, in other people's time. In the past," Katherine said. She tilted her head back and called out loudly toward the sky, "Nobody's supposed to go messing around with *my* time, you hear?"

Her time, Jonah thought. It bothered him that she hadn't said "our." But why would she? Katherine wasn't adopted like he was; she wasn't a missing child of history like him. She could be sure that their parents were her real parents; she could be sure that the twenty-first century was exactly where she belonged.

Jonah couldn't be sure of any of that. He didn't have any idea when or where he really belonged. He had no clue whose DNA he shared.

He looked around nervously, all his worries about the stopped time getting mixed up with his fears about finding out who he really was.

No, not just mixing, he thought. *Multiplying.*

Katherine playfully whacked him on the arm.

"Stop freaking out!" she told him. "Nobody's going to catch us! You know those rumors about how Mr. Richey stands out here watching for kids who sneak out? None of that's true. Kayla told me that Marina told her that Abdul told her that Mr. Richey started those rumors himself!"

Mr. Richey was the assistant principal.

Jonah slugged her back.

"What about Second catching us?" he asked, rounding the corner of the building. "Or Gary and Hodge? Or—"

Suddenly Katherine jerked back on his arm, barely stopping him from slamming into somebody frozen in place, pressed against the side of the building.

No, make that two somebodies.

Kissing.

"Is that . . . one of the cafeteria ladies?" Katherine asked, peeking beneath a hairnet.

"And . . . the janitor?" Jonah asked, recognizing the olive-colored shirt and the side of a gray-streaked beard.

Katherine gingerly pulled up the employee ID tags from the cafeteria lady's apron and the janitor's shirt pocket.

"Norma Jones and Martin Jones," she read out loud. "Oh, I bet they're married! Isn't that romantic? They're both, like, sixty, and they've probably been married forever, and they still sneak out in the middle of the day to—"

"Gross everyone out," Jonah finished. He tugged on his sister's arm, pulling her away from the kissing couple. "They really should hide better than that."

"Do you suppose they met on the job, like, forty years ago?" Katherine asked as they walked on. "Do you suppose he figured out she was in love with him because she kept giving him double servings of the Johnny Marzetti?"

Jonah saw what Katherine was doing. She was yammering on and on about the cafeteria lady and the janitor to distract herself from scarier questions. Katherine had done the same kind of thing when they'd been in danger in 1483 and 1485 and 1600 and 1611. But Jonah wasn't any good at yammering. The scary questions kept flooding his mind:

Are *we in danger?*

Are *Andrea and Chip and Alex and all the other missing kids from history roaming around unfrozen and terrified and in danger too?*

If *JB couldn't answer us, does that mean he's in danger somewhere else?*

Who *stopped time?*

If *JB isn't around to watch over us and keep us safe, then is somebody else maybe keeping track of our every move?*

Somebody . . . *malevolent?*

They pressed on, Jonah barely listening to Katherine's babbling. He stopped paying much attention to their surroundings, either, because it was too unnerving to see so many frozen people and frozen cars and frozen birds and even frozen smoke, hovering above chimneys. Automatically he turned out of the neighborhood surrounding the school. He stepped off the sidewalk to cross the lane leading to the library.

And then, out of nowhere, a car sped toward them, so suddenly that Jonah could only think in spurts:

Why *isn't it stopped like everything else?*

Why *isn't it stopping now?*

Is *it going to run over us?*

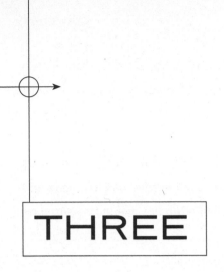

THREE

Jonah dived off to the side of the lane, into the ditch that ran along the street. He hit the ground shoulder-first but immediately rolled back up into a crouch. He strained to see where Katherine had gone. Why wasn't she diving into the ditch beside him? Had she just dived in the other direction, landing in the ditch on the other side of the lane?

No. Katherine was still standing in the middle of the lane. She'd put her hands on her hips and was squinting toward the speeding car as if she could stare it down.

"Katherine!" Jonah screamed. "Move!"

Katherine didn't even turn her head. The car kept speeding toward her. Closer, closer, closer . . . There wasn't time for Jonah to save her.

And then at the last moment the car stopped, right beside Katherine.

Katherine flipped her hair back and glanced over her shoulder toward Jonah.

"Did you really think *Angela* would do anything to hurt us?" she asked.

"Um . . . er . . ."

For the first time, Jonah looked to see who was driving the car. It was a tall, statuesque African-American woman: their friend Angela, the only adult in the twenty-first century who knew about the time-travel trips Jonah and Katherine had made. Who, actually, was the only adult from this time period who had taken any time-travel trips of her own. At one point she'd been the only adult involved with the whole time-travel mess whom Jonah trusted.

Embarrassed, Jonah stood up and tried to brush dirt and dried grass off his shirt.

"Hi, Angela," he said sheepishly. "I couldn't see who was driving. And it looked like you were coming right toward us. I guess my perspective was a little off . . . ."

"No worries," Angela said. "Better safe than sorry."

But the right corner of her mouth inched up ever so slightly.

Jonah wondered how ridiculous he'd looked, diving into the ditch.

Then a new thought struck him—a good distraction.

"Wait—how'd you get a car to work in stopped time,

when I couldn't even make a phone call?" he asked.

"Elucidator," Angela said, holding up a black rectangular device that seemed to be attached to her dashboard with a cable. It looked as if she were just charging a cell phone. But Jonah knew that this was one of those times when looks were deceiving. Elucidators were like that. They always took on the appearance of some ordinary object: a rock in the fifteenth century, a candleholder in the seventeenth, a cell phone in the twenty-first. But Elucidators had provided a way for Jonah to communicate across time, to turn invisible when it was too dangerous for him to be seen, and to travel through time in the first place.

Elucidators were great—when you knew how to use them.

"JB gave you your own Elucidator?" Katherine asked, a hint of jealousy in her voice.

"Only so I could watch out for the two of you," Angela said. "Only to be used in case of emergency. Like now."

Any trace of humor was gone from her voice.

"So call him already," Katherine said. "Make him tell you what's going on!"

Angela shook her head grimly.

"He's vanished," she said. "Him and Hadley and every other time agent I could think of to call. Last I heard

Hadley was dealing with some new crisis in the past. But I don't know where any of them went."

"They weren't going to make any more trips to the past," Jonah said stubbornly. "Not until it was safe."

Angela frowned at him.

"Hadley said it wasn't safe for them *not* to go," she murmured.

Angela's eyes flooded with tears, and Jonah remembered that Angela and Hadley had become . . . what was that stupid term that Katherine used sometimes for kids who had crushes on each other? "Special friends"?

Jonah grimaced. He had too many other problems to try to figure out grown-ups' relationships.

"Hey, hey, I'm sure Hadley and JB and the others will have everything under control soon," Angela said, misinterpreting Jonah's grimace. She made it sound as if he were some little kid who had to be comforted.

Even if it meant lying.

Katherine flapped her hands, as if trying to fight the unnerving stillness around them. Or as if she could wave away all the dangers of the past and present.

"Can we talk about all this on our way to Chip's house?" Katherine asked impatiently. "Come *on*, Jonah, get in the car."

Jonah noticed that Katherine hadn't exactly stopped

to ask Angela if she minded taking them to Chip's. But Angela was already reaching around to unlock the car's back door.

Jonah scrambled up and jumped in. Katherine slid in on the passenger side in front.

"Hurry!" Katherine begged as Angela shifted the car into gear.

Angela hit the gas, urging the car faster, faster, faster . . .

All the way to twenty-five miles per hour.

"I don't think you need to worry about obeying speed limits right now," Jonah said.

"The Elucidator is probably defying several laws of physics just to get the car to move at all," Angela said. "This is the best I can do."

Jonah realized that his notion of the car as speeding toward him and Katherine before had been a relative thing. It had only *seemed* to be going fast because everything else around them was completely still.

And it did feel wrong to be moving inside the car— more wrong than when he and Katherine had just been walking. It was as if even the air molecules around him were fighting against the motion.

Is it because the air molecules are traveling with us? Jonah wondered. *Or are we displacing them and then they go back where they belong after we pass by? Or . . .*

Those kinds of problems always tied his brain in knots, even without the complication of stopped time.

The strain showed on Angela's face, too.

"You drove like this all the way from your house?" Jonah asked. Angela lived on the other side of the city.

Angela shook her head.

"Only the last mile or so was in stopped time," she said. "I was already on my way here. Hadley told me to come find you two when he left for the past."

"What—were you going to show up at school and pretend to be our long-lost aunt or something?" Katherine asked.

"I was still figuring out a good story," Angela said. "I don't think the 'aunt' thing would work very well."

"White kids can have African-American aunts! It happens all the time!" Katherine protested, her voice going a little squeaky. Typical Katherine—she got upset when she thought people were being racist or sexist. Even when they weren't, actually.

"Yeah, but it doesn't help the story," Angela said with a shrug.

Jonah was still caught on something else Angela had said.

"Hold on," he interrupted. "You said Hadley and JB wanted you to watch over me and Katherine. Why us?

Why not Chip or Andrea or any of the other missing children from history? Or—is someone else watching over them?"

"You and Katherine have traveled through time a lot more than any of the other kids," Angela said. "You've had the most contact with JB. That puts you in the most . . ."

Jonah was pretty sure that the next word she was going to say was "danger." But then she glanced over at Katherine and in the rearview mirror toward Jonah.

"Oh, you know how those time agents are," Angela said, her tone suddenly too light and teasing. "They're always so concerned about being logical and fair, and keeping things balanced and equal. But you *know* you're their favorites."

"But—," Katherine began.

"Do I turn here to get to Chip's, or is it the next street?" Angela asked.

For the rest of the way to Chip's, Angela acted as if she needed the most specific directions ever. Did "turn after the blue house" mean the light blue house on the corner or the turquoise one farther down? Was Chip's house five or six houses away from Jonah and Katherine's house?

"When JB said you should watch over us, did he mean—," Jonah tried once.

"What?" Angela said, swerving up onto the sidewalk to

avoid a stopped car blocking the street. "Sorry, Jonah, I've really got to concentrate on driving. This is like something from a car-chase movie, where you have to keep going from lane to lane."

It was true that she had to go straight from driving on the sidewalk to driving in the lane on the opposite side of the street, going the wrong way. But the problem was that all of the other cars around her were stopped, not that they were darting around her.

This isn't like a car-chase movie, Jonah thought. *It's like one of those prehistoric video games my dad has from when he was a kid, where everything moves too slow.*

Finally they arrived at Chip's. Katherine immediately shoved open her door and began rushing up the front walk.

"No—wait! Maybe I should go first—," Angela called after her.

When Katherine didn't stop, Angela scrambled out and ran to catch up.

"Shouldn't we keep the Elucidator with us?" Jonah asked. Neither Angela nor Katherine answered him, but Jonah leaned over the front seat and yanked the connecting cable away from the Elucidator.

As soon as the link to the car was broken, the Elucidator began to make a crackling noise.

"JB? Hadley?" Jonah asked.

Through the crackling static Jonah thought he heard a voice. Was the Elucidator working as a communications device again, now that it wasn't powering a car?

Jonah lifted the Elucidator closer to his ear.

"Angela, Kath—," he started to call out to the others. But then he got scared that the Elucidator might work only briefly, and he didn't want to waste any time.

"Hello?" he said into the Elucidator. "JB? Is that you?"

"Angela? Jonah? Katherine? Are you there?" JB's voice floated weakly from amidst the static. "Are you there? Angela?"

Jonah realized that even though he could hear JB, JB couldn't hear him. He began fumbling with the controls on the side of the Elucidator.

"JB?" he said.

"Jonah? Is that you?" The relief in JB's voice practically drowned out the static. "Are you okay?"

"Uh, sure," Jonah said.

"Oh, thank you! Thank you, Angela! Thank God!" JB might have gone on with his listing of thanks, but the Elucidator blanked out for a moment. When the sound came back on, he was saying, ". . . was so worried . . ."

"JB, I can't hear you very well," Jonah said. "Are *you* okay? Where are you?"

". . . in a time hollow . . . watching . . . early nineteen- . . . he's not thinking about the right things. He . . . I thought . . ."

It was so frustrating, trying to make sense of the few bits and pieces of JB's explanation that came through. Maybe Jonah should have Angela and Katherine listen to this too. Quickly he slipped out of the car and began walking toward them. They'd reached the doorstep of Chip's house, and Katherine had just started pounding her hand against the door.

"Chip! Chip!" Katherine was yelling.

"Shh," Jonah hissed. "JB's talking on the Elucidator!"

Angela whirled around.

". . . was afraid that . . . ," crackled out of the Elucidator. "But you haven't seen anything strange . . . ?"

"Strange?" Jonah repeated. "JB, time's stopped."

For a moment the Elucidator was completely silent.

Then JB wailed, "Stopped? No! It can't be! Your time is stopped? The twenty-first century?"

Jonah reached the front step of Chip's house and climbed up the stairs behind Katherine and Angela. Angela reached out and put her hand on his shoulder.

"Hey, we're still okay," Jonah said. "Angela came and got me and Katherine, and now we're at Chip's house, and—"

"Chip's house? No! Stay away from Chip! Run!" JB's

voice screamed from the Elucidator. "Run away!"

Several things happened almost at once. Chip's door scraped back, revealing Chip looking pale and clammy-skinned. Katherine reached out and brushed Chip's hand with her fingers just as Jonah grabbed her arm to pull her back. Angela reached up to feel Chip's forehead with the back of her wrist. In that one second they were all linked, each of them touching the person on either side.

In the next second everything went black.

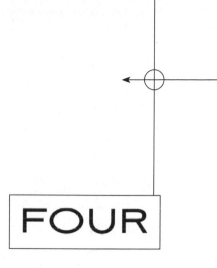

FOUR

For a long moment Jonah couldn't think. His mind remained as blank as the scenery around him.

Then he heard Katherine's voice.

"Is it just the two of us?" she asked weakly. "Just the two of us, floating through time?"

Through time, Jonah thought.

He was relieved that Katherine had put a name to what they were doing. This did indeed feel like all the other times they'd traveled to the past. Just as before, there was nothing but a dark void around them, an emptiness that seemed infinite. But neither he nor Katherine had shouted out a command to travel to another time; he didn't think Angela or JB or Hadley had preprogrammed secret coding into the Elucidator to . . .

The Elucidator, he thought.

He clenched his left hand—the one that wasn't wrapped around Katherine's arm—and was relieved to feel the smooth edge of the Elucidator against his palm and fingers. He tightened his grip. He and Katherine and Andrea had lost their Elucidator on their trip to 1600, and Jonah had no desire to repeat that experience.

"It's you and me and the Elucidator," Jonah told Katherine.

"Oh, goody," Katherine said, a bit too much sarcasm in her voice. "Why didn't Chip and Angela come, too? I was touching Chip's hand. Angela was touching your shoulder."

"Just touching," Jonah said apologetically. "Not holding on. No one was holding on but me."

"Gee, thanks," Katherine said.

They floated on in silence for a moment, and then Katherine asked, a little plaintively, "Where do you think we're going?"

"JB said he was in a time hollow," Jonah told her. "Maybe we're just going where he went. Or, he said he was watching someone in the early nineteen . . . nineteen hundreds, do you think? Or nineteenth century?"

"It could be nineteenth century BC, for all we know," Katherine said bitterly. Jonah sensed movement beside him—it seemed that Katherine had plunged the top half of her body forward. "Hello? Hello? JB?" she hollered into the Elucidator in Jonah's hand.

The Elucidator remained silent.

"Great," Katherine muttered. "Now it's broken again."

Jonah shrugged.

"We've managed before without a working Elucidator," he said, but his voice chose that moment to squeak. He sounded like a terrified mouse.

Katherine was still hunched forward, poking at the Elucidator.

"Can we switch over to voice commands?" she asked it. "Can't you let us hear JB again?"

"Jonah? Is that you? Are you okay?" came out of the Elucidator.

"No, it's Katherine now," she shouted back. "Kath-er-ine!"

"Oh, thank you! Thank you, Angela! Thank God!" JB replied, the same way he had before. And then, just as before, there was a pause before JB said, ". . . was so worried . . ."

"Katherine, I don't think JB can hear you," Jonah said. "The Elucidator is just playing back his conversation from before. Oh—it's giving you what you asked for—to hear JB again."

"You know that's not what I meant!" Katherine wailed,

as if it would do any good to scold the Elucidator.

"Yeah, but you have to be really precise with the—," Jonah broke off, because the repeated conversation coming from the Elucidator had reached the part where JB was describing where he was:

". . . in a time hollow by mistake . . . trapped watching . . ."

"Did you hear that?" Jonah asked excitedly. "I can make out more of his words this time around. Elucidator, can you play that part back for us again?"

The Elucidator fell silent for a moment and then repeated JB's words. Jonah held his breath and strained his ears, listening as hard as he could. Maybe it was because they were traveling through a near vacuum, but JB's voice came out sounding clearer and purer now:

"I'm stuck in a time hollow by mistake. I'm trapped watching . . . in the early nineteen hundreds . . ."

"There!" Jonah exclaimed. "We've got a time period!"

"Shh," Katherine shushed him. "You made me miss the rest of it!"

They had the Elucidator play JB's lines again:

". . . trapped watching . . . in the early nineteen hundreds. His daughter is one of the missing children of history. We had to return her. We had to. He's not thinking about the right things. He . . . I thought . . ."

"They returned another missing child to history?"

Jonah asked. "When JB said they weren't going to do that anymore?"

"But if they had to . . . ," Katherine mumbled. "Elucidator, let's hear that again."

Jonah strained his ears harder than ever. He held his breath again. He listened so intently that he could hear his own pulse pounding in his veins. But he couldn't make sense of whatever JB said between "trapped watching" and "in the early nineteen hundreds."

"I got it! I got it!" Katherine shrieked. "JB's watching Albert Einstein. Albert Einstein!"

"Albert Einstein?" Jonah repeated. "No way. You're making that up!"

But they replayed JB's words again, and this time Jonah heard the name too, faint but distinct.

Albert Einstein? Jonah thought. *Albert Einstein and time travel? Albert Einstein and a missing daughter?*

He relaxed through the next section of JB's words, the part they'd already figured out. And then, maybe hearing was kind of like eyesight, where sometimes you could see things better when you weren't looking directly at them. This time, when he wasn't listening so hard, Jonah could make out what JB had said after "He's not thinking about the right things."

It was: "He could ruin everything."

FIVE

"But—Albert Einstein's a good guy. Isn't he?" Jonah asked. "How could he ruin everything?"

The words were snatched from his mouth by a sudden rush of air around his face. Jonah had been so intent on trying to figure out JB's words on the Elucidator that he'd stopped paying attention to their journey through time. But now lights rushed up at them, and it felt as if every cell and molecule and atom of Jonah's body were being torn apart.

They were about to land.

"Katherine!" Jonah screamed. "Shouldn't we get the Elucidator to make us invisible? Just in case?"

His words were whipped away from him so quickly that he knew Katherine couldn't have heard. But he tried to curl forward, bending his head toward the Elucidator even as he struggled to bring the Elucidator up toward his mouth.

"In-vi-si-ble!" he cried out. "Make me and Katherine invisible!"

In the bone-crushing, teeth-jarring pressure of gravity and time crashing down on him, he couldn't tell if his request had worked or not. He couldn't see the Elucidator in his hand, but he couldn't see anything else, either. He couldn't hear; he couldn't speak; he couldn't feel.

And then everything was still. Jonah braced himself for the usual waves of timesickness. On every other substantive trip he'd ever made through time, the brief period after landing had always left him feeling brainless and senseless.

Wouldn't it . . . be awful . . . to be . . . brainless . . . around . . . Albert Einstein? he thought jerkily.

He choked back a chuckle at the silliness of his own brain, but his timesick reflexes were so slow that some sound escaped: "Heh-h . . ."

"Shh!" Katherine hissed beside him. "Got to be . . . quiet . . . I think I see . . . Einstein . . ."

"Where? Must . . . hide . . . then . . . ," Jonah whispered back.

Slowly—very slowly—Jonah remembered that he'd asked the Elucidator to make them invisible. He let go of

Katherine's arm and lifted his right hand toward his face. Slowly, slowly, slowly . . . He blinked, trying to force his eyes to work. Something crystalline swung in and out of focus. Something hand-shaped and crystalline.

Oh, yeah, he remembered. *That's how a time traveler's body looks to his own eyes—and to any other time traveler's eyes. But people who really belong in this time period won't be able to see me at all.*

His request for invisibility had worked.

Jonah barely managed to keep from letting out an audible sigh of relief.

"Where did you see Einstein?" he whispered to Katherine.

"Sitting . . . over . . . at that table," she whispered back.

Evidently she didn't have the energy yet to lift her arm and point. But she jerked her nearly invisible chin up and to the right, and Jonah guessed that meant he should look in that direction. He turned his head and tried to blink his eyes into focus for medium-distance vision. He saw lace—a lace tablecloth, maybe? Yes, there was wood showing through the lace. A moment later Jonah figured out that he could see the bars of chair backs on three sides of the table. And beyond that? Was there a fourth chair?

Jonah blinked again, and propped himself up on his wobbly elbows.

A man sat in the fourth chair. A young man, with thick dark hair and a dark moustache.

"Silly." Jonah leaned down to whisper into Katherine's ear. "That's not Einstein. Einstein's old. Don't you remember? Bushy white hair? White moustache?"

"Don't you think he had to be young before he got old?" Katherine whispered back.

It took a ridiculous amount of time for Jonah to consider this. He hoped that just meant that his brain wasn't over the timesickness yet.

But really, he told himself. *There are just some people who don't seem like they ever could have been young. It's like trying to imagine my grandparents as little kids. Or—like the guy who played Dumbledore in the Harry Potter movies. No way he was ever young.*

Albert Einstein was like that too. It seemed as if he must have been born old.

Unless Katherine was right, and this really was a young Albert Einstein.

Jonah squinted, trying to imagine the dark hair replaced by a wild white thicket, the neatly trimmed dark moustache replaced by a walruslike white thatch.

Maybe it was still the timesickness working on him, but he couldn't do it. He couldn't see Albert Einstein in this young man's face.

This could be anyone.

"Do you suppose we're seeing him before anyone knows who he is?" Katherine hissed excitedly. "Before he's even famous? How old was Einstein when he got famous?"

Jonah sincerely hoped this wasn't one of the things that Mr. Stanley had been telling them in science class when Jonah was zoning out.

"Don't know," Jonah whispered back to Katherine. "I guess we can snoop around and find out."

Dizzily, Jonah sat all the way up, going from propping himself on his elbows to supporting himself on his knuckles, pressed against the floor. He had to tuck the Elucidator in his jeans pocket, because he didn't trust himself not to drop it. But then, swaying slightly, he bent his knees, preparing to crouch and stand. Up, up, up . . .

He lost his balance and fell over backward.

He would have been able to catch himself, to keep himself from crashing onto the floor and making a horrible racket. But the floor rushed up at him quicker than he expected.

No. His perceptions were off again. He hadn't hit the floor. He'd hit something else.

Or—someone.

SIX

Jonah felt a pair of arms steadying him. But he jerked back, scrambling away. He tripped over his own feet, and it was all he could do to regain his balance without crashing to the floor in the other direction. It was a long moment before he dared to turn his head to look back at the person he'd fallen against.

First he saw Katherine scrambling out of the way alongside him. For a moment he felt a flare of hope: Maybe his perceptions were way off, and all he'd done was bump into her. But even as she moved, she was glaring at him, a look of horror on her see-through face. She was mouthing something, a silent scream: *Get out of the way!*

Jonah turned his head as far back as he could. Behind him stood a young woman, frozen in place. She was standing so still that Jonah had a split second of wondering if time had stopped again. Then he noticed a dark lock of hair that had escaped from the bun on top of her head. That strand was swaying back and forth—proof that time kept moving, even though she had stopped.

And it was proof that she had been moving forward a moment earlier—until Jonah had fallen against her.

Even as Jonah watched, a look of astonishment spread across her face.

Well, yeah, Jonah thought. *Her brain's telling her that some kid just slammed against her. But her eyes are telling her there's no one there.*

Surprisingly, the young woman didn't cry out, didn't shriek—didn't even gasp. Instead, after a long moment, she closed her eyes and took a slow step forward, gently waving her arms in front of her.

Not the best way to try to catch someone, Jonah thought.

But he was almost hypnotized by the grace of her movements. Her expression was different now too—was she *praying?* Was that what all the hope and wonder and yearning on her face meant?

It took Katherine yanking on his arm to remind Jonah that he couldn't just stand there watching.

"This way!" she hissed in his ear.

She pulled him to the side, past a stiff dark couch to a corner beside an open window. He guessed she thought they could jump out if they had to.

But the woman had stopped moving forward. She let her arms drop. She turned her head to gaze at the young man sitting at the table. He hadn't changed his pose in the slightest since the woman had come in. He still had his head bent over a stack of papers.

"My Johnnie," the woman said softly.

"See! That isn't Albert Einstein!" Jonah whispered to Katherine. "It's Johnnie somebody!"

But the man didn't look up.

"Albert," the woman said, louder. "Albert, listen!"

The man jerked to attention, reacting with such shock that he knocked a whole stack of papers to the floor.

"Mitsa! My Dollie!" he cried. "My urchin! My little witch! I didn't hear you come in! I—" He bent over to pick up the papers from the floor, and stopped talking. Distractedly, he gazed at the papers in his hand. He squinted. "No, wait. Did I square that? Should I?" he mumbled.

The woman—Mitsa? Dollie?—shook her head fondly.

"Albert, I swear, you haven't heard anything anyone's said to you since you started this new project," she said. "Someone could set off a cannon right beside you and you wouldn't notice."

"Or, if it's cubed, that would mean . . . ," Albert mumbled, completely engrossed in his papers again.

The woman sighed and walked to the table. Her body

dipped down every other step, dragging the bottom of her long skirt on the floor.

She has a limp, Jonah thought. It was strange that he hadn't noticed that before. Even with the limp, he still thought she moved gracefully.

When the woman reached the table, she eased the papers out of Albert's hand.

"Mileva!" Albert protested.

He sounded so serious, Jonah guessed that had to be the woman's real name.

"Maybe you should try using the square root," Mileva said, looking down at a long string of calculations.

"Really?" Albert said eagerly. "You think that's the answer?"

"No," Mileva said, holding the papers out of his reach behind her back. "I really don't know. But I know you'll try it if you haven't already. And—I'll help you. Later on. After—"

Albert interrupted her by springing up and trying to reach around her back for the papers. She slid the papers onto the table and caught him in her arms, hugging him close.

"This is just what I wanted for our marriage," Mileva whispered into his shoulder. "You, me, our calculations and formulas, our grand ideas . . . But I didn't know the devil's bargain I'd have to make to get this. Are you *sure* there isn't some other way?"

Albert didn't seem to hear her. He was looking past her to the papers on the table, and still mumbling: "Square root . . . proportional distance . . . time . . . time . . . space . . . time split in half . . . But what changed in 1611?"

Jonah felt Katherine bolt completely upright behind him, smashed into the corner. He turned and looked at his sister, and her wide, alarmed eyes told him she was thinking the same thing as he was.

Jonah didn't know if Albert Einstein was famous yet or not, in whatever early nineteen-hundreds year they'd arrived in. He didn't know what "devil's bargain" Mileva was talking about; he didn't know why there was no sign in this room of the missing daughter that JB had supposedly returned to them. He didn't know what "right things" Albert Einstein was supposed to be thinking about.

But he knew what Einstein was thinking about instead, why his thoughts were capable of ruining everything.

Einstein was thinking about them—Jonah and Katherine. Somehow he knew what they'd done on their last trip through time.

SEVEN

The awful thing was, Jonah couldn't scream. He couldn't rant or rave or pound his fist against the wall or moan, "Noooo . . ." He had to stand there, still as a rock, without making a single sound.

"Calm down," Katherine whispered in his ear, as if she knew how close he was to losing it.

"But—he knows . . . he found out . . . ," Jonah dared to whisper back.

"Shh," Katherine hissed. "We don't know how much he knows. Listen. And watch. Do you see any tracers?"

Tracers. Jonah had been so stressed and scattered since they'd arrived that he'd forgotten all about watching for tracers. He'd seen plenty of tracers on his previous trips through time—they were ghostly representations of how time would have gone if time travelers hadn't intervened. They were invisible to people in their native time period, but could be a helpful guide to time travelers. On their trip to 1600, Jonah had grown to hate tracers, since time was so messed up there, and the tracers had seemed like taunts. Then, soon after they'd arrived in 1611, all the tracers had disappeared, and he'd realized that that was even worse.

Please don't let time be that far off track here, he thought. *Please let there be tracers.*

Something like a whimper escaped from deep in his throat. Mileva's head immediately shot up from Albert's shoulder, and she peered straight in Jonah's direction.

A dim light glowed near her chin. Jonah shifted positions, to see it better—yes. It was a second, ghostly version of her head: its tracer. If Jonah hadn't made that sound, Mileva would have kept her head nestled against Albert's shoulder.

So why didn't I see any tracer lights before, even when I bumped into her and she started waving her arms around? Jonah wondered. *Was I just not paying attention? Or would she have stood there waving her arms anyway? Why would she have done that in original time?*

Unlike Mileva, Albert didn't move at all. He kept staring down at the papers on the table.

After a few seconds Mileva seemed to give up on both Albert and any possibility of figuring out where the noise had come from. She took a step back from Albert, and all the tracer light disappeared, so Jonah knew she would have done that regardless.

"Albert, I know you want to sit here all night thinking about your project. But you promised the Hallers that you'd play your violin for them this evening," she said.

"My violin, ah, yes, yes," Albert said distractedly. But he kept staring down at the papers.

Mileva tugged on his arm, pulling him away from the table. He'd just begun leaning down to scrawl something on the top page, and the sudden motion jerked the paper sideways.

Is there a tracer left behind by any of the papers? Jonah wondered. *Er—how could there be, if these aren't the papers he would have been working on in original time?*

Jonah was confusing himself again.

Albert only laughed at Mileva's persistence.

"My little urchin keeps her Johnnie boy in line," Albert chuckled. "If the Hallers want music tonight, music they shall have! Don't worry about the project—you know I've gotten some of my best ideas while playing."

He knelt down and picked up a violin case Jonah hadn't noticed before. He offered Mileva his arm so they could stroll out of the room together.

"Should we follow them?" Katherine whispered as soon as the door shut behind the couple.

"Are you crazy? No!" Jonah said. "We should look at those papers!"

EIGHT

They were in German.

"What? No!" Katherine protested, as she and Jonah peered down at the papers scattered across the table. "Aren't our translation vaccines still working?"

Way back before one of their early trips through time—to 1485—JB had made it so they could understand other languages on their travels. So far Jonah and Katherine had been able to understand older versions of English in 1485 and 1611, Algonquin in 1600, and an Inuit language in 1611.

"We could understand Albert and his wife, and I'm pretty sure they were speaking German," Jonah said, though he wasn't quite sure how he'd figured that out. "Maybe it only works on spoken language, not written. Here." He picked up one of the pages at random and handed it to Katherine. "Read it out loud."

"Supposing ze something, something, something, weird zigzagging figure, thingy that's kind of like an S, then—," Katherine began.

Jonah sighed.

"I don't think the problem is that we don't understand German," Jonah said. "I think it's that we don't understand enough physics. I mean, I'm barely surviving seventh-grade science. And these are *Albert Einstein's* thoughts."

"Yeah, his *wrong* thoughts," Katherine grumbled, starting to lower the paper toward the table again. "His thoughts that are going to ruin everything, because he found out—"

She stopped suddenly, the paper frozen in her hand.

"What's wrong?" Jonah whispered.

"The tracer," Katherine whispered back in a panicky voice. "The paper left a tracer!"

She was right. A ghostly, almost see-through page lay atop the other papers on the table.

"Well, duh," Jonah said. "You're a time traveler. You changed something in time when you picked up the paper. So the tracer's there to show where the paper belongs, where it would have been if *you* hadn't disturbed it."

"But Albert Einstein's thinking about the wrong things," Katherine said. "These are the wrong papers! Time's already disturbed!"

Jonah looked back and forth between the paper in Katherine's hand and the tracer version on the table.

"It's not the same paper," he said slowly. "See, the tracer page has that squiggly sign at the top of it, and then a triangle—and look, all the numbers are different."

"Let's look at all the papers," Katherine suggested.

One by one, they lifted all the pages on the table and looked at the tracer versions that remained.

Every single paper was totally different from its tracer.

And every single paper was totally indecipherable to Jonah and Katherine.

"This is impossible," Katherine complained, as they sagged down into the wooden chairs. "We know it's all wrong, but we don't know what any of it means. Could these different numbers"—she gestured at the piles of papers strewn across the table—"be the reason all of time froze back home? Is Albert Einstein that important?"

"I guess," Jonah said. "He might be."

"What was he supposed to be thinking about in the early nineteen hundreds?" Katherine asked.

"I don't know," Jonah said. "Relativity? E equals MC squared? Quantum . . . uh, quantum physics?"

"What does any of that *mean*?" Katherine asked.

"You got me," Jonah said.

Really, when he thought about Albert Einstein, he

mostly thought about things that didn't have much to do with science. A poster hung in the guidance office at school that showed the old-man Albert Einstein riding a bicycle. The caption on the poster said: "Try new things! You might discover a new talent!" And wasn't there some famous picture of Albert Einstein sticking his tongue out at the camera? Weren't there stories about how, when he was an old man, he'd help neighborhood kids with their math homework if they brought him brownies?

What could Jonah and Katherine do to make sure the young Albert Einstein they'd seen in this room was going to turn into the bike-riding, tongue-sticking-out, homework-helping old man that everybody loved? What could they do to make sure time went right?

And, oh, yeah—what was the deal with Einstein's daughter? How did she fit in with all of this?

Jonah shifted nervously in his seat, and something jabbed him from his jeans pocket.

The Elucidator.

"Hey, maybe we can ask JB all our questions," he told Katherine. "We haven't tried talking to him since we got here—maybe that will work now."

"It's worth a shot," Katherine said, shrugging.

Jonah drew the Elucidator from his pocket. When he'd begged for invisibility in the last moments of their trip through time, he'd neglected to ask the Elucidator to make itself invisible, too. So once it was out of his pocket, the Elucidator was fully visible. For a few seconds he amused himself by covering it with his hands—making it disappear completely—and then holding it flat in his crystalline palm. All he had to do was squint, and it looked as if the Elucidator were appearing from nowhere and floating in midair.

"You are such a *boy*," Katherine snorted. "Playing games when we've got serious problems to deal with!"

Why was it okay to insult males, but totally wrong and sexist to say anything bad about females?

Jonah knew better than to ask this question out loud.

"This isn't a game," he said in an offended tone. "It's a science experiment. I bet Albert Einstein would be doing the same thing if he was me."

"Only if his IQ fell into negative numbers," Katherine said. "Oh, wait—that *is* you!"

She snatched the Elucidator out of his hand the next time he opened his palm.

"Interesting," she said, rubbing her fingers over its carved surface. "What's it imitating now?"

When they'd left the twenty-first century, the Elucidator had been black and sleek, resembling the most updated cell phone Jonah had ever seen. But somehow on the trip through time it had transformed itself into an old-fashioned wooden-and-leather case.

That's probably what cell phones would have looked like if they'd had cell phones in the Victorian era, Jonah thought. *But—they didn't. They barely even had phones.*

Katherine flipped a clasp at the front of the Elucidator, and the lid sprang open, revealing a layer of glass and a needle and face below.

"Oh—it's a compass," Jonah said.

"I guess that's a step up from a rock or a candleholder," Katherine said, making a face. "But how do we talk on it?" She tapped the glass. "Hello? JB? Hello? Are you there? Are you somewhere with Einstein's daughter?"

There was a noise behind them—a gasp. And then the sound of running: *thump-slide-thump-slide-thump-slide . . .*

Jonah whirled around to see Mileva dashing toward them.

She can't see us. We're invisible, he reminded himself. *But— the Elucidator—*

He put his hand out to cover over the Elucidator, to hide it. But he was too late.

Mileva had already snatched the Elucidator from Katherine's grasp.

NINE

Jonah immediately tried to grab the Elucidator back from Mileva. But he had to be careful not to touch her hand, only the wooden case. He darted around, waiting for the exact right moment, the exact right angle.

Greedily, Mileva encircled the entire compass case with both hands, effectively killing all of Jonah's best chances.

Beside him, Katherine shot him an anguished look, mouthing the words, *What do we do? What do we do?*

Jonah held up his hand warningly.

Wait, he mouthed back. But how long had Mileva been behind them? How much had she seen? How much had she heard? What did *she* know?

Mileva huddled on the floor and bent down over the Elucidator/compass case.

"What do you know about Lieserl?" she shouted at it. "You haven't harmed her, have you? Please, God, no . . . Why would you? We're nobodies. Unless . . ."

The Elucidator lay silent in her hands. She stared at it, and tears began streaming down her face.

"Please," she whispered.

Jonah held his breath. Beside him Katherine stood equally frozen. The Elucidator stayed silent. After a moment Mileva rocked back on her heels, her expression a mix of craftiness and confusion.

"Albert would think me mad, trying to talk to a compass," she murmured. She blinked, and then wiped her face with the back of her hand. She kept her tight grip on the Elucidator but began looking carefully about the room, studying the open window, the pictures on the wall, the papers scattered on the table, the chairs that Katherine and Jonah had knocked askew when they were scrambling around Mileva. She looked right through Katherine and Jonah, then turned her head and looked straight through them again.

"Madness or not, I *know* someone's here," she said. "I heard you. I feel your presence. Are you angels? Demons? Ghosts?" Something changed in her face, a curtain of fear falling across it. "No, no—I know you're not Lieserl's ghost, come to haunt her poor, sad mama. Lieserl's alive.

They would tell me if anything happened to Lieserl." She shook her head, as if trying to clear it. "But I am not some ignorant village girl, her mind awash in superstition. I am a scientist, regardless of my last exam grades. I will solve this with rationality. I will look at the empirical data."

She stood up. She still clung tightly to the Elucidator, but Jonah noticed that her hands were trembling. He took a step back, trying to stay out of her way, and a floorboard creaked beneath his feet.

Mileva instantly jerked her head down to glare at the offending floorboard. She pressed her foot down in the same spot, making the floorboard creak again in the same way. And again. And again.

She pulled a chair out from the table and sat down. Jonah saw the chair separate completely from its tracer version. Mileva was here, now, only because of them.

"Fact," Mileva whispered, still gazing about. "This afternoon I could have sworn I felt a living, breathing child fall into my arms when there was no such child in sight."

She paused.

"Fact," she continued. She was grim-faced now, her jaw clenched. "I lied to my husband and told him I had a headache so I could come back to the apartment and check out my suspicions. When I arrived at the apartment, I heard voices. I heard a floorboard creak when no one trod upon it. I saw this compass floating through the air." She lifted the Elucidator in the air, studying it carefully, from all angles. "And I have never seen this compass before in my life. It does not belong in our apartment."

Should Jonah snatch the Elucidator away now? Across the table, he saw Katherine silently shaking her head at him.

She's right, Jonah thought. *If the Elucidator disappeared from Mileva's hands, that would just give her another suspicious fact for her list.*

He lifted his hands in the air, a gesture of helplessness.

Mileva was frowning now. She pressed her hands tightly around the Elucidator again.

"All the male scientists would add an additional 'fact,'" she said bitterly. "That I am a female, and therefore prone to hysterics and hallucinations. And I am a female who has been under great strain lately, through great emotional turmoil. Even my own husband would not believe me if I told him what I just witnessed! I cannot tell even him!"

Behind her, Jonah heard a key rattling in the door.

"Mileva! *Mein Liebchen!* The musical evening was no fun without you, so I came back too," Albert called, his entrance as loud and clumsy as Mileva's had been silent and stealthy. "Who are you talking to?"

Mileva instantly closed her hand around the Elucidator, lowering it toward the table.

"No one," she called back in a quavery voice. "Only myself."

And before Albert had stepped across the threshold into the room, Mileva had the Elucidator tucked into her skirt pocket, completely out of sight.

And completely out of Jonah and Katherine's reach.

TEN

"We'll get the Elucidator back in the morning," Jonah whispered to Katherine.

Albert and Mileva had gone off to bed, Albert seeming not to notice that Mileva had kept her hand firmly over her skirt pocket the entire rest of the evening.

"She's got to let go of it sometime," Jonah muttered.

"Yeah, and how are we going to make her forget that she ever saw it?" Katherine countered. "How are we going to make her forget whatever she heard us say? How are we going to get Einstein to stop thinking about time splitting in 1611? How are we ever going to get home again?"

"How about if we just focus on figuring out where to sleep tonight?" Jonah asked weakly. He looked around the small room. "It should be somewhere out of the way, where no one's going to step on us. . . . Is there space for both of us to fit under that couch?"

"*I'm* not sleeping under any couch," Katherine said crankily. "I'm not sleeping at all. I'm going to look for clues."

Jonah had been on enough of these time-travel adventures with Katherine to know: She was always grumpiest when she was the most terrified. Still, he felt like he had to point out the obvious.

"It's too dark to see any 'clues,'" he muttered. "If you turn a light on, you might wake up Albert or Mileva."

"They've been using, like, kerosene lamps," Katherine said. "If we turn one on really low, they'll never know."

Jonah cast a worried glance at the bedroom door, but didn't say anything else.

Katherine lit a lamp and carried it toward a desk in the corner. She set the lamp on the floor and sat down behind it, trying to hide the light.

"You go through the top drawer," she whispered. "I'll take the middle drawer."

Jonah sat down beside her, a little closer to the desk.

At first, all the papers they found were like the ones they'd seen on the table: covered with incomprehensible scientific scrawling. The only difference was that these papers left behind identical tracers when Jonah and Katherine picked them up.

"So, when Albert wrote these papers, whatever they are, he was thinking about the right things," Jonah muttered. "He wasn't ruining anything."

"Yeah, that'd be a great clue—if we knew what any of it meant," Katherine said glumly.

"And if we knew how old these papers are," Jonah said. "Didn't Albert ever have teachers who told him to put dates on all his work? Mr. Stanley would have given him an F, just for that."

He snorted, imagining this: Albert Einstein showing up as a kid in Mr. Stanley's class somehow, Mr. Stanley flunking him, Einstein instantly growing a moustache and a headful of white hair in some sort of time-lapse sequence and sneering at Mr. Stanley, "Don't you know who I am?"

"Jonah, I don't think all this is for any class," Katherine said, still sorting through papers. "I think this is what Albert Einstein does for fun. Oh—here's a date on something!"

She held up a stiff, formal-looking certificate with the names Albert Einstein and Mileva Maric written on it in a flowery script.

"I think this is their marriage license," Katherine said. "Looks like they got married on January 6, 1903. So we know that much!"

"Yeah, and what good does that do us, when we don't know what year it is now?" Jonah countered.

"Do you have to be so negative about everything?" Katherine complained, waving the certificate scoldingly at him.

Jonah shoved her away. Unfortunately, he pushed a little too hard, and her elbow knocked against the kerosene lamp. It wobbled back and forth, and Jonah could just see what was about to happen: *Kerosene splashing out, flame leaping from the lamp to the papers . . . oh, yeah, if Katherine and I set Albert Einstein's apartment on fire—that will really help history!*

He reached out and grabbed the top rim of the lamp, steadying it. But the glass was unbearably hot. He jerked back, his head slamming against the top edge of the desk. There was a soft click, and the ornate carving that ran along the edge sagged down.

"You broke it!" Katherine accused.

Jonah stared at the damage he'd done. Then he blinked, and it didn't look like damage after all.

"No," he whispered. "I found a secret compartment!"

ELEVEN

Katherine held the lamp up—very carefully—and then Jonah could see to reach into the secret compartment. It was a small space, with barely enough room to slide his fingers in and sweep to the right and left. Would he find some original formula that Einstein hadn't yet revealed to the world? Would he get to see the famous "$E = mc^2$" in Einstein's original writing?

Jonah's fingertips brushed a single paper. No, not a paper—a picture.

He dislodged it, knocking it out of the secret compartment into his other hand. He held it up to Katherine's lamp, and they both stared at it.

The picture showed a little girl, barely more than a baby. She wore a frilly dress and had a huge white bow in her hair, and she was standing in a field of flowers. It was hard to tell what the flowers were because it was all in black and white—or, what was that tint that old photos sometimes had? Sepia? It was hard to make out colors in the flickering lamplight; it was hard to make out much of anything in the fuzzy photograph. But something about the girl's steady gaze made Jonah think that she would be an interesting person when she grew up.

"Look at what's written at the bottom—'Lieserl,'" Katherine whispered. "That's the same name Mileva said before. Think this is their daughter?"

"Who keeps their kid's picture hidden in a secret compartment?" Jonah asked.

He thought about all the pictures his parents had of him and Katherine on display back home: every single one of their school pictures since kindergarten lining the stairway; all his soccer team pictures on the bookcase in the family room; pictures of Katherine's piano recitals in the living room; a formal, posed picture of the whole family and various family vacation photos in the upstairs hallway.

Was the early twentieth century that incredibly different from the early twenty-first century? Was that the only reason Lieserl Einstein's picture was hidden away in a secret compartment instead of hanging on the Einsteins' wall?

Jonah didn't think so.

"I wonder—," Katherine began.

Just then they heard the bedroom door rattle. In a flash Katherine turned the knob to put out their lamp.

"Put everything back where it was!" Jonah hissed in her ear.

Fumbling in the darkness, he shoved the picture of Lieserl back into the secret compartment and eased the carved wood back into place. Then he began throwing papers back into the drawer.

The bedroom door opened, revealing Albert Einstein holding a lamp of his own.

"What if the square root is the answer?" he mumbled.

He stepped forward and pulled the bedroom door shut behind him. Then he walked to the table and sat down. He turned the knob on his lamp to make it brighter, the flame illuminating a wider and wider circle. Jonah and Katherine were only a few feet away from him—Jonah could see the light glowing right through Katherine, clearly revealing all the papers she hadn't been able to put away yet.

But Albert kept his head bent over the papers on the table, completely unaware.

"I think, if we just finish cleaning up without making any noise, we'll be okay," Jonah whispered as softly as he could.

Katherine nodded and went back to sliding papers into the drawer. This time she was careful to match them up with their tracers. She slid the drawer silently back into the desk, and Jonah did the same with his.

As far as Jonah could tell, Albert didn't look up even once. He didn't move at all, except to send his pen flying across the paper.

"I guess we might as well sleep, if he's going to work all night," Katherine whispered.

Jonah nodded.

The couch turned out to be too low to sleep under, so the best they could do was to press themselves as close to the wall as possible. Jonah thought he'd be out the minute he closed his eyes, but lowering his eyelids meant that he could see all the horrific images of the day, all over again: Jonah's entire science class sitting frozen in time, Angela's car barreling toward Katherine, Chip's clammy face appearing and vanishing, Mileva's hands closing over the Elucidator.

What does any of it mean? Jonah wondered. *What are we supposed to do?*

He wasn't aware of actually falling asleep—it was more that he kept seeing the images play and replay in his head, and after a while they seemed to be parts of nightmares more than actual memories.

It was a relief when he woke up to bright sunshine streaming in through the window.

Well, there, he thought. *We survived the night. And today's got to be better. We'll find some way to get the Elucidator back from Mileva. We'll figure out some way to solve everything and go home.*

That was when he heard the screaming.

TWELVE

It was a female voice, so Jonah looked around immediately for Katherine.

She was right beside him, and also jerking her head frantically back and forth, trying to see what was wrong. The sunlight streamed right through her—her body left no shadow on the floor—so Jonah could cross off "We must have lost our invisibility, and someone saw us!" as a reason for the screaming.

He looked toward the table where Albert Einstein had been working the night before, but it was deserted now. Jonah looked toward the desk he and Katherine had searched—had they left something out? Had they completely messed up?

No—the desk looked just as it had the night before, the drawers lined up perfectly.

Jonah listened harder, and could make out actual words in the screaming: "Albert! Oh, Albert!"

Was the screaming coming from outside the apartment? Maybe even from the street down below?

Jonah heard a sound of feet pounding their way unevenly up the stairs. The door leading out of the apartment slammed open, just as a sleepy-looking Albert stumbled out of the bedroom. With his hair mashed to the side and a look of confusion on his face, he looked even less like the venerable old-man Einstein than before.

"Did I oversleep?" he asked. "Am I late for work?"

Mileva tripped coming into the apartment.

"No, no, it's Lieserl," she sobbed.

Albert moved quickly across the floor, shutting the apartment door behind his wife.

"What about Lieserl?" he said cautiously. His voice was quiet, and he put his hand on Mileva's shoulder in a way that seemed to be intended to quiet her down too.

Mileva shook his hand away.

"I went down to get the milk and there was a telegram—" She held up a tattered-looking piece of paper. "She has scarlet fever."

Mileva sagged against the wall.

Albert started to reach for her again, hesitated, and then drew his hand back.

"Scarlet fever can be . . . difficult," he said, wincing painfully. "This is a new variable to deal with."

Jonah wasn't quite sure what scarlet fever was, but even he could tell: That had been the wrong thing to say.

Mileva buried her face in her hands.

"No, no," she wailed, shaking her head hard.

Albert tried to hug her, but she jerked away.

"I'm going there," she announced, limping furiously toward the bedroom. "I'll pack now and take the first train out—a child should have her mother with her when she's ill."

Where is this Lieserl? Jonah wondered. *Some kind of boarding school?*

Albert and Mileva didn't look quite old enough to have a child off at boarding school—well, Albert didn't. And, anyhow, Jonah kind of thought that if Lieserl was old enough to be away at boarding school, he would have found more pictures in the secret compartment showing her as she'd grown up.

Albert trailed after Mileva.

"You don't know . . . how she'll be . . . when you get there," he said, standing on the threshold. "It's such a long train ride. It could take days. And what will I tell people about where you've gone? Or why?"

"I—don't—care!" Mileva said, and slammed the bedroom door in his face.

Albert just stood there looking stunned.

Jonah probably had the same expression on his face, because Katherine jabbed him in the side.

"What are *we* going to do?" she asked in a whisper.

"Huh?" Jonah said.

Then he realized what she was asking. Mileva was going somewhere that could be days away. Should he and Katherine stay here, with Albert Einstein, who was thinking the wrong thoughts?

Or should they go with Mileva, who had their Elucidator?

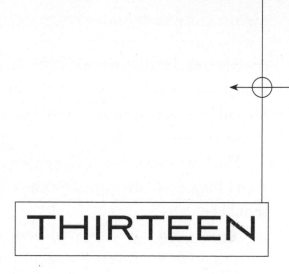

THIRTEEN

They chose Mileva.

"Because of Lieserl, too," Katherine argued in a whisper, as the sounds of frantic packing drifted out from the bedroom. "If she's one of the missing children of history, then she's connected to us. Well, you, anyway. She might need us to save her."

Jonah sank down onto the couch, feeling oddly nostalgic for 1483. When they'd gone back to that year on their very first trip through time, the only thing Jonah had cared about was rescuing his friends Chip and Alex. Period. He'd barely been aware of what it meant to preserve time; he hadn't thought much about the consequences his actions might have within the next five minutes, let alone centuries later.

Since then, all of their trips through time had been

complicated. He'd seen time buckle and crack, splinter and split. He'd seen the results of his smallest actions ripple forward, and decisions he'd made in a heartbeat become matters of life or death.

This time around—why were they here? Who had sent them? How could they possibly know what their priorities should be?

"Besides, even if we stayed here, we wouldn't know what to do to get Albert Einstein to stop thinking about the wrong things," Katherine argued. "We need to get that Elucidator back, and we need it to work!"

Crystalline tears glistened in the corners of her eyes, and Jonah saw that, no matter how certain she sounded, she was worried too.

"And we need something to eat," Jonah said. "I've been starving since science class yesterday."

"How can you think about food at a time like this?" Katherine asked.

"How can you not?" Jonah countered.

Just then Mileva opened the bedroom door again and struggled out, carrying a worn bag. It reminded Jonah of something Mary Poppins would carry.

"If I hurry I can make the eight o'clock train to Zurich," she said.

"Bern to Zurich—that's an easy trip," Albert agreed.

"But then, won't you have to change trains in Munich and Salzburg and Vienna and Budapest?"

Katherine elbowed Jonah.

"Bern's in Switzerland, right?" she whispered. "So we're in Europe again! Europe!"

"Duh!" Jonah whispered back. "Don't you think that's why we've been listening to Albert and Mileva speaking German all this time?"

But he hadn't thought about their geographical location until now either. All that had mattered was the time.

Albert was still trying to talk to Mileva.

"When will you even get to Novi Sad?" he asked.

"As soon as I can!" Mileva snapped, jerking the bag past him.

"But—can you manage the trip alone?" Albert asked.

"I'll have to, won't I?" Mileva answered. "You can't take time off work. Not for this. Not for Lieserl."

There was a sob hidden behind the words, but, to Jonah's surprise, Mileva didn't start crying. She bent her head and seemed to be concentrating only on moving the bag forward, moving her limping leg forward, moving her bag forward . . .

"I can walk you to the station," Albert said, making it sound as though he'd just made a huge decision. He took the bag from Mileva's hands and then, a second later, put it down on the table in the middle of the room. "And, here. Let's pack some food for you to have on the train."

He darted into the kitchen and began pulling out bread and sausages and cheese. Jonah scrambled in behind him and managed to grab two large chunks of bread while Albert and Mileva weren't looking. Jonah grinned triumphantly at Katherine and demonstrated how it was possible to hide one of the chunks with his hand while he was eating it.

She rolled her eyes at him. But Jonah noticed that she did step into the kitchen to take the other chunk from him.

Albert began bringing out more and more food.

"There's not time for that!" Mileva protested. "Let's just go!"

Albert wrapped all the food in a dish towel and went back to the table to tuck the bundle into Mileva's bag. He quickly added a few books and several of the papers that he'd left strewn across the table.

"So you'll have something to think about on the train," he explained.

"I already have plenty to think about," Mileva said sadly, turning away from the desk. Had she been getting something out of the desk while Jonah was watching Albert?

Or—putting something into it?

An awful thought struck Jonah.

"What if Mileva's not taking the Elucidator with her?" he muttered to Katherine. "What if she's just put it in the desk? Or left it in the bedroom? How would we know? We should have followed her into that bedroom. We should have—"

"Walked through a closed door? How?" Katherine argued. But she grimaced in dismay. "We should have searched the bedroom while they were in the kitchen. We'll have to do it now, before they're gone! Then we can look in the desk and follow them . . ."

But Albert had already shouldered the bag, put on a hat, and walked out of the apartment. He was holding the door for Mileva to step out behind him.

"We'll lose them!" Jonah hissed back at Katherine. "We won't know which way to go!"

Mileva stopped on the threshold and looked back.

"Yes, that's right," Albert murmured behind her. "Memorize every detail of our happy home. Carry it in your heart while you're away."

He bent to kiss her, but the kiss only brushed her cheek. She kept her head turned, her eyes darting about.

And then, while Albert wasn't looking, she pulled something partway out of her skirt pocket, palming it in a way that showed it only to the room behind her.

It was the Elucidator. She was showing them that she still had the Elucidator.

FOURTEEN

A moment later Albert and Mileva were gone.

Jonah couldn't move.

"Did she hear us whispering?" he asked Katherine. "Did she know we were wondering about the Elucidator?"

"She couldn't have," Katherine said. "We weren't that loud. *Albert* didn't hear us."

"But she knows . . . something," Jonah said, still rattled.

"And that's why we've got to follow her," Katherine said.

They waited a few more seconds to make sure that Albert and Mileva were far enough ahead that they wouldn't see the apartment door opening and closing, seemingly all by itself. They tiptoed down the stairs, and had to slip out another door to get to the street.

"Albert and Mileva both put on hats, right before they

walked out the door," Katherine whispered. "We'll just watch for the hats!"

They opened the door to outside—and everyone on the street was wearing a hat.

"Got any other ideas?" Jonah asked.

He didn't wait for Katherine to answer, because he'd thought of something himself. He darted over to a lamppost and shimmied up it. He looked right and left, staring out over the tops of dozens of hats. And then, in the next block up, he saw a feather on a hat bobbing up and down unevenly, as if the person wearing the hat was limping.

"That way," he mouthed to Katherine, and pointed.

He climbed down, and the two of them began making their way along the crowded sidewalk. It wasn't easy. He'd walked invisibly through a crowd before—in the fifteenth century—but people hadn't seemed packed in together so tightly then.

Maybe because they were all afraid of catching lice or fleas or the creeping crud from each other? Jonah thought, remembering how grotesque the people in fifteenth-century London had seemed to him.

The people around him here seemed clean and healthy and orderly—and that was the problem. They were always stepping politely out of the way for someone: "After you."

"Oh, no, by all means, you go first." And that meant that Jonah was constantly in danger of bumping into one of them.

"Let's just walk in the street," he whispered to Katherine. "It'll be easier."

"They still have some horses and carriages out there, along with the cars and trolleys," Katherine whispered back. "And that means we might step in some—"

"We'll just have to dodge it," Jonah insisted.

He tugged on her arm, pulling her out into the street with him. And it was easier to dodge the occasional car and carriage and horse dropping than all the people on the sidewalk. He had space to look around now too.

So this is Switzerland in the early nineteen hundreds? he thought. He stared up at rows of neatly tended, interconnected buildings, all with window boxes at every window, overflowing with flowers.

Mom would love this, Jonah thought. *She'd be saying, "Oh, it's so picturesque! It's beautiful!"*

He swallowed a lump in his throat that he probably couldn't blame on the dry bread he'd eaten without anything to drink. He never liked thinking about his parents when he was in a different time period, because those thoughts always had an echo: *What if I never see them again? What if this is the time period I get stuck in?*

They had to get the Elucidator back from Mileva.

"There! We caught up with Albert and Mileva!" Katherine whispered, looking over to the sidewalk beside them. "They're turning the corner—"

"We can't lose them!" Jonah hissed. "Hurry!"

He grabbed Katherine's arm and pulled her along with him. In the rush he forgot to watch the street beneath his feet.

Squish.

"Ugh, Jonah, did you just step in—"

"I'll scrape it off. No big deal," Jonah muttered back. He hurriedly rubbed the side of his dirty Nike against a bare spot in the street, but it wasn't a perfect method. He could still smell a rather unpleasant odor rising from his shoe.

This is why people invented cars, Jonah thought. He'd had a nasty encounter with horse manure in the fifteenth century too. It was kind of depressing that they were in the twentieth century now, and it was *still* a problem.

Jonah and Katherine managed to keep up with Albert and Mileva—and stay out of any more horse droppings— the rest of the way to the train station. It was a huge, cavernous building, and Mileva kept glancing around as if something in it frightened her.

Or is she looking for me and Katherine? Jonah wondered.

She couldn't be. They were invisible.

Albert and Mileva stood in line to buy a ticket, and then he walked her to her platform, with Jonah and Katherine right behind them. The train wasn't there yet.

"You should go now," Mileva said, touching her husband's cheek. "You can't be late for work."

"I don't want to leave you," Albert murmured. "I don't want you to leave me."

He drew her into a hug. Katherine leaned closer and sighed dramatically, as if she were watching some stupid romantic movie. Jonah wondered if he was going to have to look away.

But then Mileva pulled away from Albert.

"Albert—I have to do this," she said. "I have to go. I couldn't live with myself if—"

Albert touched a finger to her lips, silencing her.

"I know," he said. He studied Mileva's face, his expression oddly analytical, as if he were watching a lab experiment instead of saying good-bye to his wife. "I—I can't say I understand. I think it's different for fathers and mothers."

"But—if you met her . . . ," Mileva murmured. "Even just once . . ."

Jonah snapped his head toward Katherine, wondering if she'd heard the same crazy thing he had. Her eyes were wide and distressed, and she was mouthing the word *What?*

Jonah shook his head. Things were even worse than he thought. It wasn't just time that was messed up. It was Einstein's family.

How could Albert Einstein never have met his own daughter?

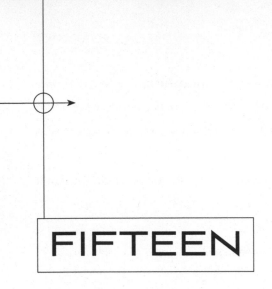

FIFTEEN

The train arrived a few moments later, and Mileva struggled into the nearest car. She sat by a window and waved and waved and waved to Albert.

Jonah and Katherine had to wait until the crush of people in front of them boarded before they could step in.

"Maybe it will be so crowded we'll have to ride on the top of the train," Jonah suggested hopefully to Katherine. He'd seen movies where people did this, and it always looked like a lot of fun.

"You're crazy," Katherine told him. "Besides, we have to keep an eye on Mileva. Something's really off, you know?"

No kidding, Jonah thought.

"And what if some moment on the train is our only chance to get the Elucidator back?" Katherine asked.

Jonah hated it when Katherine was right.

Getting onto the train and staying near Mileva was even harder than Jonah expected. Just walking down the aisle without touching someone was like walking a tightrope. All the seats were taken, so at first Jonah and Katherine tried standing in the aisle near Mileva's seat. But other people kept walking up and down the aisle: the ticket taker, a bunch of squirmy little kids, the little kids' mother chasing them, and then travelers getting on and off at every stop. Jonah and Katherine constantly had to scurry out of the way to the end of the train car, press themselves against the wall so nobody touched them, and then hurry back so they didn't miss anything with Mileva.

"I'm not going to be able to stand this for another minute, let alone all the way to Zurich and wherever else we're going," Katherine said after they'd had to squeeze themselves tightly against the wall to avoid being hit by a large man's protruding stomach. He'd come within a button's width of brushing Jonah's arm.

"So you do want to ride on top of the train," Jonah said.

"No," Katherine said emphatically. She looked at her brother, then squinted thoughtfully toward Mileva's seat. "But maybe . . . Spot me."

Tugging Jonah along with her, she went back down the aisle to Mileva's row.

Holding first on to Jonah's shoulder, then the overhead

luggage rack, she climbed onto the back of the row of seats opposite Mileva's. The people sitting there—a man in a fancy suit and a woman in a lacy blouse—must have felt the pressure on the seats, because they both looked around curiously. But, seeing nothing unusual behind or above them, then they only shrugged and went back to facing forward.

Still holding on to the luggage rack for balance, Katherine tucked her legs under her body so she was half sitting, half crouching sideways on the top of the seats.

She pointed triumphantly at her own pose and then at Jonah, clearly trying to say, *See? My idea worked! Now it's your turn.*

Jonah rolled his eyes, but he started gingerly trying to climb onto the back of the row Mileva was in. It was a little harder for him because he didn't have anyone's shoulder to hang on to. He couldn't reach the luggage rack from the aisle, so he resorted to stepping onto the seat between Mileva and the elderly woman sitting beside her. It was only for an instant, and he made sure that his shoe didn't touch either one of them.

Seconds later he, like Katherine, had reached a precarious perch atop the seat.

He looked at Katherine, and she was frowning and pointing at the seat where he'd stepped.

A small pile of dried mud clumps—*er, no, dried manure,* he

thought—lay on the seat below him. It had clearly fallen off his shoe, and turned visible again once it was apart from him. In fact, the clumps were practically arranged in a shoe-shaped pattern.

Jonah shrugged and shook his head and mouthed back to Katherine, *That doesn't matter. No one's going to notice.*

But Mileva was already turning her head and looking down at the mud clumps. She looked carefully at the woman beside her, looked all around the train, frowned thoughtfully, and then brushed the mud away.

See? Jonah mouthed to Katherine. *No problem.*

What's she looking at now? Katherine mouthed back to him. At least that's what Jonah thought she was trying to say, because she pointed down at Mileva's lap and, in a questioning way, held up the hand that wasn't clinging to the luggage rack.

Jonah looked down.

Mileva had pulled something out of her bag, something in a dark paper frame.

It was the picture of Lieserl that had been hidden in the desk's secret compartment back at the Einsteins' home.

That's what she was doing, standing over by the desk right before we left. So it's okay for that picture to be seen on a train, but not in their own apartment? Jonah wondered. *What does that mean?*

He tried to mouth, *It's the picture,* to Katherine, but she didn't understand and kept mouthing back, *What? What?*

Finally Jonah just mouthed, *I'll tell you later,* and went back to watching Mileva.

She was studying the picture as if trying to memorize every detail.

"What a lovely child," the old woman beside her said. Or maybe she wasn't that old—she just had white hair and was wearing an old-fashioned dark dress. (*Duh*, Jonah thought. *Everything's old-fashioned in the past.*)

He was pretty sure that this woman hadn't been sitting there since Bern, but had gotten on at one of the smaller stations.

Mileva jolted back, as if she hadn't realized that the older woman was looking in her direction.

Still, she nodded politely.

"Thank you," Mileva said quietly. She looked around once more, and then added, "It's my daughter. Lieserl."

There was something odd about the way she said that. Jonah had heard his own parents talk about him and Katherine a million times: "Yeah, we have two kids," "Yeah, those two little monkeys are ours," "That was our son who just scored that goal!" "Looks like we have to claim the one who's covered in the most mud" . . . and whether they sounded proud or embarrassed by what he and Katherine were doing at that particular moment, there was always something offhand in their voices, some easy assumption that they completely took for granted.

Why did Mileva sound as if she were doing something very daring, just saying, "It's my daughter"?

The woman beside her didn't seem to notice anything unusual.

"How old is she?" she asked.

"She was fifteen months when this picture was taken," Mileva said. "She's nineteen months now."

Really? Jonah thought. He looked over at Katherine to see if she'd caught that bit of information.

She had. She was leaning forward, intent on Mileva's every word.

"Oh, they change so fast at that age," the old woman said.

"Yes, I—I'm going home to see her," Mileva said. "I miss her so much. She's been staying with my parents until . . . until . . ."

So that's where Lieserl is, Jonah thought. *That's where we're going.*

He looked over at Katherine again, and she was leaning so far forward that it was a wonder she hadn't fallen off her seat.

The old woman next to Mileva was in a similarly eager pose.

"Until?" she prompted.

Something in Mileva's face closed down.

"Nothing," she said. "Never mind. My husband and I just have to work out a . . . a situation."

"At least you *have* a husband," the old woman said, in a way that implied she wasn't quite sure she believed Mileva. "So many girls nowadays get themselves into trouble, having babies without—"

"Of course I have a husband!" Mileva said, a bit too shrilly. "I have a husband, but we've had such bad luck, and now my little girl is sick, and . . . "

"Oh, you poor dear," the old woman said, patting Mileva's shoulder in a way that Jonah thought was more creepy than comforting. "Tell me all about it."

Jonah didn't exactly *mean* to kick the woman in the head at that precise moment, but he didn't quite mind it. His left foot slipped off the top of the seat, sliding down and knocking the woman's velvet hat askew.

"What was that?" the woman cried, looking all around. She turned and felt behind herself on the seat back, but by then Jonah had managed to scamper away, pressing himself between the luggage rack and the top of Mileva's seat.

"There's something wrong with my seat," the woman told Mileva indignantly. "I'm going to inform the conductor."

She stood up and rushed away, leaving behind a tracer version of herself leaning vulture-like toward Mileva.

Now Mileva looked around too.

"I don't know how you did that," she murmured. "But thank you."

Her words were so soft that Katherine and the man and woman sitting nearby couldn't possibly have heard. Mileva might have been praying. She might have been talking to herself or to Lieserl's picture or to some saint Jonah had never heard of who protected people from nosy old women on trains.

But Jonah knew: She was really talking to him.

SIXTEEN

Time travel had put Jonah in the middle of a battle in 1485, and in the middle of a mutiny and in danger of freezing or starving to death in 1611. He'd faced a potentially fatal bear attack on that trip too.

So on the trains rattling across Switzerland—and then Germany and Austria—Jonah kept telling himself that things could be worse. The scenery was actually kind of amazing: mountains and more mountains, some of them capped in snow even though the air in the train cars was so hot that Jonah was pretty sure that it was summertime right now.

But it was tedious and uncomfortable, crouching and standing and sitting and huddling and cowering on one train after another, for hours on end. His muscles ached from the crouching-above-seats position he and Katherine had to assume whenever the train cars were crowded. His stomach ached from the minimal, questionable food they managed to pick up—mostly leftovers abandoned in train-station restaurants, which Katherine at first refused to eat and then, when she got hungrier, began gobbling down as eagerly as Jonah. And he worried every time he stepped off a train for a transfer that this would be the station where they lost Mileva completely, and they'd have to find their way to Novi Sad—wherever that was—on their own.

He worried, too, that they might never get the Elucidator back or that Mileva might even lose it as she limped unsteadily from platform to platform, dragging her bag along with her.

Once, in Vienna, he gave in to an impulse and lifted the back end of her bag behind her, to make it lighter for her to carry.

"Jonah! You can't do that!" Katherine scolded him in a whisper. "I mean, I know it's nice, but . . ."

Jonah knew the rest of what she wanted to say: *It's nice, but isn't it more important to save time than to be nice? It's nice, but what if that one action ruins time forever?*

"I'm not sure she's going to make it if we don't help at least a little," Jonah whispered back.

For, as miserable as Jonah and Katherine felt on the long, long train trip, Mileva seemed to be taking it even harder. She'd started looking as though it might kill her.

Twice she got off the train to throw up.

The first time it happened, Jonah had insisted that Katherine follow Mileva into the bathroom.

"What—you want me to go into the stall with her?" Katherine had protested. "Jonah, that's sick!"

"What if she flushes the Elucidator down the toilet?" Jonah asked. "What if—"

"Okay, okay," Katherine agreed.

When she came back out of the bathroom, she looked almost as sick as Mileva, only in a nearly invisible way.

"Don't you *ever* ask me to watch someone puke again," Katherine said, half gagging herself.

"Do you think Mileva has scarlet fever too?" Jonah asked. "Is vomiting one of the symptoms?"

"Isn't scarlet fever kind of like strep throat with a rash?" Katherine asked. "Isn't that what Makenna Bryant had back in second grade?"

How did Katherine remember these things?

"She vomited *a lot*, that time," Katherine continued.

"Oh, wait—was she the kid who threw up all over her table in the cafeteria?" Jonah asked. "And then on the school secretary's desk, on her way to the nurse?" He guessed he remembered stuff too.

But this news made him relax a little.

"So, if scarlet fever is just bad strep throat, then Mileva is kind of overreacting about her daughter having it, right?" Jonah asked.

Katherine grimaced.

"I've been trying to remember—I think scarlet fever is what Mary Ingalls had in the Little House books," Katherine said. "Remember Mom and Dad reading them to us when we were little?"

"Only I didn't like them as much as you did, so Dad started reading Captain Underpants books with me instead," Jonah said, making a face. "Mary was the one who always sat quietly and did what she was told, right? The one who drove her sister crazy, being such a goody-goody?"

"Yeah—until she caught scarlet fever and went blind," Katherine said.

Blind, Jonah thought.

Mileva wasn't overreacting, being so worried about her daughter.

Mileva came out of the bathroom then, and they followed her onto another train.

It got dark, and still they kept traveling. Jonah was hoping for a nice hotel room and a long night's sleep. But when they got onto yet another train in Vienna, Mileva said to the conductor, "We'll be in Budapest by morning, right?"

What? Jonah thought. *We're going to be on this train all night long?*

"That's what the *schedule* says, yes," the conductor was replying. He leaned in conspiratorially. "But it could be afternoon. You know, over in those areas they're not so good about tending the tracks. Civilization is wasted on some people."

Mileva gritted her teeth.

"I'm going to see my family," she told the conductor in a hostile voice. "In Novi Sad. I'm Serbian."

The conductor didn't even flinch.

"Well, then," he said. "You know what I'm talking about."

Jonah could tell Mileva had been insulted, but he wasn't sure: Was this just like people back home in Ohio making fun of Michigan because of college football—a mostly friendly rivalry? Or was it something worse?

Jonah decided it was worse because of the way Mileva sank into her seat and buried her face in her hands. She was crying.

"Oh, Albert, what am I doing?" she moaned. "Why didn't I stay home with you and . . ." She began shaking her head. "No. Why aren't we all together—you and me and Lieserl—all together as a family?"

Good question, Jonah thought. *What's the answer?*

She didn't give an answer. She just kept shaking her head. After a few moments she pulled out the papers Albert had given her.

"Work," she muttered. "I will work, and then at least some good can come of this time. I will check Albert's math, like he wanted me to . . ."

But she seemed to be staring at the cluster of numbers and symbols without even seeing them.

Jonah realized that while he and Katherine had been watching Mileva, the train had pulled away from the station. No one had come to sit near Mileva, and she was in something like a private compartment. Her seat and the five empty ones nearby were separated from the rest of the train car by a sliding door.

"Looks like at least we'll have somewhere to sleep," Katherine whispered, pointing at the empty seats.

"If no one gets on in the middle of the night," Jonah whispered back.

He'd thought their voices were quiet enough to get lost in the rumbling of the train wheels against the rails. But Mileva jerked to alertness suddenly and narrowed her eyes, peering right in their direction. Jonah might have expected her to be hysterically afraid—after all, she'd been sobbing moments before. But she only sat calmly, her head cocked to the side. Listening. Watching.

"You're still with me," she said after a few seconds. "You've followed me all the way from Bern. And now we're alone. You can talk to me. Who are you? Where are you from? What are you doing here?"

Jonah and Katherine stood frozen. Jonah was afraid that if he even took a breath, Mileva would be able to hear him.

"I know you're there," Mileva said. "Albert, my husband, he's an incredible scientist because he's so good at thinking. The ideas that come out of his head! He's a genius, you know? Someday the whole world is going to know it."

Mileva waited only a second to see if they would respond. Then she went on.

"But Albert could walk through a blizzard and not know it was snowing. He was terrible at observations with lab experiments—he never would have gotten through university if the rest of us hadn't helped him," she said. She shifted slightly in her seat. "But me—I'm good at observation. All day today I've been watching the doors that stay open a moment too long, because you're walking through them. I've seen the food disappear off tables in train-station restaurants."

Katherine looked at Jonah and frowned.

Hey! We had to eat! he thought fiercely in her direction.

She only scowled.

Silently.

Mileva kept listing all the ways they'd failed to be completely invisible, completely unnoticeable.

"I've felt my train seat move like someone was climbing on top of it," she said. "I saw mud that you must have left behind. I've smelled your . . . was it perspiration? Ordinary old human sweat?"

Jonah began surreptitiously sniffing his underarms until he saw that Katherine was glaring even harder at him and making chopping motions with her hands to say, *Stop it! Just—stop!*

He glared back at her, hoping she was getting the message: *I couldn't help it! I'm a teenage boy! It was hot! Excuse me if I didn't think to bring deodorant with me when we got zapped back in time!*

Jonah looked back at Mileva and saw that while he and Katherine had been holding their glaring match, Mileva had slipped her papers back into her bag and pulled out the compass instead. She was holding it up in the air, turning it over and over, examining it. She clicked it open and shut, again and again.

"Can spirits get muddy and smell like sweat?" Mileva asked. "Do they carry compasses? *Is* this really a compass?"

The way she was holding it just with her fingertips, Jonah realized he could lunge at her and grab it away from her in an instant. He braced himself up on his toes, ready to dive—and in the next second Mileva was clutching the Elucidator with both hands again, holding it tightly against her skirt.

She'd realized the possibilities too.

"The people I grew up with were so superstitious," she said. "They put brooms upside down outside their bedroom doors to sweep away nightmares. They believed beeswax was sacred. They would only want to know what *kind* of spirits you are—evil or good? Do you mean me harm or benefit?"

Jonah looked at Katherine. Back in the 1480s, on their first trips through time, they'd talked to people from that era: monks, the king of England . . . But they'd been so ignorant then—they'd just been lucky that their conversations hadn't caused serious damage to time.

Katherine was shaking her head at Jonah even as he was shaking his head at her. They were agreeing: Neither one of them would answer Mileva's questions.

"The people I met at school—my Albert and everyone else—they don't believe in ghosts or spirits or superstitions," Mileva continued, looking toward Jonah and Katherine again. "And yet they put their faith in other unseeable things: atoms and molecules and ether, the everlasting ether that surrounds us all. Is *that* what you're made of? Are you something scientific? Something . . . maybe . . . straight out of my husband's thought experiments with time?"

Jonah shot Katherine a horrified look. How could Mileva have hit upon a guess so close to the truth?

"Just give us the compass and we'll leave you alone," Jonah blurted. "You'll never have to worry about us again."

But even as he spoke those words, he knew: They were lies. Jonah couldn't figure out what was going on with Lieserl and her parents, but if she was like all of the other missing children in history he'd dealt with, her life was in danger. And if Jonah and Katherine tried to save her, that would probably mean taking her away from Mileva forever.

That was definitely something Mileva would worry about, if she knew.

Mileva tightened her grip on the compass.

"No," she said. "That's not enough. I need answers. I have to understand what's going on."

Jonah and Katherine exchanged glances. Once again they were in silent agreement: This had gone far enough. Mileva already knew too much. As soon as her guard was down—maybe when she fell asleep?—Jonah and Katherine would just have to wrestle the Elucidator out of her hands. It wouldn't matter that she'd notice it missing. It wouldn't matter that she'd know they'd taken it. They couldn't make her forget anything. All they could do was keep her from learning more.

Mileva was still peering in their direction, clutching the compass-Elucidator with all her might.

"And don't think that you can just overpower me and take this from me," she said. "If you do that . . . if you do that, I'll tell everyone I know about you. Or, if you harm me in order to take it away, to keep me silent—my Albert loves me too much. He'd investigate. He'd figure out everything. He's that smart.

"And what would you think of that, when you're trying so hard to stay secret and hidden and out of sight?" Mileva finished.

Jonah and Katherine said nothing. They did nothing.

What other choice did they have?

SEVENTEEN

It was a long night.

Jonah and Katherine huddled in the two seats in the compartment that were farthest from Mileva, on either side of the door.

You just need to go to sleep, Jonah told himself. *It'll be okay. If anyone comes in, you'll hear the door and wake up. Or if Mileva gets up and heads this way and trips over my feet—well, so what? She already knows I'm here!*

He still couldn't sleep.

His mind kept replaying everything that had happened since the moment they'd arrived in the Einsteins' time—no, since time itself had frozen back in the twenty-first century. What should he and Katherine have done differently?

Not lost Chip and Angela. Not let Mileva see the Elucidator. Stayed hidden better . . .

He remembered a Bible passage that he'd heard in

church, usually during confession—something like, *I did the things I shouldn't have done; I didn't do the things I ought to have.*

That fit.

Still, he couldn't make himself regret everything. Kicking the gossipy woman in the head, for instance. Or helping Mileva carry her bag through the Vienna train station.

But what good was anything nice I did for Mileva, if I'm just going to help make it so she probably won't ever see her daughter again? Jonah wondered. *I don't mean her harm but—how can I not hurt her?*

Maybe he should just concentrate on watching for tracers, and trying to make sure that time stayed as close to its original version as possible. He was sure he'd done things all day long that had created extra tracers, but he hadn't paid very close attention. He hated watching for tracers—they just made him feel guilty.

Like now. Over by the window, Mileva was awash in tracer lights. In original time, it seemed, she was supposed to have fallen asleep over Albert's papers and the picture of Lieserl. Her tracer lay sprawled in her seat, disturbed only by an occasional grimace that probably just meant she was having bad dreams.

But the real Mileva was still wide awake, sitting upright and poking and prodding the Elucidator, muttering under her breath.

What if she broke it?

What if she figured it out?

She seemed smart—maybe not Albert Einstein smart, but determined and strong-willed enough to possibly make up the difference.

Jonah wished he could shut his own brain off entirely.

Hours passed. Eventually Katherine kicked him, and Jonah realized that, whether he'd managed to sleep or not, the night was coming to an end. Dim light crept in through the window, and Jonah could just barely make out lumps in the near-darkness that might be buildings outside. They seemed to be in a city again—was it Budapest?

Jonah had already forgotten that Katherine had kicked him. She seemed to be trying again to get his attention—jarring his shoulder this time.

"Mileva's writing something," Katherine hissed in his ear. "Can you lean over without her knowing and make sure it's not anything about the Elucidator or us?"

Jonah nodded silently. He leaned just far enough that he could see the words on the card in Mileva's lap:

Dear Johnnie,

I'm already in Budapest. It's going quickly, but badly. I'm not feeling well at all. What are you up to, little Johnnie? Write me soon, okay?

Your poor

Dollie

Mileva moved her hand, and Jonah realized she was adding a date in the top right corner: *August 27, 190 . . .* Before he could quite read the last digit, she was folding the letter and slipping it into an envelope. No portion of her body glowed with tracer light, so Jonah knew that nothing she was doing had been changed by contact with him and Katherine.

"It's not about us," Jonah whispered back to Katherine. "It's just a love letter to Albert."

Now, why had he called it that? There hadn't been a single "I love you" or "I miss you" in the whole letter. But it was as if every word had that as its secret meaning.

For the first time since they'd left the twenty-first century, Jonah let himself think about Andrea, the girl he'd had a crush on ever since their trip to 1600. He didn't like remembering the "let's just be friends" talk she'd given him when they got back to the twenty-first century. But he could see writing a letter to her—or, well, a text message or e-mail, anyhow—almost like Mileva's.

> *Dear Andrea,*
>
> *I'm in 190—well, something. I can't tell how this trip is going, because I can't figure anything out. But how are you? Are you frozen like everyone else in the twenty-first century? Or are you somewhere worrying about me? If you could, would you let me know how you are? And . . .*

Katherine jostled Jonah's shoulder again.

"You're not going to make fun of love letters?" she asked incredulously. "Have you actually grown up, or something?"

"I haven't gotten enough sleep to do anything," Jonah mumbled.

The train stopped, and Mileva got out, mailed her letter—and vomited once again. Jonah hoped scarlet fever wasn't terribly contagious, or that it was one of those diseases that he and Katherine had been vaccinated against as infants.

The rest of the day passed in a sleep-deprived blur of waiting in train stations and waiting on trains. Finally, in the late afternoon, Jonah heard the conductor walking through the train car calling out, "Next stop, Novi Sad. Novi Sad, next stop."

Jonah looked out the window at acres and acres of farm fields turning brown in the August sun. It was as if all the mountains they'd seen back in Switzerland and Germany and Austria had been ironed out flat. He nudged Katherine beside him.

"This is going to be like *Little House on the Prairie*," he whispered. "The prairie part, anyway."

But when the train pulled into Novi Sad, it was a bunch of old, elegant buildings, not American-style frontier shacks.

Jonah's mom would have called this place picturesque too.

Mileva had sent a telegram from the last station, so there was a carriage waiting for her when they arrived. An older man in a formal outfit met her at the platform and took her bag from her.

He hugged her and murmured into her hair, "My baby's come home," so Jonah guessed that this was her father, not some servant.

Mileva hugged him back—quickly—and then held him at arm's length and watched his face as she asked, "How is she? Is she any better?"

The man's face turned grim.

"She's very sick," he said. "It is good that you're here, with all your scientific knowledge."

"You know I studied physics, not medicine," Mileva said impatiently. "You know I am no good at—"

"Your papa will always think you are good at everything, no matter what," the man said. "The best."

Jonah and Katherine couldn't figure out how to climb into the carriage without spooking the horses or alerting Mileva's father—as well as Mileva—to their presence. So the best they could do was just jog alongside the carriage.

Mileva looked around as soon as she had settled into the carriage seat.

"It is good that our house is not far," she said, speaking

more loudly than she needed to if she meant the words only for her father's ears.

Still, Jonah was winded—and trying desperately not to draw attention to himself by panting—when the carriage finally stopped in front of an imposing house on what seemed to be the nicest street in town.

"We—huff—can't—huff—follow right—huff—behind them," Katherine whispered to him. "Not—huff—until we—huff—catch our breath."

"Right," Jonah agreed. "Let's just—huff—dodge around the side of the house . . . "

People were pouring out the front door, crying out, "Mileva!" and, "She's here!" Jonah held his breath and detoured around them. Once he turned the corner, he let himself take in huge gulps of air.

"Feeling . . . better now," Katherine mumbled, leaning over to get deeper breaths. "Not going to . . . pass out . . . after all."

Jonah reminded himself that they should still be cautious, even though everyone from the house seemed to be standing in the street out front, greeting Mileva. He peered down the side of the building. Filmy curtains blew out a window, the breeze tangling them into odd shapes.

Then Jonah realized it wasn't the breeze doing that: There were two men climbing through the curtains—two men who were almost completely see-through.

Time travelers, Jonah thought excitedly. *JB? Hadley?*

Jonah caught a glimpse of the men's faces. He saw what they were doing, who they were carrying.

These men weren't JB and Hadley, Jonah's friends. They were Gary and Hodge, his enemies.

And Gary and Hodge were in the midst of kidnapping Lieserl Einstein.

EIGHTEEN

Stop! Jonah started to yell. He turned, ready to run toward Gary and Hodge, ready to tackle them and wrestle little Lieserl out of their hands if he had to.

But something tugged him backward—Katherine's hand. And she clapped her other hand over his mouth, cutting off his shout at "St—"

This completely confused Jonah. He froze. Katherine yanked him around the corner of the house, back to the front, where everyone was clustered around Mileva.

"What'd you do that for?" he demanded, struggling against her grip. "Didn't you see who that was? They're kidnapping Lieserl! Mileva's going to go into her little girl's room and she'll have vanished and—"

"But—think!" Katherine commanded, her face twisting in distress. "We know Gary and Hodge really did kidnap

Lieserl Einstein. They do. Otherwise, how could she be one of the missing kids? What if this is meant to happen? And—if you let them see you, then they'll recognize you back in our time, in the cave. We can't even try to stop them, because, I guess, we didn't already do that. If we had, as soon as Gary and Hodge saw us at that adoption conference, they would have recognized us. They would have said, 'Hey, we remember you!'"

Jonah stared at his sister. He thought about complaining that he couldn't understand anything she was saying when she kept switching around verb tenses like that. But it was time travel confusing him, not Katherine. It just didn't make sense that the twenty-first century adoption conference where Jonah and Katherine would meet the other missing children of history had already happened for them, but was still in the future for Gary and Hodge and little Lieserl.

The past is the future is our past is their future is . . . Crud, how can I figure out the right thing to do? he wondered. *What if a "right thing" isn't even possible?*

"At least I'm going to watch them," Jonah told Katherine stubbornly. "I'm going to watch, and if they do anything to hurt Lieserl—"

"They're not going to hurt her," Katherine muttered. "They're planning to make a bajillion dollars selling her to some family in the future who wants a kid with Albert Einstein's DNA. They don't have any reason to hurt her."

"Still," Jonah said stubbornly.

Katherine bit her lip, but she didn't try to stop him when he crouched down and slipped back around the corner. Instead she followed him.

Both of them stayed low to the ground and tight against the building. They were lucky that a stand of tall grass hid them from the window where Gary and Hodge were climbing out. But Jonah and Katherine could peek through the grass.

The two men seemed not to have heard Jonah's brief "St—." It must have been completely covered by the noise of the family greeting Mileva out front.

Gary jumped down to the ground and glanced past Jonah and Katherine toward the ruckus out in the street.

"Sounds like a party," he said. "Sure you don't want to stay and sample some of the time-native treats? Secretly, of course."

"Eh, it's just one of the family members getting back," Hodge replied, even as he handed the toddler Lieserl down to Gary. She was wrapped in a blanket and seemed to be asleep—or drugged. "Time-primitives celebrate the stupidest things. You know that. And the food's never as good as the nutrition tourists like to make it sound."

Jonah looked over at Katherine and shook his head angrily. How could Gary and Hodge be so casual about everything? How could they not even know—or care— that the "family member" who'd just arrived was the mother of the child they were taking away? A mother who would soon be walking into an empty nursery, and crying out, and . . .

Jonah clenched his fists.

Katherine put a warning hand on Jonah's arm, and pointed.

"Remember Gary's muscles?" she hissed in his ear.

Jonah grimaced, staring at his enemy's bulging, muscular arms. It was true that back in the time cave Jonah had had no prayer of overpowering Gary. In fact he'd lost every time whenever it came down to strength and prowess.

But he didn't want Katherine reminding him of that.

I could still outsmart him, Jonah thought. *I kind of did that before.*

Of course, he'd also had a lot of help from JB and Angela and the other kids.

Gary was looking down at the child in his arms with a disgusted expression on his face.

"I don't know why we didn't just take her time-forward directly from the house," he said. "No one would have seen us."

"With a kid who's worth as much as that one, you take a few extra precautions," Hodge said. He jumped to the ground beside Gary and took Lieserl from him.

"Yes, sir," Gary said mockingly. "That's why I'm looking around so carefully in case any time agents are watching us."

He began walking away from the window, with his hand on his brow in a mocking imitation of someone on the lookout for spies.

But he was walking right toward Jonah and Katherine.

Jonah ducked down close to the ground and reached over and pulled Katherine's head down, too.

"Should we run?" Katherine whispered into Jonah's ear.

"He'd hear us," Jonah whispered back. "He'd see us."

Jonah didn't dare to look back up. What if Gary heard or saw them anyway? What would that do to time? Would it mess everything up?

No—more important question—what would Gary do to us? How badly would he mess up our faces?

Jonah's heart pounded. He could hear Gary's footsteps coming closer . . . closer . . . closer . . .

Back in Hodge's arms Lieserl coughed, and the sound turned into the beginning of a thin, agonizing wail.

"Quit your clowning around, and let's get out of here," Hodge commanded. "This kid's not worth anything to us if she dies. Look at her—she needs an antibiotic drip, stat."

Jonah heard Gary's footfalls recede, back toward Hodge and the window.

"I hate germy kids," Gary complained, and his voice was more distant now.

Jonah dared to peek through the grass again. Hodge was holding the blanket near Lieserl's face, muffling the sound of her cries. Gary, standing beside him, seemed to be consulting a compass.

No, Jonah thought. *Programming an Elucidator.*

It was now or never. If Jonah was going to do anything to interfere with Lieserl's kidnapping, he had to do it now.

He started to rise up—but Hodge's voice stopped him.

"This one's lucky we're taking her," he said. "A kid this sick, no way she'd survive if we left her here."

Jonah blinked. And in that instant Gary, Hodge, and Lieserl all vanished.

NINETEEN

Jonah let his body do what he'd almost done in the moment before Gary and Hodge disappeared. He jumped up and ran to the spot under the open window where the two men had been standing only a split second earlier.

"No!" he cried, waving his arms uselessly, as though he still thought he could catch them. "No! How could we have let that happen!"

"Jonah, shh," Katherine said beside him. "We had to. Don't make a scene. You'll just make things worse. They'll hear us in the front."

Jonah stood still for a second—and realized that the noise coming from the street out front had stopped.

"Mileva's about to see—," he began, and couldn't even finish the sentence. He turned around and gripped the bottom of the window frame Gary and Hodge had climbed out.

"Jonah, wait—," Katherine began.

Jonah ignored her and hoisted himself up on the frame. He pulled first one leg then the other across the sill, and slid down into the house.

He was in a dim, muffled room. The curtains were drawn on all four of the other windows, and the door was shut. A bit of light glowed from a low wooden bed. Jonah tiptoed closer—it was Lieserl's tracer on the bed, a tracer blanket kicked to the side.

But Mileva won't even see the tracer of her daughter when she comes in, Jonah thought. *She'll just see that she's gone.*

He heard a voice outside the door saying, "She's in your old room . . . ," and he took a step back from the bed, bumping into Katherine, who'd evidently climbed in through the window behind him.

"Watch where you're going, stu—," Katherine began, but then she stopped. Her eyes widened in surprise, and she whispered, "Who's that?"

Jonah followed his sister's gaze, staring back toward the bed again.

Just in the moment Jonah had spent glancing away, a girl had appeared beside the bed. She had long, wavy dark hair.

And she seemed to be wearing blue jeans.

"Is that—," Katherine began. The girl turned around,

her face pale in the dim glow from the tracer Lieserl. *"Emily?"* Katherine asked. "Emily from the time cave back home?"

The girl—Emily?—squinted.

"I don't understand," she said, almost as if she were apologizing.

It *was* Emily. Emily was one of the missing kids from history stranded in the twenty-first century. Jonah had met her in the time cave where Gary and Hodge had herded them all together when the two men were trying to re-kidnap them.

So if Emily's here now . . . that must mean her original identity was Lieserl Einstein, Jonah thought, trying to get his brain to catch up. *JB already told us he'd sent the real Lieserl back in time—we've just seen and heard things all out of sequence. We saw the teenage Emily in the twenty-first century and then we heard that JB had sent her back in time and then we saw Gary and Hodge kidnap her in the first place. And now we're seeing her return.*

This was like one of those stupid language arts activities his teachers had been so fond of back in elementary school: Put the story in order. What happened first? What happened second? What happened third? What's the end?

Jonah decided he didn't care that much about figuring out the sequence of what had already happened. He just wanted to know what came next.

"Hi, Emily. Did JB come back in time with you?" Jonah asked eagerly. "Or—is he going to?"

Emily glanced around the room. She still looked calm, but her bafflement seemed to be growing.

"I don't think so," she said. "He said I'd be alone, but . . . now you two are here, right?" She didn't quite seem certain that they were real. "Everything happened so fast, and it was so confusing. He said there wasn't time to explain. He said I'd know exactly what to do when I got here."

Jonah heard the doorknob rattle, and someone saying, "Is Lieserl awake now? Is that her talking? She's well enough to talk?"

Jonah realized they should have been whispering more softly, or not talking at all.

And he realized that Mileva was on the verge of seeing her daughter as a twenty-first-century American thirteen-year-old rather than a twentieth-century Serbian toddler.

"Lie down on top of that tracer," Jonah said. "Hurry!"

Emily only looked at him blankly.

"The glowing light on the bed—"

The door was opening.

Jonah took two quick steps toward Emily and gave her a push. His friends who'd seen their own tracers had told him they felt an almost irresistible pull tugging them in. Undoubtedly, JB had been counting on that pull working on Emily, too. And it probably would have, if Jonah and

Katherine hadn't distracted her. But Jonah remembered what she'd been like back in the time cave. She wasn't someone who'd jump into anything without thinking about it first. He'd had to push her.

But had he pushed her too late?

Jonah looked down and saw Emily lying down on the bed, drawing her knees up into the same pose as Lieserl's tracer. But Emily was practically adult-sized, and Lieserl's tracer wasn't even half as tall. Emily's arms hung over the side of the bed.

"My poor baby," Mileva was whispering, advancing toward the bed, a cluster of other women and girls behind her.

Jonah stepped aside, reminding himself, *They won't have the tracer lights to see by. Only time travelers can see the tracer lights. So it will be a few minutes before anyone realizes that something's wrong . . .*

And then he realized that he couldn't see the tracer lights anymore, either.

He peered down at the bed, and Emily was gone, the tracer was gone . . .

"Somebody give me a lamp," Mileva begged.

One of the other women handed her a softly glowing lantern, and now Jonah could see well too. He heard Katherine gasp softly in his ear.

For just a second, Jonah thought he could see evidence

of Emily's twenty-first-century, thirteen-year-old self ever so dimly in the toddler on the bed. There was just the slightest hint of blue jeans encircling her legs, just the barest suggestion of tangled strands of long, dark hair across her face. And then that evidence faded away—or maybe Jonah stopped noticing it, because other details stood out so much more: the flushed, feverish face; the sandpapery rash on every bit of exposed skin on her arms and legs; the way the little child's chest rose and fell so laboriously, as if every breath were a struggle. Even in sleep Emily/Lieserl kept wincing, the pain and agony seeming to mount until she screwed up her face and let out a tortured-sounding "Waaaaah . . ."

Jonah remembered the words Hodge had spoken only moments before: *A kid this sick, no way she'd survive if we left her here.*

They hadn't left her, but JB had put her back. And Jonah had given her the final push.

Had he truly helped Emily? Or had he just condemned her to die?

TWENTY

Jonah stumbled back away from the bed, and Katherine caught him.

"We've got to pull her back out," Jonah whispered. "We've got to!"

"Not with all these people gathered around," Katherine whispered back.

Jonah didn't care if Mileva or any of the other women heard them talking. Maybe the women would think there were ghosts and they'd run away, and then Jonah and Katherine could do what they needed to do.

"Maybe she's not as sick as she looks," Katherine whispered. "I took that babysitting class, remember? With little kids, sometimes they can look terrible and then the next day they're running around and perfectly fine. Or—was it the other way around? That they can be really sick and not look that bad?"

Mileva wasn't acting as if she thought Lieserl would be running around and perfectly fine anytime soon. She was scooping the little girl into her arms and moaning, "Oh, my poor little baby. My poor dear girl." Tears streamed down her face. "How could it come to this? Haven't we been punished enough? And—why should you be the one in pain? Poor, dear, innocent baby . . ."

She was sobbing so hard, Jonah wasn't sure he'd understood all her words correctly.

Punished? What does that have to do with anything?

"I promise you," Mileva wailed into her daughter's short, wispy curls—such a contrast to Emily's wealth of thick hair. "I promise you that I'll do everything in my power to help you recover. Please, God, let there be a way. Please, please, don't take my baby away to punish me . . ."

Now the other women in the room were clustering around Mileva, comforting her. They patted her head and arms and Lieserl's head and arms with equal sympathy.

"Don't worry. They'll give her medicine," Katherine whispered to Jonah. "Antibiotics, like Hodge was talking about. Remember all those bottles of pink stuff we had to take when we were little? What was it called? Amoxi— something?"

Jonah frowned at his sister.

"I don't think that's been invented yet," he said.

He had a vague memory of watching a TV show last year in science class about the invention of antibiotics: something about moldy bread (some of the kids in his class had made gagging noises over that) and then a scientist dude looking down at a petri dish, going, "Hey, this kills bacteria! Is that great or what?" And then the medicine being used for rows and rows of injured soldiers in hospital beds during some big war.

World War I? World War II?

Jonah thought about the cars and tanks and airplanes they'd shown in the war. There'd been swastikas on the enemy's equipment.

Definitely World War II.

Definitely after 190-whatever-year-this-was.

Jonah grabbed his sister's arm and pulled her out into the deserted hallway, away from the crowd of women keening over Mileva and Lieserl Einstein.

"JB, you've got to be watching this," he hissed. "This has to be as important as Einstein thinking about the wrong things. Why aren't you here helping us? What are we supposed to do now?"

Jonah's whispering echoed around him, his own words coming back to taunt him. The hallway stayed empty and dim.

JB didn't answer.

TWENTY-ONE

Mileva refused to leave Lieserl's side. She sat in the dim room for hours on end, barely eating, barely sleeping, barely even glancing away from her daughter.

Outside the August sun shone brightly—and then maybe the September sun too? How many days were passing? Had it been a week? Even more than that?

Jonah wasn't sure. He felt too lightheaded and stupid to keep track. He and Katherine were surviving only on the food they thought they could filch from sickroom trays without being noticed. After a while, even Katherine didn't bother complaining about wearing the same clothes day after day, washing up in quick sponge baths just to keep themselves from reeking, and making hurried bathroom trips, always in fear of being discovered.

If we walked just a little distance from Mileva's parents' house, we could probably find lots of food that no one would see us taking, Jonah thought. *We might pull fresh clothes from a clothesline, we might find a lake to completely cool off in, we might use the train station bathrooms and lock the doors and nobody would think it was strange . . .*

But he didn't suggest any of those ideas to Katherine, and she didn't suggest any of them to him.

Neither of them wanted to leave Lieserl/Emily's side, either.

A man with a black bag showed up to examine Lieserl— was he a doctor? When he finished, he just shook his head and muttered, "Yes, it's a very bad case. There's nothing else to be done. Only time will tell . . ."

Jonah and Katherine invisibly trailed the doctor to the front door and heard him tell Mileva's father, "Six more died last night."

Mileva's father blanched under his dark beard.

"Will Novi Sad have any children left when this is over?" he asked mournfully.

"Only the strongest ones," the doctor said wearily. "The strongest and the luckiest and the most blessed . . ."

Mileva's father tensed.

"My granddaughter is a blessing," he said. "She is a gift from God."

"I didn't say otherwise," the doctor replied, which wasn't the same as agreeing.

"Good day," Mileva's father said, and practically shoved him out the door.

Now, what was that all about? Jonah wondered.

He looked at Katherine, who shrugged. They went back to Lieserl's room, where Mileva and a servant girl were trying to bring down the little girl's fever by sponging her forehead with a cool cloth. It was clear that no pink bottles of amoxicillin were going to materialize. The most advanced medicine Jonah had seen anyone use was honey thinned with water.

The last time Jonah had watched Mileva put a wet cloth against her daughter's flushed face, the little girl had screamed and squirmed fitfully away. But now she didn't move, didn't make a peep. Was she just sleeping? Or was she so close to death she'd stopped feeling anything?

"Jonah," Katherine whispered. "We can't just stand here and watch her die. We've got to pull Emily out. No matter who sees us. No matter what it does to time."

Jonah nodded.

But before he or Katherine could move, Mileva turned to the servant girl and said in a choked voice, "Leave us."

The girl looked startled, but backed away.

Jonah heard the door click softly behind the girl, and then he saw Mileva reach into her pocket. Her hand emerged with the Elucidator tightly in her grip. She turned, revealing the Elucidator to every corner of the room like a lawyer showing evidence to a jury.

"Follow me," she said.

She put the Elucidator back in her pocket and scooped up Lieserl's limp body from the bed.

Struggling with the child's weight and her usual unbalanced gait, Mileva made her way through the door and down the hallway.

"We have to follow, don't we?" Katherine asked in a wavering voice.

Jonah nodded.

By the time they caught up with Mileva, she was weaving her way down an unfamiliar corridor. She went out a door at the back of the house and kept walking.

Outside, the bright sunshine of earlier in the day had faded to dusk. Shadows stretched across the alleys Mileva walked through. Dimly, Jonah wondered if Mileva had chosen this time of day on purpose—a time when streets would be deserted and no one would see her because everyone had gone home to eat the evening meal.

Or would the streets be deserted anyway? Jonah wondered. *Deserted because the children of Novi Sad are dying? Deserted because nobody wants to go out and risk being exposed to a deadly disease?*

Mileva kept limping along, Jonah and Katherine right behind her.

Finally they reached the outskirts of the city. Mileva stumbled into a stand of trees. She braced herself against one of them, pausing to catch her breath. Then, very, very gently, she rearranged the blankets wrapped around Lieserl and laid the child on the ground. She pulled the Elucidator out of her pocket once more.

"You will save my daughter's life," she announced, turning her face from tree to tree. But Jonah knew she was really talking to him and Katherine.

"You will save my daughter's life," she repeated, her voice gaining strength. It was steely and firm and unyielding. "You will make it so that she and Albert and I can live together happily for the rest of our lives. Or—" Now she bent over, placing the Elucidator beneath the heel of her boot. She began to lower her heel. "Or I will destroy your treasure."

TWENTY-TWO

"Stop!" Jonah hollered. "Don't!"

Katherine turned and glared at him.

She's only bluffing! Don't let her know we're here! she seemed to be thinking at him. Or maybe she was really just thinking, *That's not the best way to react when someone threatens you! Don't sound so panicky!* Because she opened her mouth and started talking, too.

"We want your daughter to live just as much as you do," Katherine said. "But if you destroy our, uh, compass, we may not be able to succeed."

She seemed to be trying to make her voice sound as steely as Mileva's. But she mostly just sounded like she did when she was bargaining with Mom and Dad to get to stay up late, or to invite more friends to her birthday parties, or to watch a TV show that Mom and Dad thought was "inappropriate." It wasn't exactly the right tone for negotiating about a matter of life and death.

"Katherine, didn't you hear what she's asking for?" Jonah asked. *"Everything* she's asking for? We can't—" Katherine clapped her hand over Jonah's mouth, but it was a moment too late. Jonah's voice had squeaked upward on the word "can't."

Mileva sagged to the ground, falling beside her motionless child.

"You're just children," she moaned. "I'm begging children to save my daughter's life, when the best doctor in Novi Sad couldn't do it."

"Well, *we* actually can," Katherine said in an offended voice. "If—"

Now it was Jonah's turn to put his hand over Katherine's mouth. Had she thought through anything she was saying? Unless JB was suddenly going to airlift bottles and bottles of antibiotics into Novi Sad—which Jonah did *not* expect to happen—then the best he and Katherine could hope for was to save Emily, the thirteen-year-old version of Mileva's daughter. Mileva wouldn't even recognize Emily.

And as for Mileva and Albert and Lieserl living together happily the rest of their lives?

If Emily/Lieserl is a missing child of history, that didn't happen, Jonah told himself. *It won't.*

Did that mean it couldn't?

Jonah hadn't had to worry about this with the other missing kids he'd seen returned to time. Either they'd been orphans, or the circumstances of their lives hadn't left Jonah feeling very sorry for the parents they'd left behind in the past.

But here was Mileva, sobbing and sobbing and sobbing beside her dying daughter . . .

She snatched up the Elucidator from beneath her shoe and held it up, squeezing it too tightly.

"I'm warning you," she said. "I will destroy this if I have to. I will."

Katherine shoved Jonah's hand away from his mouth just as he shoved her hand away from his. Both of them lunged for the Elucidator in Mileva's hand. In a flash, Mileva tucked the Elucidator under her knee and began blindly waving her arms about, grabbing at air, trying to catch . . .

Jonah and Katherine.

Jonah instantly reversed course, scrambling away over a downed tree. Mileva's hand brushed his shirt sleeve, but he pulled back, diving past her. This was like being back in elementary school, playing tag or sharks and minnows. Jonah almost wanted to say, *Nyah, nyah, nyah, nyah, nyah. You can't catch me!*

Then he looked back.

Mileva wasn't chasing him.

She'd already caught Katherine.

TWENTY-THREE

Mileva had her fingers circled around Katherine's wrist. With her other hand, she was feeling her way up Katherine's arm, patting her hair, touching her face.

"You *are* an invisible child," Mileva was saying. "A little girl."

"Not that little," Katherine muttered.

When she saw Jonah looking back at her, she mouthed other words: *What am I supposed to do?*

Katherine probably could have just yanked her arm away. Certainly Jonah and Katherine together could have overpowered Mileva and escaped. For that matter, Jonah could have swooped in, snatched up the sleeping Lieserl, and threatened to carry her away if Mileva didn't let Katherine go.

The problem was, second by second, Jonah and

Katherine could feel time changing. No matter what they did now, they could see by the expression on Mileva's face that her whole understanding of the universe had been rearranged.

It is possible for people to walk around invisibly.

It is possible for a child to have a solid body, with skin that feels like anyone else's, and yet have light flow right through her, as if she isn't even there.

What else is possible?

"Please," Katherine whimpered. "Let me go. You can't know too much. It'll ruin time."

"Time," Mileva said thoughtfully. "My husband has been quite preoccupied of late thinking about time."

"Katherine, that was the exact wrong thing to say!" Jonah complained.

Mileva glanced toward Lieserl, making sure she was safe. Then Mileva looked back and forth between the spot where Katherine sat, invisibly trapped, and where Jonah stood, just as invisibly frozen in indecision.

"I have a theory," Mileva said, and now she sounded calm and analytical—like a scientist, not a distraught mother. "Last night, when I could hear both of you breathing deeply, as if asleep, I studied your 'compass' once again. And it is my hypothesis that that is the device by which you are able to render yourselves visible or invisible.

It is not that you possess magical powers, but that you have harnessed the magic of science."

"Uh . . . possibly," Jonah said slowly, looking at Katherine to see if she thought it was safe to admit this. She shrugged helplessly.

"Are you asking us to tell you if you're right or wrong?" Katherine asked. "What good would that do? You're hiding the 'compass' under your knee. We can't do anything with it right now."

"But—if you give it back to us, we could demonstrate some of its powers for you," Jonah said. Even as he spoke, he could hear the craftiness in his own voice, the deceit. He tried again. "We swear, we wouldn't do anything bad. Nothing that would hurt you or Lieserl."

Katherine made a face at him—a grimace that said either *You are a terrible negotiator* or even *You are a terrible liar.*

Jonah shook his head at her and mouthed back, *I'm not lying.* But was that quite true? The first thing he'd want to do with the Elucidator was contact JB. And what would JB do? On Jonah and Katherine's most recent time travel trips, to 1600 and 1611 and 1605, JB's concern for saving people had edged out his desire to preserve time in its original form, no matter what. But he still wanted to keep time on track. And it seemed pretty clear that time was about to bring Mileva plenty of pain in the near future.

"I don't believe I need you to operate the 'compass,'" Mileva said. She lifted one eyebrow in a way that made her look smug. "I believe I've figured out how to use it myself."

Jonah and Katherine exchanged glances. Jonah could tell that his sister was as skeptical as he was.

Sure Mileva knows how to operate the Elucidator, Jonah thought. *Just like back home when Mom said she knew how to use her new cell phone, but she spent the whole first week asking Katherine and me, "How do I change the ring tone?" "How do I set the alarm clock?"*

"Voice commands," Mileva said confidently. "Make them visible again. Katherine and the other one. The boy."

Jonah looked at Katherine again, and what registered first was the horrified look on her face. Only then did he realize that he could no longer see trees through her face—instead he could see the freckles on her cheeks, the blue of her eyes, even a leaf stuck in her blond hair.

She was visible again. And—he looked down at blue jeans, at a gray Ohio State University soccer camp T-shirt—so was he.

Mileva looked calmly back and forth between the two of them.

"From the look of your clothes, I'm guessing that you're not from around here originally," she said dryly.

Jonah realized that of course that would be one of the things she'd notice right away. All the females they'd seen so far in Mileva's time wore skirts or dresses, mostly with aprons and kerchiefs or hats. The males went for baggy shirts and pants—though more in an "I could be Amish" way than an "I'm a hip-hop star" kind of way. Of course blue jeans and T-shirts would look weird to her. But Jonah and Katherine had managed to pass off their fashions in the fifteenth century by saying that they were from another country. Mileva had just given them that excuse to use now, too.

Mileva glanced to the side, checking on the sleeping Lieserl again.

"What? There are three of you?" she asked, sounding startled.

What's she talking about? Jonah wondered. *Or—who?*

Katherine shifted positions, so Jonah had no hope of seeing past her and Mileva. Jonah dashed forward, hoping that somehow JB had managed to come to them—not that Gary or Hodge had returned.

Jonah caught a glimpse of blue jeans and running shoes. Whoever it was, was lying on the ground and had just rolled toward Mileva.

Mileva jumped to her feet.

"Where's Lieserl?" she screamed. "What happened to

my daughter? She was right here! How could she have vanished?"

Mileva dived past the figure on the ground, feeling around in the twigs and leaves where she'd placed her daughter only moments earlier. Nothing was there.

Except a tracer.

Jonah saw a strand of long, dark hair stretching back into the same space as the tracer's head. He saw Lieserl's blanket clumped around the blue jeans. And finally he understood.

Lieserl hadn't vanished.

She'd just turned back into Emily.

TWENTY-FOUR

"Where's my little girl?" Mileva shrieked again, even louder. "What have you done to Lieserl?"

"Chip and Alex didn't separate from their tracers that easily," Katherine said.

"But if time's really messed up . . . ," Jonah began.

He saw a glint of something on the ground, and realized that Mileva had left the Elucidator behind when she'd jumped up to search for Lieserl. He scrambled toward it, but Mileva did too. Her hand closed over it and she brought it up to her mouth.

"Bring Lieserl back," she commanded. "Give me back my daughter. Please. Please. I beg of you . . ."

Her words turned into wails. Jonah cast a nervous glance back toward Novi Sad. What if someone heard her?

Emily sat up, looking groggily around.

"Emily," Jonah said quickly. "You have to get back together with your tracer. Just until we can get Mileva calmed down."

Emily blinked at him. She seemed to be struggling to draw air into her lungs.

"Couldn't . . . breathe," she finally said. "Can't . . . go back. Felt like I was going to . . . die."

"No," Jonah said. "Not that. Not yet. You can't . . ."

He glanced toward the tracer lying on the ground. The light glowing from the tiny figure seemed to be growing dimmer and dimmer.

"She's really dying?" he gasped. He'd seen this happen with a tracer deer back in 1600, its glow vanishing completely after a tracer arrow pierced its heart. That's what happened when tracers died. But that had just been a deer. This was a little girl.

No, Jonah reminded himself. *Lieserl's not going to die. Just her tracer. Gary and Hodge kidnapped the real girl. She grew up and became Emily. Emily's right here. She's fine. She doesn't even look sick.*

But somehow, even through her own wailing, Mileva had heard the horrible word.

"Dying?" Mileva moaned. "Where? How? What can I do? How can I stop it? Please! Please! Tell me!"

She went back to feeling around on the ground again, as if she believed that there'd been some sort of trade—as if she'd lost the ability to see her daughter when she'd gained the ability to see Katherine and Jonah.

And, in a way, wasn't that how it happened? Jonah thought. *Was it just a coincidence of timing? Or is everything connected? Us becoming visible, talking to Mileva . . . did that mess up time just enough that Emily could easily break free from her tracer?*

And then Jonah couldn't think, because Mileva's anguish was too awful to watch. Her hands flailed about through the tracer's dimming outlines again and again and again.

Katherine put her hand comfortingly on Mileva's shoulder.

"Mileva," she said. "Lieserl's not going to die. She's just . . ." Katherine looked helplessly at Jonah. "Changed," she finished feebly.

"Grown up," Jonah said. He couldn't watch Mileva's pain and grief a second longer without trying to help. "You could say it happened through the miracle of science."

He put his hands on both sides of Mileva's head and turned it so she couldn't help but stare directly into Emily's eyes.

"Mileva," he said firmly, without a hint of squeakiness, his voice carrying the ring of truth, "meet your daughter as a teenager."

TWENTY-FIVE

Jonah instantly had second thoughts.

For one thing—though, in the scheme of things, it was a really a minor point—did people even use the word "teenager" in the early nineteen hundreds?

For another thing, there was the way both Katherine and Emily were staring at him: their jaws dropped, their eyes bugging out, their faces drained of color.

Jonah couldn't remember Katherine looking that horrified by anything he'd ever done before. Not dropping spiders down her shirt, not putting peanut butter in her hair, not secretly booby-trapping her closet with knotted string . . . They'd been brother and sister for almost a dozen years. They'd traveled through centuries' worth of time together. He'd shocked and outraged and horrified her plenty.

Just not ever quite this badly.

Jonah glanced around quickly, pretty much expecting the world to be ending around him: the ground shaking, trees collapsing on his head, the Elucidator shrieking out an alarm, perhaps even the voice of God himself proclaiming from the heavens above, "That's it. Game over. Let there be darkness. . . ."

Jonah and Katherine had experienced something like that—only without the voice of God—back in 1600 when things really got messed up. They'd experienced the sensation that time itself was splitting in half back in 1611, at the moment that they now worried that Albert Einstein had discovered.

But the world around Jonah right now didn't seem to have changed that much. A gentle breeze rustled the leaves high overhead. Otherwise, everything was quiet.

Quiet? Jonah thought.

Mileva had stopped shrieking.

She was staring straight at Emily, her eyes burning with intensity.

"You look . . . a little like Albert," Mileva said softly. "Around the mouth. And maybe the nose. And . . ." She laid her hand gently on Emily's head. "Your hair is just like mine was at your age." She turned back to Jonah and Katherine. "How? She survived the scarlet fever and then . . . how could this even be possible?"

"You believe it?" Katherine asked incredulously.

"Is this any more incredible than invisibility? Or my child, who is too ill to walk, vanishing from my side in the blink of an eye?" Mileva asked. "Or than scientists saying the whole universe is bathed in an invisible ether, which light flows through?"

"Is that a yes or a no?" Jonah asked.

Mileva made a sound that might have been a chuckle, if she hadn't looked so serious.

"Let's just say that I am suspending disbelief until I hear all the explanations," she said. "I will listen with an open mind."

Jonah and Katherine both opened their mouths. Then, just as quickly, they both shut them.

"Well?" Mileva asked, narrowing her eyes. "Explain."

"I think," Emily said slowly, "this is such a strange situation, we are all trying to figure it out. To figure out *how* to explain."

Mileva looked back at Emily again, seeming to drink in the sight of her.

"She can even speak—was that *English?*" Mileva asked.

Jonah realized that Emily hadn't gotten the translation vaccines that eliminated language problems for him and Katherine. He hadn't really bothered to think about how many languages and dialects they'd managed to understand since they'd started following Mileva across Europe. He'd barely noticed that they'd been talking with Mileva in German all along. But that would explain part of the reason that Emily kept looking at them with such a dazed expression.

"I only know as much Serbian as Lieserl would have, at eighteen months," Emily explained apologetically. "But I do know some German from school. I just don't speak it very well."

Somehow, she'd managed to switch into German to say that.

"My daughter heard little but Serbian from my family. But—German school?" Mileva asked, looking puzzled all over again. "Where—?"

"Oh, brother," Jonah muttered, because this added a whole other layer of complications to explain.

Mileva seemed to have decided to focus on the emotion of the moment, rather than the explanations. She reached out to touch Emily's cheek.

"To think that I agonized over missing so much of your first year and a half," Mileva murmured. "Your first tooth, your first step, your first word . . . This is better than losing you entirely, but—how much more have I missed? How old are you?"

"Thirteen," Emily said softly.

"Thirteen," Mileva repeated. "Another eleven and a half years gone . . ." Alarm broke over her face. "Did that much time pass somehow while I thought I spent only moments out in these woods?" She glanced quickly back at Jonah and Katherine. "The two of you did not seem to age, but you are strange beings, perhaps not subject to the rules of time . . ." Her panic seemed to grow. She pressed her hands to her own face in dismay. "Did eleven and a half years pass for the whole rest of the world while I was here? Have I been away from my family that long? Away from my Albert?"

Jonah saw that she was working out a Rip van Winkle– type theory to explain Emily's appearance. He couldn't let her keep thinking that.

"No," he assured. "Eleven and a half years didn't pass for anyone but, uh, Lieserl. And that's not exactly the right explanation about her but, uh, it's close enough. Just don't worry. It's still nineteen-oh . . ." He realized he still didn't know exactly which year they were in. "You know," he said. "It's still the same year it was when we left your parents' house and walked out here. It's still the same day."

"It's 1903, then," Mileva said, peering at him closely. "It's still 1903, right?"

Something bothered him about that date, but he didn't have time to analyze it. He concentrated on looking truthful and honest and trustworthy as he gazed back at Mileva and said, "Right."

"Then . . . ," Mileva said, her gaze jerking back to Emily once more. "This might make things easier. You can come back to Switzerland and live with me and Albert, and no one would ever suspect. . . . We can say you're a different relative. A cousin, a niece . . ."

"Um, well, that's not quite . . . ," Jonah began. How did you tell someone that living with her own daughter would probably ruin time forever?

"Don't worry," Mileva said. "If you can't figure out how to explain any of this, Albert can. He'll understand it."

"No!" Jonah and Katherine said together.

"You can't tell any of this to Albert Einstein!" Jonah added for emphasis.

"But—he is my husband," Mileva said. "How could I keep this secret? About our own child?"

"He's too important," Jonah tried to explain.

Mileva's expression soured.

"You're someone else who believes that everything must be sacrificed for the good of a *man*?" she asked. "Even his own daughter?"

Jonah squinted at her. That wasn't what he'd been saying. Was she calling him sexist or something? Did she think he meant it was just because Einstein was male?

"No, I—," Jonah began. He shook his head. With that motion and his narrowed eyes, the glow of the Lieserl tracer on the ground seemed to intensify. Was she getting better?

No, wait, Jonah thought. *I'm not just seeing Lieserl's tracer. I'm seeing Mileva's, too, bent over her.*

Mileva's tracer was gathering her daughter into her arms. She held the child tightly against her chest and rocked back and forth. She had her head tilted back, tears streaming down her face. Though Jonah couldn't hear a sound, he could tell that the tracer was sobbing and wailing and screaming at the top of her lungs.

Oh, no, Jonah thought. *Oh, no. Did Lieserl's tracer just die?*

No—that wasn't it. The glow of Lieserl's tracer was dim, but it was still there. And the tracer child was moving its arms and feebly turning its head and—however soundlessly—crying along with its mother.

Jonah turned back to the real, flesh-and-blood Mileva.

"You came out here just to lure me and Katherine away from the house and bargain with us in private, right?" he asked her.

"Uh, right," she said, puzzled all over again.

Now Jonah turned to Katherine.

"So why are we seeing tracers?" he asked.

TWENTY-SIX

"I guess the tracers must mean that Mileva would have brought Lieserl out here even if we hadn't been around," Katherine said slowly. "But—why?"

"What are you two talking about?" Emily asked.

Jonah remembered that this was Emily's first trip to the past, and so far she'd spent almost all of it as a deathly ill toddler. He glanced at Mileva, then switched to English to explain.

"Tracers—those glowing versions of Lieserl and Mileva—they show what people would have been doing if no time travelers had intervened," he said. "So what else would Mileva have come here for, besides talking to us?"

"That tracer person—she was reading a letter to her little girl a minute ago," Emily said.

Jonah guessed that Emily must have inherited her mother's powers of observation rather than her father's.

Jonah himself certainly hadn't noticed such a tiny detail in the midst of real people yelling and jumping around and, oh yeah, meeting a barely recognizable daughter under very odd circumstances. But the Mileva tracer was indeed clutching a tracer letter against her child's back. A tracer envelope lay crumpled on the ground.

"That's Albert Einstein's handwriting, isn't it?" Katherine asked, glancing at it.

The real Mileva opened her mouth, and Jonah could tell that she was about to complain about them speaking English, which she didn't understand. She was looking as if she didn't trust them again.

"Did you just get a letter from your husband?" Jonah asked her, switching back to German.

"Yes, the maid brought it to me when the doctor left," Mileva said. "It's right here in my pocket." She patted her skirt, and for the first time Jonah noticed the white edge of an envelope sticking out slightly. "I haven't read it yet. I was saving it. I think my husband will be happy. I'd just told him that I—"

Just then Jonah heard a shout from the direction of the road.

"Mileva! Mileva, where are you?"

"That's my father," Mileva said. She glanced around quickly, as if to remind herself that Jonah and Katherine—and Emily—were fully visible right now, and could easily be discovered. She looked down at the Elucidator still clutched in her hand, then shook her head. She seemed to be deciding that she didn't want to make them invisible again. Maybe she just didn't think she had time for that.

"I'll go send him away," she said, struggling to her feet. "All of you—hide!" Her eyes lingered on Emily. "As much as he'd love to see you . . ." She stepped away, holding out the Elucidator for a moment as if to remind them that she still had something they wanted, and they couldn't just run away.

Jonah saw a tracer version of Mileva's father rushing toward them, arriving much faster than the actual man.

So in original time he must have heard Mileva wailing. Something in that letter made her cry so hard he heard her from the roadside.

Mileva limped past Jonah, so close that the bottom of her skirt brushed his ankles. Jonah thought about grabbing the Elucidator from her hands and demanding to be made invisible again. But Mileva would undoubtedly start screaming and fighting against him—he couldn't risk causing such a huge disturbance with Mileva's father so close by.

Maybe there's something else I can do, he thought. *Not about the invisibility, but . . .*

He inched his hand out, below her line of view.

It wasn't the Elucidator he was reaching for.

It was the letter.

TWENTY-SEVEN

Jonah closed his fingers over the corner of the letter that showed at the edge of Mileva's pocket. He drew his hand back—slowly, slowly . . .

This was like pick-up sticks or Kerplunk or Jenga—one of those little-kid games where you had to take what you wanted without making the whole game collapse.

She's going to turn around, Jonah thought. *I'll have to make up some lie about just catching the letter when I saw it falling out of her pocket.*

But Mileva didn't turn around. She took the next step, putting a huge space between her and Jonah. And then she just kept rushing on, scurrying toward her father's shouting.

But Katherine and Emily both saw what Jonah had done. They gaped at him, horrified once more.

"Jonah!" Katherine exclaimed. "When she finds out that you stole—"

"It's just going to make her cry," Jonah said, pointing at the sobbing tracer Mileva. The tracer version of her father huddled over her, trying to comfort her.

Katherine frowned, but didn't say anything else as all three kids crouched down behind the downed log, hiding from the real version of Mileva's father and anyone else who might approach from the road. Once they were in a safe position, Katherine yanked the letter from Jonah's fingers.

"Let me see that," she said. "Since you're going to get us in trouble anyhow, we might as well read it."

Jonah could tell she was dying of curiosity.

"Read it out loud, so we can all hear," Jonah said. He flipped over onto his stomach so he could see over the log. That way he could watch for Mileva or her father coming close even as he listened to Katherine. She had the letter out of the envelope and was unfolding it.

"'Dear Dollie,'" she began in a whisper. Dimly, Jonah realized she was translating it into English as she read, for Emily's benefit. Katherine looked up and explained to Emily, "He means Mileva. She and Albert call each other these silly pet names—it's going to be way embarrassing if they're still doing that when their kids are teenagers."

"Katherine!" Jonah said. "Their kid *is* a teenager now! Emily!"

"Oh, right. Sorry," Katherine said.

"Never mind," Emily said. "I feel like . . . Do you really think we should be reading her mail?"

"Yes," Jonah and Katherine said together.

"But—it's private," Emily objected. "Personal."

Jonah wondered if maybe she was a little too nice to cope with time travel. He wondered how she'd survived middle school back home.

"Yeah, well, the fate of the world could depend on us knowing what's in that letter," Jonah said.

He expected Katherine to roll her eyes and tell Emily, *See how full of it my brother is?* The fact that neither girl challenged him made him feel even worse about their situation.

Katherine went back to reading out loud.

"'I'm not the least bit angry that poor Dollie is hatching a new chick,'" she continued in a hushed voice. She'd adopted a bit of a German accent to imitate Albert's voice. "'In fact, I'm happy about it and had already given some thought to whether I shouldn't see to it that you get a new Lieserl. After all, you shouldn't be denied that which is the right of all women. Don't worry about it, and come back content. Brood on it very carefully so that something good will come of it.'"

Katherine almost dropped the letter.

"Is he for real?" she muttered.

"Hold on, hold on—'hatching a new chick'? Getting 'a new Lieserl'?" Jonah asked. "Does he mean Mileva's going to have another baby?"

"I bet that's what she'd just told Albert. And that's why she kept throwing up on the way here," Katherine said. "She's pregnant."

"She threw up by my bedside, too," Emily said thoughtfully. "I remember thinking, as Lieserl, 'Mama sick too? Mama sick too?'"

Jonah shot her a puzzled look.

"Look, you try thinking with the brain and vocabulary of a toddler," Emily said. "It's not easy."

"But do you see how Albert talks about this?" Katherine said, shaking the letter for emphasis. "'I'm not the least bit angry'—that's not what a man should say when his wife tells him she's pregnant! That's, like, just asking for trouble!"

Great, Jonah thought. *Katherine's in sixth grade and she just got her first boyfriend—and she thinks she's qualified to be a marriage counselor?*

Katherine was still ranting.

"And talking about getting a 'new Lieserl' and how Mileva should 'come back content,' when the original

Lieserl is really, really sick and, for all Albert knows, on the verge of death?" she asked.

"Lieserl *is* on the verge of death," Jonah said, glancing quickly toward the still-sobbing tracers. "She was. Er— would have been."

"What kind of mother is going to come back content from her own child's deathbed?" Emily asked. "What kind of father acts like one kid is pretty much interchangeable with another?"

"You said it!" Katherine agreed fiercely. Then she clapped her hands over her mouth. "I'm sorry! I'm sorry! I forgot, these really are your parents—"

"No," Emily said. "My real mother is a special-ed teacher. My real father works in a factory."

"Back home," Jonah said, because Katherine still didn't look as if she understood. "In the twenty-first century."

"Right," Katherine said.

"Does the letter say anything else?" Jonah asked, because he wasn't sure how long it would take Mileva to send her father away. Their tracer versions were still huddled together right beside the downed log. But he could see nothing of the real people except, far off in the distance, one small corner of Mileva's skirt that wasn't blocked by all the trees.

Katherine looked back at the paper in her hands.

"The second paragraph is all about Lieserl, but I don't quite understand it," she said. "Listen. It says: 'I'm very sorry about what has befallen Lieserl. It's so easy to suffer lasting effects from scarlet fever. If only this will pass. As what is the child registered? We must take precautions that problems don't arise with her later.'"

"So he is worried about Lieserl, after all," Jonah said. "But what does he mean, asking how she's registered? What 'problems' could he be talking about?"

"Scarlet fever can lead to blindness, deafness, brain fever, rheumatic fever, heart problems, kidney problems . . . ," Emily began reciting.

Jonah and Katherine turned to stare at her.

"What?" she said. "I heard the servants talking."

Jonah shook his head.

"I don't think that's what Albert means," he said. He pointed at the letter in Katherine's hand. "It sounds more like he thinks they need to take precautions so that problems don't arise because of how she's registered."

"Registered," Emily said thoughtfully. "What's that mean? A birth certificate? A passport? Why would it matter?"

"Maybe it's in the next paragraph," Katherine said, looking back at the letter and starting to read again. "'Now, come to me again soon . . . ,'" She skimmed ahead, picking out bits and pieces: "'A good little wife shouldn't leave her husband alone any longer. Things don't yet look nearly as bad at home as you think. You'll be able to clean up in short order.'" She jerked her head back. "Sheesh, is he a jerk or what? Sexist! She's here taking care of their deathly ill child and he wants her to, what, come home to clean up his dirty dishes? Wash his socks? 'A good little wife shouldn't leave her husband alone'—bleh! What century does he think this is?"

"The twentieth," Jonah said, rolling his eyes. "It's 1903. I think pretty much everyone was sexist in 1903."

Katherine slugged his arm with a little bit too much force.

"Yeah, well, he's Albert Einstein," she said. "He should be smarter than that."

Jonah didn't want to get into that debate.

"And if we were smarter, we'd know why Albert's never seen his daughter," he said. "We'd know why Lieserl's living with her grandparents."

"I think . . . ," Emily began. She tilted her head thoughtfully to the side. "I think there's something wrong with me. Something the servants whisper about that I don't understand. Some reason the family is ashamed of me. Or—they should be."

Jonah realized she was talking about herself as Lieserl now, and drawing on the little girl's memories. He remembered the defensive way Mileva's father had spoken to the doctor: *My granddaughter is a blessing. She is a gift from God.*

"Oh, no," Katherine said, shaking her head. "Oh, no. Is this one of those times and places where almost nobody values little girl babies? Is that why Albert Einstein's never bothered meeting his daughter—because she's not a son?"

"Shh," Jonah said, because she wasn't being careful to keep her voice down anymore.

"Don't you tell me to be quiet," Katherine said. "This is an outrage!"

She wasn't even keeping her head down now. Jonah pulled her back out of sight behind the log.

"Katherine, you're just guessing. You don't know what any of this means," Jonah protested.

"There," Katherine said, pointing at the paper in her hand. "There in Albert's letter. He says, 'Brood on it very carefully so that something good will come of it.' Don't you think that's code for, 'Make sure you have a boy this time'?"

"*No*," Jonah said emphatically. "Because then why would he talk about giving her a new Lieserl? They wouldn't name a boy Lieserl!"

"But—," Katherine started to object. Emily put her hand over Katherine's mouth.

"Shh!" Emily hissed. "They're coming this way!"

They were. In the few moments that Jonah and Katherine had spent arguing about the meaning of Albert's letter, Mileva and her father had gotten so close that Jonah could hear their voices.

"Papa, really, you don't have to worry," Mileva said.

"Mileva, my child, you're not strong," her father said. "In your condition, you shouldn't carry Lieserl around the house, let alone—"

His voice stopped so suddenly Jonah couldn't stand it. He had to know what had happened. Had Gary or Hodge or JB or some other time traveler suddenly appeared out of nowhere? Had Mileva accidentally let him see the Elucidator? Had Jonah or Katherine or Emily left behind some evidence of the twenty-first century when they'd scrambled behind the log? A shoelace, a scattering of glitter from Katherine's shirt, an iPod or cell phone one of them had forgotten they were carrying?

Jonah dared to raise his head just a little, just enough to peek over the top of the log.

Mileva's father was bending over, picking up something from the ground: a blanket. The blanket that had been wrapped around Lieserl. The blanket that Emily had left behind when she'd separated from her tracer.

"Where is she?" he asked, sounding completely

bewildered. "She couldn't have crawled away—somebody stole her!"

"Papa, no, there's something else going on—I can't really explain, but—you have to trust me on this!" Mileva begged.

Mileva's father touched his daughter's forehead.

"You're feverish," he said. "You don't know what you're saying. We have to organize a search party. We'll have every able-bodied man in the village search every inch of ground for miles around . . ."

Katherine grabbed Jonah's arm. He turned and saw the panicked look on her face. He could tell she was thinking, *What are we going to do? We're not invisible anymore! If they have people searching every inch of ground for miles around, someone's bound to find us!*

He shook his head at her. He hoped she could tell that he was thinking, *Don't worry. Mileva will figure out some lie to tell her father, some way to keep him from starting that search party. Or, if she has to, she'll make us invisible again.*

But he didn't hear Mileva speaking up or objecting. He peeked over the edge of the log just in time to see why not.

Mileva was swaying side to side. She had her mouth open slightly, as if she wanted to say something. But she was so pale—ghostly pale, practically tracer pale. Her eyes rolled back in her head.

And then she fell to the ground in a dead faint.

TWENTY-EIGHT

"Mileva!" her father cried. "Oh, my poor child!"

He bent over and picked her up.

Okay, at least we'll have some time to figure out what to do while he's taking care of her, Jonah thought.

But, with Mileva in his arms, he immediately began running back toward the road and screaming out, "Help! Somebody help us! My granddaughter is missing! My daughter is ill!"

He'd barely paused to take a breath before Jonah could hear someone shouting back to him.

"Milos! Milos Maric, is that you?" a voice cried.

And then another: "What can we do?"

And another: "I'll alert the others!"

I guess this is how 911 worked before there was a 911, Jonah thought.

He scrambled up, hoping nobody was close enough yet to see him.

"Hurry!" he told Emily and Katherine. "We're going to have to run!"

He glanced back toward the road. Already he could see someone advancing toward them with a torch, an eerie glow in the darkening gloom.

"No," Emily said, shaking her head stubbornly. "We run, we'll make too much noise. They'll chase us. And when they catch us . . ."

She only had a small child's memories of what it was like to live in this place in 1903. But did she know something about how they'd treat strangely dressed outsiders suspected of kidnapping Albert Einstein's daughter?

Jonah really wished it were Gary and Hodge facing that fate, not him.

"So if we don't run, what are we going to do?" Katherine asked. "There's nowhere around here to hide. Not well enough."

"What about Lieserl's tracer?" Jonah said reluctantly. "If Emily just rejoins it long enough to let the villagers find her, they'll call off the search. We can pull her out again right afterward. It's a gamble, but . . ."

But when he glanced toward the place where Mileva's

tracer had been sobbing and clutching Lieserl's tracer, both of them had vanished.

"Oh, no. Oh, no," he muttered. "Did *both* tracers die?"

"No," Katherine said, shaking her head emphatically. "Didn't you see? Mileva rejoined her own tracer right before she fainted. And when her father carried her off, there was just the faintest bit of tracer light with them—in original time, he would have been carrying Lieserl, too."

"I saw it too," Emily murmured.

Jonah shook his head, trying to clear it. But that only allowed him to focus better on the crowd gathering in the distance. He could see several torches now.

"We have to run," he said. "It's the only thing we can do."

"No," Emily said. "We can climb." She pointed toward the tops of the trees around them. "Nobody's going to look for a missing toddler up there."

It made sense.

"Right," Jonah said. He flicked Katherine's shoulder. "Why didn't we think of that?"

"Maybe because we're not related to Albert Einstein?" Katherine said.

Now that they had a plan, they were almost leisurely selecting the best trees to climb, the best strategies for getting to the top. Jonah gave Emily and Katherine each a leg up to reach the first branch of the tallest, broadest tree they could find. He chose a neighboring tree with low-hanging branches.

"Psst, Jonah!" Katherine hissed across to him. "Just don't think about the crow's nest back on the *Discovery*!"

"I wasn't going to—until you mentioned it!" Jonah grumbled.

On their trip to 1611 they'd found themselves on a sailing ship, and twice Jonah had been forced to climb to the crow's nest near the top of the tallest mast.

Jonah hated heights. On his first climb in 1611 he'd managed to reach the top only because he was so annoyed with Katherine, and that had distracted him from his fear.

Jonah realized he'd gotten halfway up this tree thinking about how annoying Katherine had been in 1611, and how annoying she was now.

Ergh! She did it again! he thought.

He decided that halfway up was far enough. The shadowy trees seemed to gather the darkness around them—or maybe that was just in contrast to the bright torches advancing toward them.

It was only a few moments after Jonah stopped climbing that he saw the first torch reach the spot directly below him. A cluster of three men circled the downed log where Jonah and Katherine and Emily had hidden when Mileva's father came near.

"Something—or someone—was squatting here," one of the men said, pointing down into the leaves. "Squatting here watching the baby lying right over . . . there?"

Jonah froze in fear, his fingers digging into the tree bark. Back in 1600 his friends Brendan and Antonio had been able to look at an indentation in a sandy beach and figure out exactly how many people had once camped there. What if these Serbs were just as talented at reading signs in nature? What if they could look at the pattern of old leaves scattered across the ground and know that three kids were hiding in the trees above them?

But the other two men were shaking their heads.

"Oh, Pavle, you and your imagination," one said. "You look at shadows and think you see signs."

"And it's just a sign your eyes aren't so good anymore," the other one sneered.

"We're not going to find that child out here," the first added. "That's not how this story ends."

"Then why are you bothering to look, Javor?" the one called Pavle asked defensively. "Why not stay home with your own sick children?"

"Because Milos is my friend," Javor replied. "He would do this for me."

"A child like that, maybe it's a mercy if she is gone," the third man said.

"Then, please, don't look too hard," Pavle snapped. He waved his torch. "You know what? I think I'll search on my own."

He moved several steps away and began methodically walking back and forth, searching the ground. The other two men shrugged and moved on.

The searchers showed up in waves, small clusters of them coming within earshot, pausing to examine a supposed footprint or a stray thread, and then moving on. The snippets of conversation Jonah heard only made him more frustrated about everything he didn't know.

"—child from my mother-in-law's village eaten by wolves—"

"Really, what were they going to tell that child once she was old enough to know?"

"—heard voices over here—?"

"Just the wind howling, but—"

Jonah's arms began to ache from holding on to the tree trunk for so long, and still the search continued. His sense of time was messed up once again—while Jonah and Katherine and Emily sat silently in their trees, how long did the searchers keep looking? Three hours? Four? Five?

The last hint of daylight had long vanished, and the torches had flickered down to stubs when Jonah saw the first group finally turn around and head back to the village. All the men walked with a hunched-over, defeated posture; Jonah didn't have to hear anything they said to know that they believed Lieserl Einstein was already dead.

It's not right for all of them to be so depressed, when they tried so hard, Jonah thought. *I wish it were safe to tell them the truth.*

But at the moment it wasn't even safe for him to breathe loudly.

Finally the woods were completely dark. Jonah began shimmying down the tree—a huge challenge in total darkness, especially since Jonah's right leg had gone to sleep and he kept thwacking it against the branches. But finally he was on the ground again. With his hands held carefully out in front of his face so he wouldn't run into anything, he began walking slowly toward the tree where the girls were hidden.

"Katherine! Emily! I think you can come down now!" he whispered. He tilted his head back, trying to aim his voice up into the tree.

"We're coming!" one of them whispered, high above him.

After a few minutes he heard first one thump, then another.

"We're down—where are you?" Katherine asked.

"Walk toward my voice," Jonah said. "It's so dark we're probably going to have to hold on to one another to stay together, getting back."

Suddenly he heard a scratching nearby—the sound of a match being struck? A light flared, yet another torch springing to life. Whoever was holding the torch thrust it toward Jonah.

"Caught you!" a voice cried.

TWENTY-NINE

Jonah sprang back, proving to himself that no one had actually caught him. Or at least—no one was holding him. He blinked, trying to get his eyes to adjust to the sudden light. Where were Katherine and Emily? Where was the person actually holding the torch?

"Give me back my granddaughter!" the voice cried. "Give her back, and leave my family alone, and I'll let you go . . ."

Mileva's father, Jonah thought. Somehow the old man had continued searching after everyone else had given up. Somehow he'd decided that sitting in darkness was the best way to catch his granddaughter's kidnappers.

The torch swung nearer and nearer to Jonah. Could Mileva's father see him?

"Run!" Jonah shouted toward Katherine and Emily.

He took off sprinting into the darkness. Staying together was impossible now.

"I'll meet you there!" he called over his shoulder, hoping Katherine and Emily could hear him. And hoping they'd know he meant back at the house.

Branches jabbed and pricked and poked at him. He was glad they wouldn't have had DNA testing in 1903, because he had to be leaving a trail of blood on the branches and leaves from all the scrapes and scratches on his arms and face. He kept his hands up, protecting his eyes from being stabbed.

And then there weren't any trees around him. The ground dipped before him. Even the grass seemed to vanish—when he stumbled and touched the ground, he felt packed dirt in front of him.

The ditch, Jonah thought. *The road.*

It was still dark, but he could see the dim lights of Novi Sad off to the side.

Jonah crouched down and looked back over his shoulder. Even in the darkness he still held on to some hope that he might catch the slightest glimpse of Katherine or Emily, racing toward him. Or he might hear them.

But all he saw was the torch coming closer and closer. All he heard was Mileva's father yelling, "Stop! Stop! I see you! You can't get away!"

Jonah turned toward Novi Sad and took off sprinting again.

It was easier running on the road and toward lights, but Jonah still kept stumbling and having to right himself, again and again. And, just before he reached the first house on the outskirts of Novi Sad, his brain decided to point out the problem with running past lit-up homes.

You're not invisible anymore, he remembered. *You step into the light, anyone can see you. . . .*

He gulped in air, wondering how he could run back into the woods or out into the fields without Mileva's father tracking him.

Shadows, his mind advised him. *Just stay in the shadows and you'll be fine.*

This part of Novi Sad wasn't like Jonah's neighborhood back home, with streetlights in front of every house and a glow from every porch light. People seemed to have nothing but candles and lamps to push back the darkness. As he ran by and glanced in windows, he could see that even inside crowded homes the flickering flames did little but cast larger shadows.

Like back home when the electricity's out, Jonah told himself. *It's not that there are ghouls or spooks or ghosts around.*

But he could see why Mileva had said the people in her hometown were so superstitious, if they sat around in candlelight every night. All sorts of bad things seemed more likely in the darkness.

Mileva's father hit the edge of the town only five or six paces behind Jonah.

"I found the kidnappers!" he screamed, waving his torch. "One of them's running into Novi Sad right now!"

If someone screamed something like that on Jonah's street back home, Jonah doubted that anyone would hear. People would have their TVs turned up too loud; they'd be on Facebook; their thick windowpanes and heavy air conditioning would shut out the sound.

But people here had their windows open. And Mileva's father's scream seemed to electrify everyone. Within seconds, dozens of people were spilling out their doors— and even their windows. They were brandishing torches again, crying out, "Where is he?" and "We'll catch him!"

How could Jonah possibly find a shadow to hide in when all the shadows were vanishing? And when an angry mob was gathering behind him?

No, make that in front of me, too, Jonah thought despairingly.

He ducked into the space between two houses— deserted houses, he guessed, since they were the only ones still totally dark, with no people spilling out their doors. He didn't know if anyone had seen him yet, but he had to get away from the crowd, had to get away from all those torches. He raced blindly forward, squinting in hopes of seeing the next street, the closest way out. The flames flickered behind him, throwing shadows onto the walls to his right and to his left. And—throwing shadows into midair, directly ahead of him? How could that be?

Jonah blinked, trying desperately to get his eyes to see things differently. But they refused. From the shadows and dim, flickering lights, his eyes kept making out walls to his left and right—and directly ahead of him as well.

He hadn't run into a gap between two houses. He'd run into the courtyard of a single house, a space enclosed by walls on three sides. The only way out was the way he'd come in—a way now blocked by dozens of angry men with flaming torches.

He was trapped.

THIRTY

Jonah was running too fast to stop even when he saw the third wall. He slammed into it, making too much noise—but what did that matter when everyone was going to see him in a few moments anyway?

Look for a window, he thought disjointedly. *Or a door.*

Weren't there any breaks at all in the wall? Any other way to get through?

Jonah spread his hands along the wall, feeling side to side. It was solid in every direction.

JB, this would be a great time to pull me out of 1903, he thought.

But how could JB suddenly have the power to do that, if he hadn't been able to get Jonah out before? What could JB do when he was trapped himself?

Oh, please, God, Jonah thought. *Can't you help?*

Jonah wasn't sure he'd prayed even once during all his

time-travel trips—it had all seemed too strange, too far from anything he'd learned about the way religion worked. But he felt a little steadier just thinking those few words. Steady enough to turn around, and prepare to be caught.

Mileva's father was in the front of the mob of torch-bearing men. He was roaring, "Stop! Stop! Just tell us where she is! Where's my granddaughter?"

Couldn't he start with an easier question? Jonah wondered.

He opened his mouth and tried to think of a good defense: *What are you talking about? I didn't kidnap anyone!* Or, *Hey, buddy. You've got the wrong dude!* (How would that sound in Serbian?) Or . . .

Jonah caught a glimpse of the fury in all the dark faces in front of him. These were men whose own children were dying. These were men who welcomed the chance to chase someone, to take out their own pain and anger on anyone who was running in front of their flaming torches—whether he was guilty or not.

Nothing Jonah might say would make the slightest bit of difference.

Jonah shut his mouth.

Mileva's father was only three steps away. He held his torch high. Some of the ash from his torch blew down onto Jonah's hair, and Jonah brushed it away. He concentrated on trying not to look scared, trying not to look guilty.

Somehow, incredibly, Mileva's father seemed not to have seen him yet. He was still running forward, still screaming. He stopped only inches away from the tip of Jonah's shoe.

"Where is he, Milos?" someone called out from the back of the crowd—too far back to see anything, probably.

"I—I don't know," Mileva's father said, looking around with a baffled expression.

What? Jonah thought. *Is he blind?*

The man's torch was practically touching the wall. Jonah could *hear* the flame roaring beside him. He could feel the heat from the flame on his right ear. There was no way Jonah wasn't completely illuminated, completely visible.

Unless . . ., Jonah thought. *Could it be . . . ?*

He looked down. In the firelight his whole body looked crystalline. The light flowed right through him, leaving no shadow on the wall behind him. Sometime during the chase—or, at least, since he'd climbed that tree and it had gotten too dark for him to see his own hands on the branches—he'd turned invisible again.

How? Jonah wondered. *Did JB do this? Did God?*

He was picturing something like the miracle of the loaves and the fishes—what was the difference between food appearing out of nowhere and Jonah disappearing into nothing?

Then a simpler explanation occurred to him.

Mileva, he thought. *She has the Elucidator. She knows how to turn Katherine and me visible or invisible. She knew her father was organizing a search party. She took care of us.*

Jonah's knees went weak with relief.

No, no, watch out for the torches, he reminded himself. *They can still harm you even if no one can see you.*

But the other men behind Mileva's father weren't rushing forward or thrusting their torches farther into the shadows. They weren't looking very closely at all.

In fact, the man closest to Mileva's father was lowering his torch, putting his arm around the other man's shoulder.

"Milos," he said. "It's been an awful day for you. You're grief-stricken. You want to believe that your granddaughter is still alive. I don't blame you. But face facts, my friend. There's nobody there!"

"I *heard* him!" Mileva's father insisted. "His footsteps running ahead of me—he was there!"

He waved his torch uselessly toward Jonah. Jonah didn't even have to bother dodging it, because there was no energy in the man's efforts now.

"Milos," the man beside him said comfortingly. "There's nowhere anyone could have gone from this courtyard. You must have been hearing things—or hearing the echo of your own running. Look, you should be with your family right now. Your daughter needs you. Let me take you home."

Mileva's father resisted for barely an instant before he let the other man lead him away.

The crowd behind them began to melt away, too. They extinguished their torches and vanished back into poorly lit houses. The darkness and shadows returned.

Jonah let himself sag back against the courtyard wall and draw in the ragged breaths he'd been stifling.

"And what do you think *that's* going to do to time?" a voice asked in his ear. "Another search that was never supposed to happen—and now everyone thinks Mileva's father is seeing and hearing imaginary things when he really isn't . . . "

It was Katherine. She and Emily stood beside him now, both of them equally translucent. Emily kept looking down at her hands in amazement.

"Look, I'm just happy nobody caught me," Jonah said. "Or the two of you. When did you notice that you were invisible?"

"As soon as we stepped out of the woods," Katherine said. "That's why *we* just started tiptoeing and trying not to make any noise."

Jonah shook his head. He really wanted to say, *Yeah, well, I would have done that too, if I'd known I was invisible.*

But—that's right—I was too busy distracting the crazy man with the torch so he wouldn't chase you!

He decided not to go into it right now.

"It had to be Mileva who changed all three of us," he said. "She knew someone would find us if we weren't invisible. Do you think this means she really trusts us now?"

"No," Katherine said. "I think it means she wants to negotiate."

When she put it that way, Jonah saw exactly what she meant. Mileva was reminding them that she had what they wanted—the Elucidator. And they had what Mileva wanted—Emily.

Jonah watched Emily, still staring at her own see-through hands in wonderment. She didn't seem to be listening. But then she spoke, her voice trembling.

"What if the only deal Mileva will make is a straight trade?" Emily asked. "You get the Elucidator, she gets to keep me here in 1903—you wouldn't do that to me, would you?"

"Of course not," Katherine said, almost too quickly. "We can't."

But she turned her face toward Jonah, and even in the shadows Jonah could tell what she was thinking. Because he was thinking the same thing.

What can we possibly do instead?

THIRTY-ONE

They went back to the house where Mileva's family lived. The three of them agreed: Anything they planned to do had to start with talking to Mileva.

They just didn't know what they were going to say.

It was a somber journey they made back through the dark, twisty streets of Novi Sad. Jonah hadn't paid much attention to directions when they were following Mileva away from the house in the first place, and he certainly hadn't been watching for street signs and landmarks dashing back into Novi Sad with an angry, torch-wielding mob behind him. If it had been up to Jonah, they might have been forced to just wander the streets all night, turning corners at random and struggling to find any familiar sight.

Fortunately, Emily seemed to have a good sense of

direction. Or maybe it was a good memory?

"Oh, this is where the servants come to pick up the laundry," she said, stopping near a house with a long row of sunflowers out front. "And I always play with Senka when we're here . . ."

A stricken look came over her face, and she pressed her hands against her cheeks.

"Oh, no!" she said. "I just realized—I must have gotten sick because of Senka! Her face and hands were so hot the last time we came. I hope she's all right!"

Emily tiptoed past the sunflowers and started to peek in one of the windows.

"Emily, no," Jonah said. "You can't do anything to help her anyhow, so—"

The sound of a woman sobbing came from inside the house. She seemed to be wailing, "My Senka! No, not my Senka!"

The doctor said six children died in Novi Sad last night, Jonah thought. *Six. And how many have died so far tonight?*

Emily froze.

"Let's just stick with going back to Mileva's, okay?" Katherine said, gently taking Emily's elbow and steering her back toward the street.

Emily nodded. She walked on for several blocks in silence.

"I'm just not used to children dying, okay?" she finally said. "Back home, you know, there might be someone killed in a car crash, or some poor child getting some awful fatal disease, but here it's like it's not even a surprise, you know? Even when I was thinking as Lieserl, just with a toddler's brain, it was like I knew kids die all the time, like I knew *I* could die . . . "

"I guess they don't have vaccines yet in 1903," Jonah said. "It wasn't that long ago, but—"

"Everything was different," Emily said bitterly. "Everything *is*."

We can't condemn Emily to being stuck in 1903, Jonah thought. *We can't.*

But what if that meant that he and Katherine were stuck there themselves?

They got back to the home of Mileva's parents, and somehow the entire house seemed darker than ever before. As soon as they got close to the front door, they heard the same kind of keening they'd heard back at Senka's. Jonah peeked in a window: Mileva's mother was hugging Mileva's father and sobbing into his shoulder. Other family members and servants clustered around them, sobbing just as hard.

"This just isn't right," Jonah mumbled.

He reached over and scratched against the door—a

sound that might have been made by a branch blowing in the breeze, or might have been someone working up the courage to knock.

A servant strode over to the door and opened it, peering out curiously.

"Tracers!" Katherine hissed in Jonah's ear.

Jonah nodded to show he understood. The servant had left a tracer version of himself huddled against a wall and rubbing his eyes. Several other people looked toward the door, creating a glow of other tracers as Jonah's knock interrupted their mourning.

So everybody would have been crying like this in original time, Jonah thought. *So—Lieserl is supposed to be dead.*

He glanced back at Emily, reassuring himself that *she* was still alive. He felt unsettled. Every other time he and Katherine had been involved with returning missing children to history, they'd pulled out and left the foreign time immediately after the original child would have died. They'd had only the briefest moments of having to watch people mourn someone who wasn't actually dead.

So—stop watching, Jonah told himself. *Get out of here as soon as you can. Go find Mileva.*

"Come on!" he whispered to Katherine and Emily. "Let's get in there while the door's still open!"

The three of them barely managed to brush past the

servant before he pulled the door shut and went back to huddling sadly against the wall. But once Jonah and the two girls were inside the house, it was easy to maneuver around all the mourners. Their actions were slow and ponderous, as if time were stopping for them, too.

No, it's because of their grief, Jonah told himself.

He'd never been to a funeral, never had anyone close to him die. So it was unnerving to be in a room so filled with sorrow. He really wanted to jump up on one of the chairs and scream, "Stop crying! She's not dead!"

You can't, he told himself. *Just focus on looking for Mileva.*

She wasn't anywhere among the mourners gathered in the front room. Jonah silently pointed down the hallway, and Katherine nodded. Emily trailed behind them.

All the doors lining the hall were shut, so they had to gently push open each door and peek in.

Darkness.

Darkness.

Darkness.

"If we ever get out of here, on my next trip through time I'm bringing night-vision goggles," Jonah muttered.

"That doesn't do us much good now, does it?" Katherine asked. She bit her lip. "If every room turns out to be dark, do you think it'd be okay to light a candle and come through here again? Or will we have to wait until morning when the sun comes up to look for Mileva?"

"I don't want to wait," Emily whispered. "Don't you feel like . . . like time is locking into place? Like our chance to change anything is ending?"

"Don't say stuff like that," Katherine scolded.

"Even if it's true?" Emily asked.

Nobody answered. Jonah turned to open the next door. And, this time, there was actually a soft glow in the room, from a lamp turned down low on a bedside table. Jonah tiptoed in.

Mileva lay on the bed. Her eyes were closed, and the light blanket draped over her rose and fell with a regular rhythm, but Jonah couldn't believe that she was truly sleeping peacefully.

He stepped closer to the bed.

"You're faking, aren't you?" he whispered.

In a flash Mileva had the Elucidator out from under the covers, and was crying into it, "Make them visible again!" She dived across the bed and grabbed Emily, wrapping her arms tightly around her daughter's waist.

"Papa!" she screamed. "Papa, come quick!"

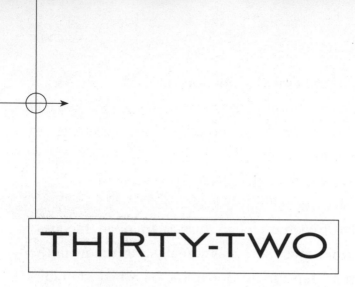

THIRTY-TWO

There was no time.

To the extent that Jonah had planned anything about how to deal with Mileva, he'd expected a long, careful conversation, inching toward getting the Elucidator back without giving away any more information. But now he had only a matter of seconds before Mileva's father—and possibly a lot of other people too—would come bursting in the door.

"Papa!" Mileva screamed again.

Emily was struggling to get away, but Mileva's grip was too tight. Katherine rushed to help, trying to peel Mileva's fingers back to let Emily escape. Jonah thought about joining in.

Wouldn't matter, he thought. *We wouldn't have time to get completely away, out of this room.*

But he didn't run away to hide. He stepped closer to Mileva.

"Please," he said. "Don't do this."

Mileva didn't even look at him. She was entirely focused on holding on to Emily. She had a wild look in her eyes; her hair stood out crazily; she had her teeth clenched in utter determination.

Well, isn't that how my mom would look if she was afraid she might lose me and Katherine? he thought.

"Please," he whispered again. "What do you care about the most? Making sure your dad sees Em—er, Lieserl? Or doing what's best for your daughter?"

Mileva looked at him this time. And then she let go of Emily.

"Hide," she said. "Quick. Crouch down by the other side of the bed. But—don't go away."

She picked up the lamp and hurried toward the door just as it opened wide, her father storming in.

"Mileva, what—"

"Bad dream," Mileva said, looking convincingly dazed.

Jonah crouched down on the opposite side of the bed, safely away from the light. He huddled with Katherine and Emily, who seemed to be shaking with fear.

"Oh, Mileva, the bad dream is real," her father moaned.

Jonah dared to raise his head to see past the tangled

blanket, just to make sure that they weren't coming back toward the bed. Mileva and her father still stood in the doorway, hugging each other.

"Nothing about her life went the way it was supposed to," Mileva mumbled. She was acting as if she couldn't even bear to say Lieserl's name.

"But she was such a gift while we had her," Mileva's father said. "A gift we still want to honor—"

"I'm going back to bed," Mileva said abruptly.

"I'll send a servant girl in to sit with you," her father said.

"No!" Mileva said, her tone sulky now. "I need to be alone! Please, just let me stay alone!"

Her father hesitated, clearly wanting his daughter to change her mind. But finally he murmured, "As you wish."

Mileva eased her father out the door and gently shut it behind him. She stood at the door with her ear pressed against the wood for a few moments—probably listening to make sure he really did walk away. Then she brought the lamp back toward the bed and slumped against the pillows.

"Everyone thinks I have gone mad with grief," she said. "They think my child is dead and I took her body out into the countryside to hide it. So—so that I could deny that she's not still alive."

Jonah had to keep himself from perking up and grinning triumphantly over at Katherine. He was thinking, *Hey, that would be a good cover story to explain why Lieserl/Emily just disappears. Why didn't we think of that?*

But then Emily asked, in the gentlest of voices in her halting German, "They wouldn't arrest you, would they? Are they accusing you of any crime?"

Okay, Jonah thought. *Maybe that's not such a great idea, after all.*

Mileva was staring so intently at Emily that it seemed as if she were trying to develop X-ray vision.

"Where have you grown up, child?" Mileva asked. "Here—or in some foreign land? What do you know of our customs and laws?" She gave a sad laugh. "And how can I know so little about my own daughter?"

Jonah wondered if Mileva really had gone mad with grief. Or, at least, crazy from the strain of having invisible people follow her around and then seeing them become visible and then having her own daughter seem to age eleven and a half years in a single moment . . . .

Emily just kept steadily looking back at Mileva.

"I didn't grow up here," she said simply. "I grew up someplace . . . safer."

"When I was a child, I thought my home was the safest place on the face of the Earth," Mileva said, but now she seemed mostly to be speaking to herself. "And the most limited. I wanted to go out into the greater world, into the world of ideas and knowledge and learning. I was always so excited to leave. I never knew I could become so . . . trapped."

Jonah heard Katherine gulp beside him.

"Then they are going to arrest you?" she asked, sounding indignant. "That's not fair! We could testify for you, if you want—"

Mileva snorted.

"I'd like to see what story you'd come up with, that anyone around here would believe," she said. She shook her head. "No one is going to arrest me. Not when my father is Milos Maric, one of the most important men in town. Not when Lieserl was . . . born the way she was born."

Jonah looked at Emily. As far as he could tell, she looked like a perfectly normal thirteen-year-old girl. Why was Mileva making it sound as if there was something strange about her? Something shameful?

"How was I born?" Emily asked softly. "What do you mean?"

Mileva gaped at her.

"You don't know?" Mileva asked. "You've lived to the age of thirteen without the shame following you, without the whispers . . . Where did we send you, Albert and I? What have we done?"

Emily squinted at Mileva.

"Where do you think that I came from?" she whispered.

Mileva waved this question aside.

"Isn't it obvious?" she asked. "My daughter, now, is not supposed to be even two years old yet. You are thirteen. So, of course. You come from the future. Or—some alternative future, from a split in time. My husband knows all about that."

Jonah glanced quickly toward Katherine. *Did* Einstein know that much?

"What if you are the proof of my husband's theories?" Mileva asked, still staring at Emily. "Was he the one who sent you back from the year nineteen . . . 1915?" She held up the Elucidator. "Did he invent this? Did I help?"

The way Mileva talked, Jonah could almost picture everything she described. It seemed likely—probable, even. More probable than Emily being kidnapped from time, growing up a century out of place, then returning as a teenager when she was supposed to still be a toddler.

A dead toddler, Jonah reminded himself, giving himself chills.

"So," Mileva continued in an even tone. "How are we all doing in 1915? How did we manage to escape the shame?"

There was that word again.

Jonah cleared his throat.

"If you've helped your husband with his time experiments, then you understand that it's dangerous to know too much about the future," he said.

Mileva ignored Jonah and kept staring at Emily.

Emily stared back.

"Shame," she repeated. "*What* shame? What's wrong with me?"

"Nothing," Mileva said sharply. "Nothing at all. It's what I did, what your father and I did . . . ." She clenched her fists. "If only . . . No, no, I can't tell you, can't let you think for an instant that *you* should be ashamed."

"What did you and Albert *do*?" Katherine asked. "Kill someone?"

"No," Mileva said, shaking her head violently. "No. It was just—"

She broke off, because someone was tapping on the door.

"Mileva," her father called softly. "Can I come in? I have some good news."

Jonah and Katherine and Emily exchanged quick glances. At once, all three of them began to scramble away from the light, toward the shadows in the corners of the room.

Good news? Jonah thought. *Good?*

For a moment he wondered if they'd misunderstood

everything. What good news was possible?

Mileva scrambled up from the bed, carrying the lamp back toward the door.

"Yes?" she said, swinging the door open.

"We sent word to Albert," Mileva's father said. "We just got his reply—he's coming to comfort you. He's on his way now. You and your husband can grieve together."

At that exact moment a tracer version of Mileva came dashing into the room and threw herself across the bed, sobbing. She clutched a thin, official-looking piece of paper. Jonah dared to inch close enough to read the boldface words on the paper:

No. I can't come —Albert

Jonah looked back and forth between the ghostly, sobbing tracer Mileva on the bed and the slightly more hopeful real version standing by the door. His head spun.

Albert isn't supposed to come here to mourn his daughter, Jonah thought.

Maybe in original time Albert hadn't thought there was anything he could do when he heard his daughter was dead. But circumstances were different now—now Albert had undoubtedly been told that Lieserl had vanished and was only presumed dead. And Mileva had supposedly gone mad with grief, and maybe wouldn't be capable of traveling back to Switzerland by herself. . . .

So those changes were enough to change Albert's plans? Jonah thought. *Is it because he's so worried about his wife and daughter? Or . . . is it because Albert is thinking about time travel now, instead of whatever he was supposed to be thinking about? Has he figured out that Lieserl's "disappearance" is connected to time travel too?*

Jonah felt prickles of dread. He remembered the long, long trip from Switzerland to Novi Sad. It seemed too far for Albert Einstein to travel out of place, out of the path of original time.

Every time he pictured Albert making that journey, he pictured him falling off the globe completely, falling out of history.

Or falling into a completely different history and taking the whole rest of the world with him.

"This isn't right," Katherine whispered behind him. "This can't happen."

"But what can we do to stop it?" Jonah whispered back.

THIRTY-THREE

"You can't tell Albert the truth," Jonah said to Mileva as soon as her father left the room again.

"Of course I'll tell him the truth," Mileva said, glaring back at Jonah. She swayed slightly, looking dizzy and nauseated and pale. She clutched the bed frame and eased herself back into a seated position, mostly blocking Jonah's view of her sobbing tracer. Now she looked strong enough to keep arguing. "This isn't like with my father . . . This is my husband we're talking about. Lieserl's father. We tell each other everything. We'll figure out what to do about all this, together. He'll understand even the details that my brain keeps tripping over."

She waved her hand vaguely, in a way that seemed to indicate Emily and the Elucidator and even the keening of the mourners still out in the front room of the house.

"But he's not supposed to understand," Jonah said. "He's not supposed to know about any of this. It could ruin everything."

"Oh, piffle," Mileva said. She seized the blanket on her bed and shook it out. "You're a child—an amazing child, even, who's known invisibility and . . . and time travel? Have you traveled through time along with my daughter?" She gazed speculatively at Jonah, but didn't wait for an answer. "You've seen and done these amazing things, and yet you sound like some of the old men in my village, who claim that humans are not meant to know the miracles of science, not meant to see by electric lights, not meant to move about by automobile, not meant to see the bones of their own hands revealed to them by X-rays . . . It's only ignorance and fear that make you think that way! Once people learn more, once people understand—you'll see! Knowledge and science will bring us such enlightenment!"

Jonah squinted at Mileva. She looked the same as she had before: a somber, plain woman who was probably more than twice Jonah's age. She was definitely a grown-up, and he was still definitely a kid. But for a moment he felt a million years older than her.

Doesn't she know about nuclear weapons? He wondered. *Doesn't she know that cars brought pollution, and even X-rays can give you cancer if you have too many of them?*

No. She wouldn't know about any of those problems.

In 1903, Mileva Einstein was still living in an age where people could believe that scientific advances would bring nothing but good.

How could Jonah tell her any different when her own husband was going to come up with ideas that helped cause some of those very advances—and problems?

Jonah looked desperately toward Emily and Katherine.

"We know your husband is a genius at science," Katherine said soothingly. "He'll do what he thinks is best for science. But are you sure he'll do what's best for your daughter?"

"He will!" Mileva said, but now her voice was shrill and defensive.

Katherine began drawing something out of the pocket of her blue jeans. Jonah realized it was the letter from Albert to Mileva that they'd read out in the woods. The letter Mileva was supposed to read and cry over with her dying daughter.

"You probably forgot about Albert's letter, with everything else that's been going on," Katherine said. Now she sounded almost apologetic, as if she regretted bringing it up. "But we saw it, and, well, he doesn't really sound like he cares that much about Lieserl."

"Give me that," Mileva said, snatching the letter from Katherine's grasp and yanking it from its envelope. She scanned it silently.

"I'm sorry," Katherine whispered.

But the letter that had sent Mileva's tracer into hysterics out in the woods didn't seem to faze Mileva in the least now.

She looked up with a shrug, her eyes completely dry.

"Albert is better with numbers than words," she said. "Sometimes when he's in a hurry, writing a letter, he doesn't say what he really means. But I know. He's coming here, isn't he? Doesn't that mean more than mere words?" She gazed toward Emily. "You'll see. When you meet him, when you meet your father . . . when the three of us are finally together . . ."

Emily was shaking her head.

"I don't think it's supposed to happen like that," she said softly. She glanced toward Jonah and Katherine. "Right?"

"This is out of your control," Jonah told Mileva. He pointed at Emily. "She can just run away if she wants to, you know?"

"If you try to force her and Albert together, that's what will happen," Katherine agreed.

Jonah felt a burst of inspiration.

"In fact," he said, "she'll run away if you don't call Albert right now and tell him not to come to Novi Sad. Tell him to go back to Bern. You have to do that."

Mileva gaped at him.

"And how am I supposed to 'call' my husband when

he's on a train hundreds of miles away?" she asked.

Emily and Katherine were both frowning and shaking their heads at Jonah.

Oh, yeah, Jonah thought. *No cell phones. There's no way to stop Albert.*

It was dizzying to think about that—the fact that Albert Einstein, in transit, was completely unreachable, completely out of touch. Jonah's parents had talked about how, before cell phones, the whole world was like that. But time travel kept reinforcing how terrifying that must have been on a daily basis.

"Never mind," Jonah mumbled.

"I could still run away," Emily said quietly, glancing uncertainly at Mileva. "I don't want to—I don't want to treat you like you're my enemy. I want us to figure out how to work things out together. But . . ."

"But what you want—you just can't have that," Katherine said. "You can't tell your husband everything you know about your daughter. You can't let him meet his daughter who's eleven years older than she should be now—you just can't. It's impossible."

"Really," Mileva said flatly. She gritted her teeth. "Did you know that when I was younger, people told me a girl would never be allowed to study physics? Did you know that people said someone like me—a girl who limped, who was too old, who'd spent her whole life studying—would never be anything but an old maid? And, certainly, someone like *Albert* would never marry me?" She clenched her fists angrily. "I don't like it when people tell me something is impossible!"

"But some things really can't happen," Jonah said. "Or— they shouldn't, because there are too many dangerous consequences."

Katherine sank down into one of the chairs near the bed.

"We've got hours and hours before Albert gets to Novi Sad," she said. "We've got all the time in the world to figure out how to handle this. There are three of us and only one of Mileva—we've got the upper hand."

"That's what you think," Mileva said.

She shoved one of her clenched fists down into the pocket of her dress. Dimly, Jonah realized that that was probably where she'd tucked the Elucidator.

What if she's so mad at us she decides to destroy it? he wondered.

"Hey, hey, don't—," Jonah began, lunging toward Mileva.

But Mileva wasn't lifting the Elucidator in order to smash it against the floor. She wasn't throwing it against the wall. She was speaking into it.

"Skip us forward in time!" she commanded the Elucidator. "Skip us forward to the moment when Albert opens that door!"

THIRTY-FOUR

Jonah hadn't even thought about that as a possibility. Never in a million years would he have thought of Mileva trying to use the Elucidator in quite that way, to outsmart them.

She'll see, he thought. *She'll find out for herself that the Elucidator is more complicated than that, that you always have to be careful about what you tell it . . .*

But even as his brain was hiccupping out that thought, his body jerked out of his control. He had a brief sense of weightlessness, of hovering in midair.

No—of falling.

I jumped, he told himself. *I was lunging to grab the Elucidator from Mileva's hand.*

That didn't explain why he seemed to take too long to land. That didn't explain why the dim, lamp-lit room was suddenly bright and airy and open, with sunlight streaming in through every window. That didn't explain why Mileva's sobbing tracer, sprawled across the bed, had completely vanished.

And that didn't explain why, a split second later, Jonah heard the doorknob rattle, the door itself creaking open.

"Hide!" he called out to Katherine and Emily, even as he himself hit the floor and rolled. He tried to scramble under the blankets hanging down from the bed.

"Albert!" Mileva cried delightedly. She leaped down from the bed and raced for the door.

Jonah couldn't help turning around to look. It was too late to get out of the way, anyhow. He might as well see what was going on.

Albert Einstein stood in the doorway looking rumpled and travel-weary. He squinted confusedly at Mileva.

Because the Elucidator sped him forward through time too and he's disoriented? Jonah wondered. *No—because he expected to find his wife sobbing over their dead daughter, not beaming like all her dearest wishes have just come true.*

"Mileva?" Albert asked hesitantly. He was looking only at his wife. He hadn't broadened his gaze to notice Jonah or Katherine or Emily. He was too focused.

He smiled uncertainly.

"I—I brought you some math problems to check," he said. "To cheer you up."

He held out a sheaf of papers.

Mileva laughed. She took the papers but didn't even look at them, throwing her arms around her husband instead.

"Thank you, but there's no need for that," she said. She kissed him. "I have something even better to show you. Someone."

She stepped to the side and took his hand, as if she planned to lead him straight to Emily.

"You finally get to meet our Lieserl," she said, tugging on his hand.

"I—," Albert began.

Jonah couldn't have said which he noticed first: the way Albert's voice just ended, the single syllable, "I," not even fully formed, or the bafflement and worry that flooded over Mileva's face.

She stopped moving forward, stopped pulling Albert toward Emily. Mileva hesitated, then turned and looked back at her husband, who had stopped halfway in and halfway out of a particularly bright sunbeam. He was close enough to Jonah that Jonah could see the way Albert's forward motion had displaced the dust motes dancing in the sunlight. But the dust motes weren't dancing anymore. They weren't moving at all. They hung suspended in midair, completely still, just as Albert stood completely still, one foot jutted out, one arm stretched toward Mileva. It wasn't natural to stop in such an unbalanced pose. Under normal circumstances Jonah didn't think anyone would be able to hold that stance for more than an instant.

But Albert held it, proving that these weren't normal circumstances. Albert stood unnaturally frozen, and the dust motes stood unnaturally frozen, and—Jonah felt certain—all of time stood frozen along with them.

Mileva began to scream.

THIRTY-FIVE

"What happened?" she shrieked. "What's wrong with him? What happened to my husband?"

"Calm down," Jonah said. "Nothing's wrong with him. Something's wrong with time."

Like that was supposed to be a comforting thought? *No, no, don't worry. Your husband's fine. It's just time itself that's ruined. No big deal.*

"Why isn't Mileva frozen too?" Katherine asked. She was still sitting in the chair on the other side of the bed. She'd evidently had no time to move at all. "Back home when time stopped, only time travelers could . . . oh."

Jonah figured things out at the same time as his sister: The reason Mileva wasn't frozen was that she was a time traveler now too. She'd become one when the Elucidator skipped all of them ahead to the moment when Albert arrived.

"Could someone please explain what's going on?" Emily asked in a small voice.

She was perched on the edge of the bed, on the side away from the door. Like Katherine, she clearly hadn't had enough time to hide. She was sitting so still that Jonah almost could have believed that Emily was as frozen as Albert.

Jonah looked back and forth between the two of them: Emily on the bed and Albert, frozen mid-turn, moving toward her.

"Hold on just a minute," Jonah said. "Emily, stay right where you are."

He got up and went over to stand behind Albert. By standing on his tiptoes, Jonah could look over Albert's shoulder and see the room exactly as Albert had seen it a moment earlier.

Emily was still out of his line of vision. But Jonah turned his head just a fraction to the left, a hair's breadth difference of positioning. And then he could see her profile—a profile that looked oddly like Albert's own.

"Time stopped to keep Albert from seeing his daughter," Jonah announced, stepping back around the man.

Mileva's screams turned into a gasp.

"No," she moaned. "So—now even time is conspiring against me? Time itself won't let me have my husband and my daughter together?"

"I don't think it's anything personal," Katherine said. "It's just that—Emily wouldn't be here if it weren't for time travel, and she certainly shouldn't be thirteen years old right now. And since some of Einstein's theories are connected to time travel, maybe it's too much of a paradox for him to see his theories proved before he's even thought of them."

Or has time changed so much that now he's never going to come up with the theories he's supposed to have? Jonah wondered. *What if that's the real reason time stopped? What if there's no way to fix it?*

Jonah didn't like scaring himself like that.

"Let's test things out," Jonah said, managing to keep his voice steady in spite of himself. "Mileva, get back into the position you were in a minute ago, when you were pulling Albert toward your daughter. Emily, when I give you the signal, could you scoot over about, I don't know—four or five inches?"

Mileva squinted at him suspiciously for a moment, but then she got back into place. Jonah stepped around behind Albert a second time. And then he motioned to Emily.

Emily leaned slowly to the side, away from Albert. At the same time, Albert leaned forward ever so slightly, his head turning toward Emily. The dust motes in the sunlight danced away from Albert. It was as if Emily's motion caused all the other movements.

And then everything stopped again, Albert's face turned just to the point where the next instant would have brought Emily into view.

Mileva yanked harder than ever on Albert's arm.

"No!" she screamed. "No! It can't be!"

She put her hands on Albert's face and seemed to be trying to turn his head. Maybe it felt like trying to move stone; maybe she was afraid of hurting him. After only a moment she changed strategies. She ran toward the bed and grabbed Emily by the arm, pulling her straight toward Albert. Mileva clutched the back of Emily's head and pressed the girl's face close to Albert's. They were nose to nose, eye to eye. If time started up again, Albert would have to be completely blind not to see his daughter before him.

If time ever starts up again . . ., Jonah thought. *If Mileva hasn't just made that impossible . . .*

He grabbed Mileva by the shoulders and jerked her away. She was still holding on to Emily, so Emily jerked back, too.

"Stop it!" Jonah yelled at Mileva. "That's just making things worse!"

"Look at her!" Mileva yelled at Albert, even as she struggled to break away from Jonah. "Look at *us*! Look at your family!"

"Mileva," Katherine said softly. "I really don't think he can."

Mileva froze momentarily, and then all the fight seemed to go out of her. She sank to the floor as if she'd suddenly lost the ability to stand. She buried her face in her arms.

"I'm going to have to choose," she wailed, her voice only slightly muffled. "I can't have both of you!"

Emily crouched beside Mileva. She stroked the woman's hair, gently smoothing down the locks that had slipped down from her topknot.

"You've always known you would have to make that choice," Emily said softly. "Ever since I was born."

Mileva turned her head and blinked up at her daughter through tear-thickened lashes.

"You know now," Mileva said.

Emily nodded.

"I think so," she said. "I think I figured it out."

Jonah stamped his foot.

"Would someone please tell me what's going on?" he asked. He'd thought time travel and stopped time and time-travel paradoxes were hard enough to keep track of. But this was incomprehensible. What were Emily and Mileva talking about? They were each staring straight into the other's eyes, and nodding sympathetically. Mileva was still crying, but she kind of looked relieved, too. And

Emily was smiling at her through tears of her own and murmuring, "It's okay. It's okay."

"Emily?" Katherine asked, and Jonah was kind of glad to see that his sister was acting as baffled as he felt.

Both Emily and Mileva ignored Jonah and Katherine.

"I thought, when Albert and I got married, then we could have you live with us," Mileva whispered to Emily. "I still hoped . . ."

"Ooooh," Katherine said. "Now I get it."

"What?" Jonah demanded.

"Jonah, we should have figured this out ourselves," Katherine said, her usual confidence back. "We saw Albert and Mileva's marriage certificate back in Bern, remember? From January 1903, right? And this is—what? September 1903? So Albert and Mileva haven't even been married a full year, but Lieserl was nineteen months old, so—she was born before her parents were married."

Katherine had a "Ta-da! Aren't I brilliant?" tone in her voice, but Mileva grimaced over every word.

"So what?" Jonah asked, feeling a little bit as if he needed to defend Mileva.

He remembered lots of awkward conversations with Mom and Dad back home, where they'd say, "When you're grown-up, you should wait until you're married to have kids"—but then follow it with, "Not that there's anything wrong with the *kids* whose parents aren't married."

Because of me, Jonah thought. *Because they figure my birth parents probably weren't married, and that's why they gave me up for adoption. They didn't want to make me feel bad.*

No wonder he'd had such a mental block about what Mileva was so ashamed of. He didn't like thinking about things like that.

"I didn't think people in 1903 had children very often who were—what's it called? 'Out of wedlock'?" Katherine said, in a way that she probably meant to sound like she was being sensitive. Or at least sophisticated.

Mileva flinched.

"Albert and I were going to lead such bohemian lives," she said sadly. She was staring up at the ceiling now, avoiding everyone's gaze. "We didn't want to be like everyone else, didn't want to follow the rules that everyone followed. And, anyhow, we couldn't afford to get married. And . . . Albert's family didn't approve of me. They didn't think I was good enough for him."

"But you're married now," Emily said softly.

"Albert's father gave us his blessing right before he died," Mileva said. She was still staring at the ceiling. "And I thought that would solve everything, but . . . Albert had such trouble finding a job! He's so much smarter than everyone else that people resent him. And . . . he really wasn't very good at job hunting. Then he got the job at the patent office, but it's a civil-service job, and the Swiss can be so prim and proper sometimes . . ." She turned her head and looked straight at Emily. "We can't have him lose that job. Do you understand? We'd have nothing!"

"What?" Katherine said, leaning in toward Emily and Mileva. "You mean that even though you're married now, Albert would be fired if his boss found out you had a baby before your wedding? That's crazy! That's, like, a violation of your rights!"

"Katherine," Jonah said. "I don't think people had those kinds of rights in 1903."

Mileva shrugged hopelessly.

"Albert is certain we can never tell anyone in Bern about Lieserl," she said. "Not without horrible consequences. But I always thought—he's so smart, Albert is, and he's going to publish brilliant papers, I just know it. And then universities will be begging him to work for them, and he can get a job in a place where nobody cares about Lieserl's birth date or our wedding date—or anything. So we were just leaving Lieserl here in Novi Sad for a little while, until things changed, until, until . . ."

"Until time stopped," Jonah said, and now it was Katherine glaring at him, as if he were the most insensitive clod on the planet.

"So I just have to stay out of Albert's sight?" Emily asked. "That's all we have to do to get time to start up again?"

"Are you in his sight lines now?" Katherine asked doubtfully. She stood up and walked toward Albert. "Or is something else messed up now too, that will have to be fixed?"

As she approached Albert, Katherine lifted her arm to the level of his eyes, as if trying to gauge the angle of his vision. She tilted her arm down, sliding it toward Emily.

"He would just be able to see the top of your head, I think," Katherine said. She crouched down beside Emily and Mileva. "Slide down a little more and we'll see—oh, wait a minute, Mileva should get back into position first—"

Katherine put her hand on Emily's shoulder, ready to push her down. At the same time, Katherine reached out her other hand toward Mileva, to help her back up.

Jonah had a sudden flash of memory: him and Katherine and Angela standing on the doorstep at Chip's house, all of them linked together. And then, a split second later, Jonah and Katherine floating back through time. He still didn't understand why that had happened. And that had been four time travelers linked together in the midst of stopped time. But what if the same effect worked when it was only three?

"No! Katherine! Stop!" Jonah screamed.

Maybe there wasn't time for her to hear him and understand and actually do what he said. Katherine wasn't that great at doing what he said under the best of circumstances. So Jonah scrambled forward, reaching for Katherine to yank her back.

Jonah wasn't planning on tripping.

The toe of his shoe caught on the edge of the carpet, and he started falling toward the others. He saw Katherine tighten her grip on Emily's shoulder, steadying herself. Katherine stopped reaching for Mileva and grabbed Jonah's arm instead. Mileva reached out for him too—defensively, because she probably thought he was going to smash down onto her.

"No!" Jonah tried to scream. "Don't touch me! Let go!"

The words were ripped from his mouth even as he felt Mileva's hand on his wrist, even as everything went black, even as he found himself falling and falling and falling . . . .

Falling through time.

Jonah had just caused the very thing he was trying to prevent.

THIRTY-SIX

"Oops," Jonah said.

"You! Are! An! Idiot!" Katherine screamed.

"Okay, okay, agreed," Jonah said meekly. "Can we just move on from you telling me what a huge mistake I made, to figuring out what we're going to do next? Are we all here together? Were we all holding on?"

He squinted into the darkness. Katherine was squeezing his arm a little too tightly on his left, and he twisted his wrist around to ease her grip. Just in case, he grabbed onto her arm, too. That gave him enough confidence to lean out and peer past her. He could just barely make out another person on her other side.

"Emily?" he called. "Mileva?"

"I'm here." Emily's voice came from the dark shape beyond Katherine. "But—I wasn't holding onto Mileva. I was just touching her hair. Did we lose her?"

Now, see, that's the way to act, Jonah wanted to tell Katherine. *Emily's really upset and worried about Mileva, but she's not screaming or anything. She didn't even raise her voice.*

Emily being so calm helped keep Jonah calm too. He looked around cautiously.

"Oh," he said after a moment. "Mileva's right beside me. Mileva?"

Everything had been a jumble from the moment Jonah tripped on the carpet, but he could kind of reconstruct the whole sequence now. They'd started falling the instant Mileva had touched his wrist—that must have been the last link connecting the four of them. But at some point after they'd begun falling through time, Mileva had let go.

Now Jonah grabbed her hand, just to be sure she didn't float away.

"Mileva?" he repeated.

He shook her gently. She didn't answer. Her legs and her free arm flopped helplessly, as limp as a rag doll's.

Jonah lost his Emily-influenced sense of calm.

"What happened to her?" Jonah asked frantically. "What if—what if this killed her?"

He was so sorry for tripping. He was so sorry for everything he'd done wrong leading up to this moment. Did it go back to him and Katherine deciding to walk out of school, back in their own time?

Sheesh, what if all those stupid lectures at school are right, and skipping school is the first step toward really awful stuff? Like killing Einstein's wife?

He realized he couldn't *really* believe that Mileva was dead, if he was thinking such flippant thoughts.

Emily—who seemed to be a natural at the weightlessness of floating through time—swung around and felt Mileva's wrist. Then she put her hand under Mileva's nose.

"She has a pulse and she's still breathing," Emily said. "So she's not dead. I think she just fainted—you know, with being pregnant, she's more susceptible to that. Remember, she fainted out in the woods, too."

"You should be a doctor," Jonah said admiringly.

"Because I can tell if someone's alive or dead?" Emily asked.

"No, because you stay calm in emergencies—unlike certain other people," Jonah said, turning to glare at Katherine.

"Well, if certain people weren't constantly causing disasters by being total klutzes—," Katherine began.

"Oh, hey, can you save that for later?" Emily asked. "We're traveling through time again, aren't we? Do either of you have any idea what we're headed toward? Can we come up with any sort of plan?"

It's easier just to argue, Jonah thought.

But Emily made him feel like a misbehaving little kid. He dutifully switched to looking around. The freaky emptiness of Outer Time was familiar to him now, but it was still unnerving.

"We're definitely going a lot farther than we did when Mileva skipped us ahead to Albert's arrival," Jonah said. "That was so quick, I barely even felt the time travel."

"Yeah, I think you're right," Emily said. "But are we going forward in time, or back?"

"I—can't tell," Jonah said, and that was unnerving too. "What do you think, Katherine?"

That was his olive branch, letting her have the chance to act smarter than him.

But she shook her head.

"I can't tell either," she said. "Doesn't it kind of feel like we're falling *sideways*?"

"That's not going forward or back in time, then," Jonah said. "That's going—"

"Out of time," Katherine finished for him. "To a time hollow." She'd accepted his peace offering. And she seemed to like the conclusion they'd both reached. Even in the near-complete darkness, Jonah could see a grin on her face. "Don't you think it will probably be the time hollow where JB—"

But before she could finish her sentence, the air rushed

up at them, the sensation of smashing through time accelerated, and all sorts of strange forces tore at Jonah's body. And then all four of them landed in a heap.

Jonah just wanted a moment to catch his breath, but Katherine was already lifting her head, looking around.

"Yes!" she cried out. "I was right! We found JB! We're in the same time hollow as him!"

That was enough to get Jonah to raise his head and look too. It kind of made sense. If JB had been watching Albert Einstein in 1903, then he must have been in the nearest time hollow. That would be a logical place for Jonah and the others to fall to, if they had to fall out of time.

As Jonah began craning his neck, an unpleasant thought struck him, one that kept him from cheering as loudly as Katherine. JB had told them that he was trapped in a time hollow. Would Jonah and the others just end up being trapped too?

JB will figure out what to do, Jonah told himself. *Now that we're all together again, we'll be fine.*

Then Jonah got his first glimpse of JB.

JB was sitting with his back to Jonah and the others. He hadn't turned around at the sound of four people falling into his room, thudding against the ground. He hadn't turned around at Katherine's triumphant shriek, "Yes! I was right!" He didn't turn around now, even as Jonah cried out, "JB? What's wrong? Can't you hear us?"

In fact, JB was sitting completely still. His shoulders didn't rise and fall with even the faintest hint of breathing. No muscle twitched; no foot tapped; not even a single hair on his head shifted position in even the tiniest breeze.

Jonah didn't know how it was possible, in a time hollow. Or how this could have happened to JB.

But it certainly looked as if time had stopped for him, too.

THIRTY-SEVEN

"No!" Katherine screamed. "JB! Wake up!"

"He isn't sleeping," Jonah said wearily.

Awkwardly, he managed to stand up and weave toward JB. Jonah couldn't have said if it was timesickness that made him feel so sluggish, or just shock. He waved his hand in front of JB's unseeing eyes. Nothing. JB looked just like Albert Einstein had, frozen back in 1903, or like Jonah's science teacher had, frozen in the twenty-first century. JB's mouth was open, as if he'd been stopped in the midst of speaking. His brown eyes seemed to be focused very precisely, but the pupils didn't shrink or grow even when Jonah shaded JB's eyes with his hand or pulled his hand back completely.

"Is *he* dead?" Emily asked, in such a small, careful voice that it jolted Jonah.

"Oh—no," Jonah said. At least they had that to be grateful for. "I'm pretty sure time has just stopped for him. Somehow."

"But we're in a time hollow, aren't we?" Katherine asked. "How can time stop in a time hollow? Time doesn't exist here, remember? It can't stop or start or move or—or do anything!"

She was screaming again. She sprang up and practically shoved Jonah out of the way so she could grab JB by the shoulders and shake him.

"Wake up!" she shrieked right in his ear.

JB didn't move. In fact, his body seemed to just absorb Katherine's shaking and her shouting into its stillness.

I've heard of antimatter, Jonah thought. *Is there such a thing as anti-motion?*

"I think you just woke up Mileva," Emily said softly.

"Oh, sorry," Katherine said, and actually had the grace to look a little ashamed.

Emily crouched down beside Mileva and brushed her hair out of her face.

"Are you okay?" Emily asked. Dimly, Jonah realized that she'd switched back to speaking German for Mileva.

"No worse than usual," Mileva said. She coughed, clearing her throat. "I don't do pregnancy very well." She sat up gingerly, a thoughtful expression on her face.

"Actually—I kind of feel better than usual. What did you do to me? Where are we? And"—she gazed around anxiously at the blank room around them, completely empty except for JB in his chair—"where's Albert?"

Jonah exchanged glances with Katherine. He wondered if they should at least tell Mileva that just as people in a time hollow couldn't feel hungry or thirsty, they probably couldn't feel nauseated or dizzy or faint either.

No. It was dangerous to tell Mileva anything.

"Maybe you should just lie down and go back to sleep," he suggested to Mileva. "Not . . . learn things that might mess up time even worse."

"Jonah," Emily said gently. "She already knows about time travel. She figured out how to use the Elucidator."

"Better than we did," Katherine muttered.

"So don't you think we might need Mileva to really know what's going on, so she can help us decide what to do?" Emily finished.

Jonah frowned. He looked down at JB. Jonah knew JB hadn't moved a hair in the past few seconds—hadn't moved at all since Jonah and the others had arrived. But it still seemed as if JB's gaze had taken on an accusatory cast, as if he were already blaming Jonah for mistakes he hadn't even made yet.

For most of Jonah's first trip through time, JB had

lectured again and again about how time needed to be left undisturbed, kept or restored as much as possible to its original state. Through their next few journeys through time, JB had come to care more about keeping the people he loved alive, rather than preserving the original flow of time. But what did it mean that he'd sent Emily back in time after promising to stop all time travel until it was safe again?

Had anything that Jonah witnessed in the year 1903 seemed safe?

"I just wish we knew what JB would want us to do," Jonah muttered.

"Why? Can't you make a decision on your own?" Katherine challenged.

Jonah shook his head.

"She's Albert Einstein's *wife*," he said, pointing at Mileva. "If she tells him even one thing she finds out about time travel, don't you think that could change the entire twentieth century? And everything after that? Like—oh, no. What if she's the reason that time froze in the twenty-first century?"

"What if she is?" Katherine argued. "The twenty-first century is already frozen. The year 1903 is already frozen. This time hollow is already frozen. What more can go wrong?"

Mileva was sitting up.

"You forget that I am also a scientist in my own right,"

she said, in a dignified voice. "And—don't you think I would do everything in my power to protect my own child?" She laid a hand on Emily's leg. She laid her other hand over her stomach. *Both* my children?"

Jonah realized that the hand that Mileva held over her stomach was still clutching the papers that Albert had handed her back in 1903. The papers covered with math formulations that she was supposed to check to help her "cheer up."

"We probably do need to go about this in a methodical, scientific way," Jonah admitted grudgingly. "Think. What if it wasn't just the danger of Albert seeing his daughter that stopped time back in 1903? What if it was something about those papers that was a problem, too? Like—that Mileva wasn't supposed to see them?"

"You want to look at these?" Mileva asked, holding the papers out toward Jonah. "See if they're dangerous? You're welcome to check the math yourself."

Was she being sarcastic or trying to be helpful? It didn't matter—even from several feet away, Jonah could see that the papers were covered with the same kind of incomprehensible scrawl that he and Katherine had seen back at Albert and Mileva's Bern apartment.

"I'm not good enough at math," Jonah admitted. "Neither's Katherine. Emily?"

Emily shook her head.

"I love math," she said. "But I don't think even my

teachers would be able to make heads or tails of that." She pointed ruefully at the scrawl on the top sheet of paper.

Jonah walked over and took the papers from Mileva's hand. She didn't resist. He put them down in JB's lap.

"Let's try to figure out how to unfreeze JB," Jonah said. "Then he can make sense of these."

Mileva opened her mouth, but shut it quickly.

Katherine took a step back, away from Jonah and JB.

"Maybe we should all be careful to stay apart from one another," she said. "There's something about time travelers clumping together in stopped time . . . Who knows what we'd fall into next?"

"It seems like four people being linked together is the magic number," Jonah mumbled. "We were always okay in stopped time until we had four people holding on to each other."

"Why?" Mileva asked. "Why four?"

Jonah shrugged.

"I'm picturing it the same way my science teacher explained gravity," he said. "He said to picture a bowling ball on a trampoline, and marbles rolling down toward the dent made by the bowling ball . . . The bowling ball stretches everything out of shape. Maybe certain events in time travel kind of work the same way."

"But are four time travelers linking together the

bowling ball in that analogy?" Mileva asked. "Or are we just marbles being acted on by forces we can't control?"

Jonah couldn't actually answer that.

"It feels like we broke *through* the whole trampoline—or space or time or whatever it's supposed to represent," Katherine muttered. "We broke through *twice.*"

"Jonah," Emily said, "I think Einstein was the person who came up with that analogy about the bowling ball on the trampoline."

Jonah winced.

"You have to promise you'll never tell him," Jonah told Mileva sternly. "If he comes out with his theories at the wrong time—it could mess up everything."

"You want me to make promises about bowling balls?" Mileva asked incredulously. "When I'm thinking I may never see my Albert again in my life?"

She had a point.

"Okay, okay," Katherine said, holding out her hands in a calming gesture. Jonah noticed that she still stayed several steps back. "We just need to slow down and think about everything. Mileva, you still have the Elucidator, right? Jonah, can you check and see where JB's Elucidator is? Even if it's frozen too, maybe we can get the two Elucidators to, I don't know, communicate with each other. That'll help us figure out why time stopped again."

"All right," Jonah said.

He hated taking orders from his sister, but he had to admit he should have thought of looking for JB's Elucidator himself.

He leaned down and looked in JB's hands. He felt in JB's shirt pocket, in his pants pockets, beside him in the chair.

Nothing.

Feeling a little creepy, Jonah bent down and felt around JB's socks and shoes. He felt along JB's belt. He patted down his shirt and sleeves.

Nothing, nothing, nothing.

"He doesn't have an Elucidator with him," Jonah announced.

"What?" Katherine asked. "He has to! He was talking to us from this time hollow—"

"You want to see for yourself?" Jonah asked, stepping back, holding his hands out, giving Katherine a chance. "An airport security pat-down couldn't find an Elucidator on JB! He doesn't have one!"

"Can't we just look at this one?" Mileva asked, holding out the Elucidator she'd been keeping in her pocket. "This is what you're calling an Elucidator, right? Isn't one enough to help us?"

Something changed in the moment that Mileva pulled out the Elucidator.

Jonah was looking in her direction. Since they were in the time hollow now, not a particular time period where any disturbance to regular time could ruin everything, he wondered: Was this the moment to just rush over to her and grab the Elucidator from her hand? To take control?

No, Jonah decided. *Not while she's cooperating and acting like she wants to help.*

While Jonah watched, Mileva's jaw dropped in what could only be stunned amazement. Beside her, Emily's face was suddenly just as transformed, providing practically a mirror image of the awe on her mother's face.

Behind Jonah, Katherine gasped.

"What?" Jonah said.

Nobody answered.

Emily and Mileva were staring just past Jonah and JB, toward a completely empty section of the room.

Jonah turned his head, following their gaze.

That part of the room wasn't empty anymore.

THIRTY-EIGHT

In the corner beside JB, another man sat in a matching high-tech chair.

"Is that . . . someone else you know?" Mileva asked faintly.

Jonah recovered from his astonishment enough to stammer out, "Y-yes. It's Hadley Correo, another time traveler who works with JB. A friend of ours."

"And he's frozen in place too?" Mileva asked.

"Looks that way," Jonah said.

He managed to gather his wits enough to walk over to Hadley and poke at his shoulder, swipe at his curly beard. Just as with JB, Hadley's body seemed to take in the movement while remaining completely still.

"But he *wasn't there*," Katherine said, sounding perplexed. "Right? It wasn't that we just didn't notice him before. Was it?"

"No," Emily said. "I saw him appear. Out of nothingness."

Jonah thought of something.

"You didn't tell the Elucidator, 'Make everyone in this room visible,' did you?" he asked Mileva. "It wasn't that he was there but invisible, until right at that moment?"

"Of course not," Mileva said. "You would have heard me."

"Then what changed?" Jonah asked. "Just, Mileva took the Elucidator out of her pocket, and boom, Hadley appeared?"

The others gave baffled shrugs and vague nods.

"Did *you* see or hear anything else?" Emily asked.

"No," Jonah said.

But something else did happen, he thought. *I decided not to tackle Mileva and grab the Elucidator from her hand.*

Did that matter? Were all three things connected? Were thoughts enough to help change time?

Er—not time, exactly, because time doesn't exist in a time hollow, and everything is stopped anyway . . .

Jonah's brain was twisting around in knots. It really creeped him out that he couldn't see any clear cause and effect. How was he supposed to decide what to do next, when he didn't know what had caused the events he'd already seen?

"Really," Katherine said in her huffiest voice, the way she always talked when she was scared but trying not to show it. "What good does it do to have Hadley here, anyway? He's just as frozen as JB! He can't tell us what's going on! He can't help us at all! This just gives us someone else to worry about!"

Jonah was still staring at Hadley, trying to get over the strangeness of seeing him appear out of nothingness and the strangeness of seeing him frozen—and the strangeness of not knowing why any of it had happened. Hadley was usually a fairly jolly person, so even though his face was frozen into a serious expression, there was still just the hint of a twinkle in his eye. Seeing that helped Jonah calm down a little, think a little more clearly.

"Oh!" he said, jolted by what he hadn't noticed before. "He's *not* just another person to worry about. Hadley has an Elucidator! I bet you anything that's what this is. Maybe it can show us an explanation for all this!"

He leaned forward and pulled out a thin piece of plastic that Hadley had been clutching in his right hand. It was like futuristic cell phone technology taken to its extreme: a tiny screen that still seemed capable of displaying vast worlds, and a keyboard that appeared only when Jonah thought, *How would you communicate on this thing?*

Maybe it appeared *because* Jonah thought that.

Ooo-kay, Jonah thought. *More creepiness. Hey, Elucidator, if you can read my mind, how about taking a hint and not freaking me out so much?*

Was it just Jonah's imagination, or did the Elucidator instantly start looking a lot more like an iPhone?

"Voice commands," Katherine said in a shaking voice. "Tell us. Why are JB and Hadley frozen? Why did Hadley appear out of nowhere like that? How can time be stopped in a time hollow, anyhow? What are we supposed to do now?"

"Hey, Katherine," Jonah complained. "How about just asking one question at a time? You're going to confuse it. Or—us."

But the Elucidator date screen was already displaying answers:

EXTREME DANGER OF CATASTROPHIC TIME DISTURBANCES. AND UNCERTAINTY—

The screen—and the entire Elucidator—suddenly vanished.

A second later the Elucidator was back in Jonah's hand.

INSTABILITY → UNPREDICTABILITY

appeared on the screen now.

Somebody screamed. Jonah couldn't tell if it was Katherine or Mileva or Emily—or maybe even himself.

The Elucidator vanished again, reappeared, vanished, reappeared . . .

"Mileva!" Jonah cried. "Is *your* Elucidator acting normal?"

Which was a joke. Because what had ever been normal about an Elucidator?

Mileva didn't answer. She just stared thoughtfully at the Elucidator flickering in and out of existence in Jonah's hand. Was the room starting to flicker around him too? Jonah could see Mileva holding the other Elucidator, the one she'd grabbed from him way back in Switzerland, way back in 1903. It looked so solid and real and unchanging. Jonah dropped the disappearing/reappearing Elucidator from his own hand and rushed toward Mileva's.

He couldn't have said if he intended to grab the other Elucidator back from her now, or if he just wanted to huddle close to something that didn't just appear and disappear at random. He didn't really think at all.

Then he saw Mileva's eyes widen in fear.

"No!" she screamed.

Jonah realized that Katherine was also running toward Mileva.

Mileva lifted her hand like an angry traffic cop. No—like someone pointing a remote control. She had the Elucidator clutched in her hand, aimed at Jonah and Katherine and even Emily, right by her side.

"Stop them!" Mileva shrieked. "Stop them all right now!"

Jonah had both feet off the ground, his right leg stretched forward, his left leg extended behind him. He was running as fast as he could. He knew how that worked, knew he'd need to push off again as soon as his right foot hit the ground.

But it didn't hit the ground. His left leg didn't cycle forward, ready for his left foot to push off next. His elbows didn't pump back and forth.

Run! his brain commanded. *Keep going!*

But his body refused to obey. In fact, it refused to do anything except stay exactly where it had been the instant Mileva yelled "Stop!" His right leg stayed stretched forward; his left leg stayed extended back; his entire body stayed suspended in midair.

He couldn't move his eyes, either, but he had a broad view. He could see Katherine on his left, Emily crouched on the floor beside Mileva.

Both girls were just like Jonah: completely frozen.

THIRTY-NINE

I can still see, Jonah told himself. *I can still hear. I can still think.*

None of that was much comfort, but it helped a little. It kept him from total despair.

Did Mileva know that we'd freeze like this? He wondered. *Did she do it on purpose? To take control, to keep the Elucidator for herself? Or . . .*

He remembered what had happened the last time the four of them had clumped together, how they'd fallen out of time. Like a bowling ball falling through the trampoline.

What if Mileva was only trying to prevent that?

Jonah watched Mileva.

For a moment it seemed as though she were frozen, too. Then she dropped the Elucidator and put her hands up to her mouth. Tears pooled in her eyes. She reached out and touched Emily's face, and the first tears spilled over the edges of Mileva's eyelids.

"Not dead," Mileva said. "She is not dead. I swear it."

Her voice sounded creaky, as if it had been a long time since she'd used it. Maybe a long time had already passed—Jonah had no way of knowing.

"I have to figure out how to fix this," Mileva said. "For Lieserl. For Albert." She touched her stomach. "For my baby . . ."

She picked up the Elucidator again. Then she gingerly stood up and edged toward JB. She walked like someone who feared that the floor might drop out from under her feet at any moment.

"I have to make myself understand," she said, and it seemed as if she was talking to Jonah and Katherine and Emily. "It's like the Hippocratic oath in medicine—first, do no harm. I can't be sure that I won't make things worse if I don't understand." She seemed to be looking particularly at Jonah now. "I *have* to do this."

She picked up the papers from JB's lap—the math papers Albert had originally brought to Mileva in Novi Sad to help her "cheer up"; the papers Jonah had feared would ruin time if Mileva saw them.

Mileva edged back across the empty floor to sit beside Emily again. Her eyes flicked across the pages.

"Oh, Albert, how can you be so careless with your math?" she murmured, shaking her head. She looked up. "And how can there not be a single pen or pencil in this room?"

The Elucidator glowed in her hand.

"Oh, there's a way to write on the Elucidator?" Mileva asked. "Why would anybody choose to do that instead of using pencil and paper?" She sighed. "I suppose I should be grateful that I don't have to use my own blood as ink."

For a long time there was no sound in the room except Mileva turning pages and tapping against what must have become a keyboard on the Elucidator. Then she exclaimed, "Oh! Oh, my! That's how time travel works?"

Jonah realized she hadn't learned just what Albert had figured out. She'd tapped into much deeper information on the Elucidator. She probably knew more than Jonah did about time travel now. Maybe even as much as JB or Hadley did.

And what's she going to do with that information? Jonah wondered.

She sat back against the nearest wall and stared off into space. Time passed. Or—maybe it didn't. It was impossible to tell, because nothing changed.

Finally Mileva shook her head.

"I have to see what was supposed to happen," she said,

and once again it seemed that she was talking to Jonah. "I have to know."

She hit something on the Elucidator, and the wall seemed to turn into a movie screen. Jonah had seen this kind of thing happen before, but Mileva hadn't. She gasped and practically fell to the floor.

"Courage," she whispered. She clutched Emily's arm. "I will be brave for you."

On the wall, Jonah saw Albert Einstein, looking as real as if he'd just walked into the room, fresh from 1903. He sat at a table Jonah recognized: the one from the Einsteins' apartment in Bern. The door behind him opened, and there stood another version of Mileva. She looked even more sick and ragged and distraught than she'd seemed on the train trip to Novi Sad. Albert just sat there looking at her for a moment; then he stood up and wrapped his arms around his wife.

"I missed you," he said.

Mileva began crying into his shoulder.

"My little witch," Albert said, almost hopefully. "My urchin."

The pet names came out sounding all wrong. Mileva cried harder.

"Look," Albert said, speaking over Mileva's head. "Perhaps it would be best if we never spoke Lieserl's name again. Pretended even to each other that she never existed. Just focused on . . . on the new baby." He put his hand over Mileva's stomach. "On the future. Not the past that's dead and gone."

The real Mileva—the one sitting on the floor of the time hollow—gasped and hit something on the Elucidator in her hand. The Mileva and Albert on the wall froze in place, stopped in time. The real Mileva studied the image.

And studied it.

And studied it.

"He doesn't know what else to do," she murmured to herself. "He's trying his best. He thinks this *is* for the best."

She kept staring at her husband's image.

"No," she said, after a long while. "He just wants everything to be easy for him. The only hard thing he ever wanted to think about was physics."

With surprising speed, she sprang up and rushed toward the wall. She began slapping her hand against her husband's image.

"You were so selfish, Albert!" she screamed at the wall. "You didn't want to give me any choice in the matter!"

Jonah had been still for so long it took him a moment to realize that he, himself, might be entitled to form an opinion about Albert. He studied the man's face even as Mileva battered it.

Albert looks . . . uncomfortable, Jonah thought. *Awkward. Uncertain. Afraid. And . . . sad. Albert's sad too. He just doesn't know what to do about it.*

Finally Mileva stopped slapping her husband's image on the wall. She slumped down to the floor.

"No," she whispered. "Those other papers. I have to look at them, too."

She hit something on the Elucidator and the images on the wall began moving forward again. Mileva seemed to have figured out how to zoom the viewpoint in and out, and she began studying the papers strewn across the Einsteins' apartment table.

"Okay," she murmured. "Yes . . ."

Jonah noticed that the images of Albert and Mileva projected on the wall were changing. Mileva's stomach shoved out farther and farther in her old-fashioned dresses. Albert's hair and moustache grew longer and messier. Mileva trimmed them. They grew back.

Maybe at a certain point Jonah stopped paying such close attention, because it was the minute-by-minute of daily life that passed by on the wall. Mileva fixed sausages, Albert ate them, Mileva walked to the store, Albert walked home from work . . .

And then suddenly things were different: The projected image of Mileva on the wall held a tiny, wizened baby.

"Hanserl," she crooned in his ear. "Our little Hans Albert. You're going to grow up so big and strong—and smart! So smart!"

The real Mileva sitting by Emily was sobbing again, but these might have been tears of joy. She rubbed her hand against her stomach.

"A little boy! Hans Albert!" she cried out. She paused. "Will you ever have a chance to live for real?"

Maybe the tears weren't tears of joy.

Albert's and Mileva's lives kept unspooling on the wall, before Mileva's eyes, before Jonah's eyes. Hans Albert was a useful addition to their family, because as he grew up, Jonah could see how much time was passing, how far ahead Mileva was watching after 1903. Little Hans Albert could sit up, he could crawl, he could walk . . . He was one, then two, then three . . .

Albert played the violin and talked boisterously with friends. He wrote letters bragging about the great scientific papers he was about to publish. He played with Hans Albert, then forgot about the little boy in the middle of their games and began writing down formulas instead . . .

The Mileva who showed up projected on the wall still checked Albert's math, when he wasn't showing it to someone else, but mostly she was cooking and cleaning and boiling Hans Albert's diapers on the stove. She seemed to be fading away before Jonah's eyes. When she and Albert went to parties, he laughed and talked and told bawdy stories. More and more, Mileva sat silently in the corner.

"Don't," the Mileva who sat on the floor of the time hollow pleaded with her own self. "Join in. What's wrong with you? Everyone there is your friend!"

But the future Mileva just looked more and more hollow-eyed, more and more angry, more and more pained.

Another Einstein child arrived, a second little boy they named Eduard but seemed to mostly call Tete. A parade of important-looking men began showing up to talk to Albert. They offered jobs at one university then another. Prague, Zurich, Berlin . . . Albert stood behind podiums and spoke, and whole auditoriums full of very serious-looking scientists listened intently.

Albert kissed a woman who wasn't Mileva.

Oh, no! Jonah thought. *Did I miss something? Did those two get divorced while I wasn't looking?*

No—that kiss also seemed to be a surprise to the real Mileva watching her future life.

"Albert Einstein!" she hissed. "How could you! With her?"

She had tears in her eyes once more.

Is that Mileva's future life? Jonah wondered. *Or just a possible future? Is there anything anyone can change—if any of us ever get out of this time hollow?*

Maybe Jonah was distracted pondering these questions, because huge gobs of time seemed to be passing on the wall before him. Little Hans Albert and baby Tete grew up. Albert and Mileva both turned gray and a little wild-haired—the change in appearance making Albert more and more recognizable. This was the man Jonah had seen pictures of all his life, the lovable genius who jokingly stuck out his tongue for photographers, who helped little kids with their math, who made forgetting to wear socks the sign of a brain that just had better things to think about.

Albert was honored in a ticker-tape parade. He won a Nobel Prize. He traveled the world.

He and Mileva fought about getting divorced. About their children.

Mileva collapsed and had to be hospitalized. She found out her brother was missing in action in World War I in Russia. She saw first her sister, then Tete, have mental breakdowns and get sent to asylums—sometimes in horrifying places. Still, Mileva visited each of them faithfully. She taught piano lessons and math, rented out apartments, scraped together money to seek better treatment for her troubled son.

Some of the time Jonah felt as if he were watching a

movie in history class, only in 3-D color rather than in black and white. Armies marched across Europe. People carted wheelbarrow-loads of money just to buy bread. Nazis threatened Albert because he was Jewish. Albert moved to America. He wrote a letter to the president of the United States about nuclear weapons, about how to win World War II.

Mileva died.

Albert died.

The wall went blank.

The real Mileva sat staring at the emptiness, breathing hard.

"And Lieserl?" she finally said in a broken voice. "What of Lieserl, if . . . "

Jonah wasn't quite sure what she meant, but evidently the Elucidator could follow her line of reasoning.

The scene on the wall came to life again, but it didn't look like history anymore. Or, rather—it looked like history that even Jonah remembered.

A phone was ringing.

Yeah, we had a cordless phone just like that when Katherine and I were little too, he thought.

Now an ordinary-looking couple clutched the telephone together. The woman had the same kind of haircut Jonah's mom had had, years ago. The father wore a T-shirt bragging that he'd volunteered at the Columbus Marathon in 1995.

"Tonight?" the woman was saying. "We get the baby tonight?"

The next scene showed the woman holding a baby in her arms.

Jonah realized he was watching Emily's childhood. She blew seeds off dandelion stems. She played an angel in a Christmas pageant. She received an A+ on a math test. She opened a birthday present that turned out to be a miniature microscope.

Mileva, watching, had tears in her eyes once more.

Now Emily-on-the-wall looked exactly the same age as Emily sitting frozen beside Mileva. She seemed to be wearing the same blue jeans, the same maroon shirt. And Jonah recognized her surroundings as well: a time hollow, possibly this very same one.

On the wall she was talking to a version of JB that wasn't frozen yet.

"I'll do it," she was telling him with quiet resolve. "I want to help."

What? Wait! Jonah thought. *Did I just miss something? What did she just agree to? Mileva—can't you back things up and show me that again?*

It was maddening not to be able to ask out loud.

Mileva let the scene keep playing, but it transitioned to a moment Jonah had actually witnessed: Emily showing up in the toddler Lieserl's room, Jonah convincing her to join with her tracer, Mileva sweeping into the room and finding her there . . .

"Oooh," Mileva said, letting out a sigh of understanding. "So that's how it worked." She started punching in commands on the Elucidator. "No, no, I want to see more of her life in the twenty-first century. I want to see what's possible for my daughter that wasn't possible for me . . ."

The scene on the wall only froze. Evidently some sort of explanation showed up on the Elucidator, because Mileva started complaining.

"Why not?" she muttered. "Why can't I see everything?" She paused. "It depends on *what*?"

Mileva looked up, squinting in distress. Jonah would have expected her to look toward the real Emily again— maybe pat her daughter's face or stroke her daughter's hair. Instead Mileva stood up and walked unsteadily toward Jonah. She lifted her arm, pointing the Elucidator at him.

"Restore him," she said. "Please."

A split second later, Jonah felt his right foot touch the ground. He stumbled, his ankle twisting.

Mileva grabbed his arm, holding him up.

"Will you help me?" she asked.

FORTY

"What?" Jonah said, his first word in an eon. "You unfroze me first? Before your own daughter? Why?"

Mileva opened her mouth to answer, but Jonah was so relieved to be able to talk again that he decided to keep asking questions.

"Is it because you thought the unfreezing might be dangerous, and you wouldn't really be that upset if it killed me?"

Mileva laughed. And then, strangely, she hugged him.

"I forgot how funny you were," she murmured. She held him by the shoulders, looking directly into his face. Her eyes gleamed. "I forgot how wonderful it could be just talking to another human being, and having them answer. After more than sixty years . . ."

"Sixty years!" Jonah exclaimed.

"Well, yes," Mileva said. "I watched the entire rest of my life, and the rest of Albert's life, and the first thirteen years of my daughter's life in the future . . . I taught myself everything I could about time travel too, and that probably took sixty years as well, just by itself. Though that's impossible to measure, since time really doesn't pass in here, and I never got hungry and I never got thirsty and"—she patted her stomach—"I never got any more pregnant . . . Oh, how Albert would love this place! He could get so fixated on his ideas, and he would forget to eat or drink or, you know, even comb his hair . . . If he were in this time hollow, he'd stay a million years!"

She sounded so merry, Jonah wondered if he'd just been hallucinating about all the sad details of her life.

"Um," he said. "When you were watching what was going to happen to you and Albert—er, I guess, what *could* happen—I saw it too. I'm sorry."

He wasn't sure if he was apologizing for watching her life—like such a stalker—or if he was apologizing for what happened in her life: Albert betraying her, and her being so sick and sad and poor, and the tragedies and failures piling up around her even as the fame and honor and glory piled up for Albert.

Something in Mileva's expression softened.

"Thank you," she said. "I do appreciate that. But I knew

you were watching all along. You and my daughter and Katherine, and those strange men I've never even met . . . It's a strange quirk of stopped time in a time hollow, that even people frozen in time aren't completely frozen. Time can't ever quite stop here, since it doesn't really exist in this place to begin with."

"That doesn't make sense," Jonah objected.

Mileva shrugged, the merriness back.

"Oh, that's just the tip of the iceberg, for the contradictions of time travel!" she joked. "But it's such a relief, that stopped time doesn't work that way in general. I was so happy to find out that Albert frozen in 1903 *isn't* aware of anything, and when you and I unfreeze him, it will seem to him that nothing happened. For him, one second of his ordinary time will just flow right into the next."

Jonah felt relieved by that detail about stopped time, too. It meant that if he ever got back to the twenty-first century, his science teacher would never know that Jonah had sneaked out of class.

Assuming Jonah was ever able to return to the twenty-first century and sneak back *in* to class.

Jonah realized he was getting ahead of himself.

"Hold on," he said to Mileva. "Did you just say that you and I are going to unfreeze Albert in 1903? Aren't you going to unfreeze Katherine and Emily and JB and Hadley first? Can't you just let the experts take care of dealing with 1903?"

Mileva bit her lip.

"No," she said. She winced a little.

"Why not?" Jonah challenged.

Mileva sighed. She patted the puff of hair around her face, still preserved in the topknot style of 1903.

"Time is very fragile right now," she explained. "I think it's possible that outside of this room, all of time is frozen. In every time period."

Jonah gaped at her.

She was watching him very carefully. Almost sympathetically.

"You should think of it like . . . I know," she said. "In the twenty-first century I saw Emily—my Lieserl—reading an article about medically induced comas. Sometimes when patients are horribly sick or have been in horrible accidents, the doctors will give them medicine to keep them comatose, so their bodies can use all their energy for healing. That's almost exactly what's happened now. Time itself is in a coma, and as far as I can tell, you and I are the only ones who can heal it. Anybody else unfrozen would be an unnecessary complication." She gulped, and shot a tense glance at Emily. "A . . . potentially fatal complication."

Jonah stared at her. Maybe another sixty years passed before he could figure out an adequate response.

"You're not supposed to know about things from the twenty-first century," he finally said. "That's dangerous."

Mileva's lips curled up into a rueful smile.

"And . . . that's why it had to be you that I unfroze," she said, shaking her head. "Because you will keep telling me things like that. And . . . I will need to hear them."

Jonah squinted at Mileva.

"Why should I trust you?" he asked. "Why should you trust me?"

Mileva glanced quickly at Emily, who still sat frozen in the exact spot where she'd huddled protectively against Mileva—when? Sixty years ago? A hundred and twenty?

Then Mileva took Jonah by the shoulders, gently turning him so he faced Katherine, still frozen mid-stride, and JB and Hadley, frozen so grimly in their chairs.

"We have to trust each other," Mileva said. "Because that is the only way to save the people we love."

FORTY-ONE

They landed in a patch of sunshine. Jonah's head was spinning, but he couldn't have said how much of that was from timesickness and how much of it was from the dizzying plans Mileva had shared with him. Jonah had tried to understand her explanations of what she'd learned about time travel and its underlying principles, but so much of it seemed nonsensical. For instance, she'd told him why three time travelers joining together in stopped time was no problem, but four could lead to disastrous unpredictability.

What was the reason, again? Oh, yeah, it has something to do with time being the fourth dimension, Jonah remembered. *But that's only an issue in stopped time, right?*

He hoped it never mattered that he couldn't remember clearly. His brain jumped to the mind-boggling array of broader topics Mileva had discussed: the speed of light, the theory of relativity, quanta, Schrödinger's cat, Heisenberg's uncertainty principle . . .

Uncertainty is right, Jonah thought, his stomach lurching. *What if Mileva is wrong about everything? What if there's some blatant error in her calculations, and I'm too stupid to figure it out? Or what if she knows I'm that stupid, and she's tricking me on purpose?*

He squeezed his eyes shut and opened them again. Familiar objects began to swim into focus. A desk. A table with a lace tablecloth. This did look like 1903—1903 in the apartment Albert and Mileva had left behind in Switzerland, not 1903 in the bedroom in Novi Sad where Albert still stood frozen.

Jonah blinked again.

"Are you *sure* we have to come here first?" he asked Mileva, who'd landed flat on the floor beside him.

"Yes—er—ah—" Mileva began gagging.

"It's just timesickness you're feeling," Jonah said encouragingly. "Swallow hard, and you'll feel fine in a few minutes."

Mileva stumbled to her feet and weaved unsteadily toward the kitchen. Jonah could hear her retching into the sink.

"I'm pregnant, remember?" she called back to him. "It's like there was more than a century of morning sickness waiting for me back here. Ohh . . ."

She leaned over the sink again.

Jonah tried not to listen for a while after that. He struggled to his feet and went to the farthest window. Looking out, he could see the picturesque scene on the street below: the flower boxes, the trolley cars, the men in suits, the women in long dresses, everyone in a hat—and everyone frozen in place.

Time was still stopped here.

"I thought people were much more open about talking about pregnancy in your time," Mileva said behind him. "In the twenty-first century."

Jonah turned around.

"Well, I guess they are, but—nobody likes hearing somebody else vomit," Jonah said. Then, just in case she wanted to talk about this a lot more, he added, "And I'm a thirteen-year-old boy. I bet there isn't any time period where thirteen-year-old boys like hearing about pregnancy symptoms."

"I guess I should have thought of that, because of my brother," Mileva said. "But I was away so much by the time he was thirteen . . ."

She looked so haunted that Jonah mumbled, "Sorry."

What was it like for Mileva to know that in a decade or so, her brother would go off to war and be missing for years? That the family would give him up for dead—and that even when they found out he wasn't dead, they'd get word that he didn't want to come home?

How could Mileva bear knowing that she was facing so many awful moments in her future?

"Maybe . . . maybe you should try to forget everything that you saw back in the time hollow," Jonah said gruffly. "You could give me the Elucidator right now, and let me freeze you in time with everyone else from 1903. Maybe that would keep you from thinking about things you shouldn't know . . ."

Mileva shook her head resolutely.

"You need me to imitate Albert's handwriting, remember?" she said.

Jonah walked toward the table in the middle of the room. Just as before, it was covered with papers full of Albert's scribbles.

"A *chicken* could imitate this handwriting," he joked.

He touched the top sheet of paper and stopped.

"What if we're wrong?" he asked. "What if this doesn't work?"

"We have to try," Mileva said. Jonah couldn't tell if she was fighting back more pregnancy nausea—or fighting back tears.

He nodded, and lifted the top sheet. He looked back and forth between the sheet in his hand and the ghostly version of it still remaining in place on the table.

The ghostly version—the paper's tracer—held completely different words, different numbers, different ideas.

He let out a deep sigh of relief.

"Is it there?" Mileva asked hopefully.

"Yep," Jonah said. It was still so weird to him that Mileva couldn't see the tracer page, since it was from her own time period. To further reassure her, he added, "It's just like when Katherine and I looked before. The tracer page shows exactly what Albert would have written, if time travelers had never intervened. If he'd hadn't gotten distracted thinking about time splitting . . ."

Mileva was already sitting at the desk, a pencil poised over paper.

"Start reading it to me," she said in a brisk, businesslike voice.

"What if I don't know some of the symbols?" Jonah asked.

"Describe them to me," Mileva said. "Or—here." She handed him a piece of paper and a pencil of his own. "If it's something that's too difficult, draw it as best you can, and we'll work it out together."

"Okay, then," Jonah said. "This one starts with the word 'capillarity'. . ."

"Capillarity?" Mileva repeated in amazement. "Albert

was supposed to be thinking about that in 1903? I don't remember him expressing the slightest shred of interest in capillarity during that time. Why would he care?"

Jonah just looked at her.

"This is never going to work if you don't trust me," he said. "And it's going to take forever if you challenge everything."

Mileva gritted her teeth.

"Right. Capillarity," she said. "Next word?"

It was long, slow, tedious work, reading every single word and symbol and equation from the papers spread across the Einsteins' table, and waiting while Mileva copied them down. She was actually uncannily good at reproducing the same cramped, careless script that Albert had used on the original papers.

They were lucky that Albert had left the papers spread across the table, only a corner here and there hiding the words written on the paper below. The only problem was that Jonah couldn't flip over any of the tracer pages to see whatever was written on the backs. He and Mileva could only hope that they caught enough of the original idea.

Of course, how good can our plan really be, Jonah thought, *when it relies on outsmarting one of the most brilliant men in history?*

FORTY-TWO

"Must not vomit," Mileva said through gritted teeth. "Must not vomit."

They had just finished using something Mileva said was officially called Ancillary Dislocation Travel in Otherwise-Originated Massive Time Stoppages—ADTOOMTS, for short. Basically, that just meant that the Elucidator had whisked them from the apartment in Bern to Mileva's room at her parents' house in Novi Sad while time was still stopped in September 1903.

"Why don't they just call it teleportation?" Jonah asked. "Or a 'beam me up, Scotty'?"

"Because it's such a precise form of teleportation, and time travelers have to be precise," Mileva said. "And— 'beam me up'? Time travelers already pay homage to that *Star Trek* phrase. They use it to refer to any return to their native time after being away . . . oh, crud," Mileva moaned. She dived under the bed and pulled out a chamber pot so she could vomit.

Jonah took the all-important papers from her sweaty hands. He sighed, and held loose strands of her hair out of the way.

She finished throwing up and slid the chamber pot back out of sight. She sat back against the wall.

"Thank you," she whispered.

"You'll have to forget everything you know about *Star Trek*," he said.

Mileva wiped the back of her hand across her clammy forehead. Her face was too pale.

"I know," she mumbled. "It's just—Emily watched so many of those old reruns with her adopted dad in the twenty-first century. And I loved watching them too, back in the time hollow. I might have made some of my favorites repeat a time or two . . . so Emily and I could watch them together. Sort of. It felt like something I could actually share with my daughter, from the portion of her childhood she had without me. The *vast* portion of childhood she had without me."

A familiar sadness crossed Mileva's face, and she shook her head. Jonah could tell she was trying hard to fight the sorrow.

"Anyhow," Mileva said, with forced cheer. "'Beam me up, Scotty'—how can anybody not love that? It's *so* much better than ADTOOMTS!"

Jonah tried to keep looking at her sternly.

"Really, I'll make myself forget!" Mileva insisted. "Or, at least, I'll never tell a single other soul about it. Not in any way that matters."

"You have to stop saying 'crud,' too," Jonah said. "That's something you picked up from me. It's not even the same word in German, is it?"

Now Mileva looked amused.

"Jonah, think! What language have I been using with you almost constantly since the time hollow?" she asked.

Jonah tilted his head to the side thoughtfully.

"English?" he asked. "You actually learned English?"

"I had to teach myself English in the time hollow, so I could understand watching Emily's life in America in the twenty-first century," Mileva explained. "I can't believe you didn't notice. You're almost as absentminded as Albert!"

"I've had a lot else on my mind," Jonah said defensively. "And—when you understand all languages, you kind of stop noticing any of it."

Mileva punched him playfully on the arm.

"Show-off," she said, treating him like a lovable younger brother. "'I understand all languages, so I don't really notice,'" she mimicked in a fake-snobby voice.

"You're the show-off, teaching yourself a complete foreign language without any of the time-traveler help I got—you'll have to forget the English, too, remember? No speaking it to anybody in your real life by mistake!" Jonah commanded.

"I know," Mileva said wistfully.

She took a deep breath, and carefully inched the papers out of Jonah's hand.

"You think we should have Albert's early thoughts about relativity near the top?" she asked in a quavering voice, as she rearranged the order of the papers. "That will draw him in right away, don't you think?"

"You know him a lot better than I do," Jonah said.

Mileva stood up and turned to face the frozen Albert. He was standing in the same awkward, ungainly position they'd left him in before zooming into the time hollow.

Mileva reached for his hand.

"Wait!" Jonah said. "How are you ever going to be able to pretend you still love him after everything you saw in the time hollow? After the way he treated you—I mean, how he will treat you—"

"Jonah, I do still love Albert, even after everything I saw," Mileva said evenly. She turned her head and looked straight at Jonah instead of her husband. "You have to understand—I'm really angry about the way he's going to treat me and Hans Albert and Tete in the next two decades, but even then I'll love him." She shook her head. "I can't blame you if you can't follow the logic there. I wouldn't have understood at thirteen either. Maybe you'll understand when you're a grown-up." She paused. "No, I hope no one in your life treats you in such a way that you'll ever have to understand."

"But, Mileva—," Jonah began.

"Here," Mileva said, pulling the Elucidator out of her pocket. "Let's turn you invisible first. Just as a precaution."

Jonah thought he could *feel* himself disappearing. He glanced down quickly to make sure it had really happened.

"Oh!" Mileva said, as if something about the process surprised her. "So *that's* what it looks like."

"What?" Jonah said.

"Since I've become a time traveler myself, I can see you now even though you're invisible—just barely, just the slightest hint . . . ," Mileva said.

"You knew it would be like that," Jonah said. "You read all the fine print about the ins and outs of time travel, the way time travelers' lives are changed forever. You probably know the rules and the explanations better than anybody else. And—"

He was about to add another stern warning: *And that's*

something else you're going to have to forget after today. Or, at least, never talk about again. But Mileva was looking at him so strangely.

"What?" he said once again.

"You look like glass," Mileva murmured. "So fragile. It just made me realize—everyone's fragile, everyone I'm trying to protect."

She touched his arm, just the slightest brush against his sleeve.

"Just to be sure you're safe, why don't you hide behind Albert?" Mileva asked in a choked voice.

Jonah thought this was as crazy overprotective as some of the things his parents told him to do, but he didn't argue. He handed her the papers he'd been holding and stepped behind Albert's back.

Mileva tucked the Elucidator back into her pocket and got into position. She took Albert's hand once again, as if ready to tug him toward the end of the bed where Emily had once sat. That spot was completely empty now, just as the chair where Katherine had once sat was completely empty.

"Voice commands, Elucidator," Mileva said. "Resume normal time."

For a moment, nothing happened. Then—

"—I-I'm worried about you," Albert said, his first word

stuttering ever so slightly, exactly like a recorded voice starting up again after being paused.

Jonah stared at the dust motes dancing in the sunshine around Albert's left arm.

Movement, Jonah thought. *Normal movement. Keep going, keep going . . .*

Albert turned his head to squint at Mileva.

"You're acting strange," he complained.

"I feel so much better, just seeing you," Mileva said, pulling him forward. She looked back at him over her shoulder. Her cheeks were rosy, almost feverish.

"What did you want to show me?" Albert asked. "I mean—who?"

Mileva stopped in the center of the floor. Jonah thought it was almost exactly the spot where he had tripped on the carpet and fallen toward Mileva and Katherine and Emily.

"Can you feel our daughter's spirit here?" Mileva whispered. "This is the spot where she left us . . . left Novi Sad . . . left this world. I miss her so. But I know she's going to be in a better place."

Albert's face twisted. Was it a sign of regret? Grief? Confusion?

Or—suspicion?

He seemed to be deciding to humor his wife.

"Perhaps . . . ," he murmured. He huddled with Mileva,

hugging her tight. They clung to each other. Albert opened his mouth, but seemed to be thinking hard for a moment before he actually spoke. "I'm sorry I never met her. Will never meet her. I wish things could have been different."

He didn't sound like a soon-to-be-famous scientist. He didn't sound like someone who'd figured out time travel and the secrets of the universe. He just sounded awkwardly, unbearably sad.

Mileva didn't answer. She grimaced, as if holding back a lifetime worth of sobs.

"Mileva?" Albert said. He pushed her away slightly, holding her at arm's length so he could look into her face. Just in time Mileva smoothed out her expression, hiding most of her anguish.

Another "tip of the iceberg" situation, Jonah thought.

"Your parents think . . . well, they think you're refusing to face the truth," Albert said slowly. "They told me you wouldn't admit that Lieserl is gone."

"I know the truth," Mileva said. Her voice was even and calm. She didn't sound at all like someone who had gone mad with grief. She sounded entirely sane and competent and more composed than Albert.

Having a century or so in the time hollow to come to terms with things had probably helped.

Also, of course, she knew the actual truth. The one where the Einsteins' daughter still had a chance at life.

"So . . . are there . . . details that need to be taken care of?" Albert looked as if he'd rather undergo a root canal than explain exactly what he meant by that.

"Are you asking, do we need to have a funeral?" Mileva said. "Do we need to bury a casket in the cemetery and fill out the paperwork with the church and dot all the i's and cross all the t's and make it look like society dealt with our little girl properly? And then years from now, when your brilliant brain brings you the fame you deserve, people will come nosing around here and snicker behind their hands as they look up the records and say, 'Oh, look, this little girl was Albert Einstein's shame.' . . . I will not have our daughter treated like that! I will not have her memory maligned!"

She was breathing hard now. For a moment Jonah was afraid that she was getting sick again, and would need to interrupt her passionate speech to throw up one more time. But she just shook her head fervently and kept going.

"I didn't have much control over what happened to Lieserl during her first year and a half of life," Mileva said. "And I couldn't protect her from the scarlet fever. But I will not have her treated disrespectfully now. I'd rather have her existence kept a secret outside of Novi Sad than give a single person the opportunity to say, 'Oh, weren't they lucky that that child died. That really solved all their problems, didn't it?' We were not lucky!"

Albert recoiled, pulling back from Mileva.

Does he think they were lucky? Jonah wondered. *Had he kind of been hoping that Lieserl would die?*

It was an awful thing to think about Albert Einstein. Jonah couldn't tell what was going on inside the man's mind, except that he looked as if he didn't want to be having this conversation.

"We . . . can keep everything secret," Albert said faintly. "You don't even have to tell me . . . all the details. But— what if anybody ever . . . finds the body?"

He spoke the last word in a whisper, as if he could barely bring himself to form the sounds.

"Our daughter is in the best place possible," Mileva said. "I swear to you, nobody will ever find our daughter's body in Novi Sad. And the people around here are loyal to my family. They won't tell. We'll be able to take this secret to our graves."

She was staring into her husband's eyes now, her own eyes burning with intensity.

He's going to ask for details, Jonah thought. *Even though he said he wouldn't, he's got to be curious. And he does think he's going to be famous someday. Won't he want to make sure that this secret never comes back to haunt him?*

But Albert looked down. He was looking, actually, at the papers clutched in Mileva's hand. He was looking at them longingly, as if he wanted nothing more than to pull completely away from Mileva and bury himself in numbers and formulas and scientific ideas. It was like seeing a man in the midst of a horrible battle catch a glimpse of an open door to a fort. Now Jonah felt as if he could read Albert's mind—he had to be thinking, *Oh, please! Let me just escape into my beloved physics* . . .

The most risky moment of Mileva's entire plan was almost upon them.

"Maybe . . . maybe we'd both feel better about all of this if we just sat down and looked at those papers," Albert said. "Leave our sorrow behind, share our happiness—why dwell on the past? Let's look to the future. I really have come up with some interesting ideas lately! I do want you to see them!"

Something flickered across Mileva's face, and for a moment Jonah thought that she would never be able to hide her true emotions. How could she be anything but furious at Albert? How could she even pretend to forgive him? How could she let him gloss over their daughter's supposed death like that?

But Mileva smiled at her husband.

"And I do so love hearing about your ideas," she said in a low voice.

Jonah could hear the pain in her voice. It wasn't just that she was acting sad because Albert needed to believe that Lieserl had died. Or because, if her plan worked, Mileva would lose her daughter to the future. It truly pained Mileva that Albert's enthusiasm for sharing ideas with her wasn't going to last. Mileva had seen their future. She knew that as soon as the important men of science started paying attention to Albert, he'd stop caring what Mileva thought.

And if I can hear that in her voice, Albert's going to notice it too, Jonah thought. *He's going to figure out that something else is wrong. This is going to ruin everything.*

But Albert was already bent over the papers.

"See, right here," he began. "I figured out that if time split into two entirely separate dimensions in 1611, as I suspect, then there'd be signs of that in nature. Subtle signs, signs you'd have to look for, but still, this would be the formula for finding them . . . "

He was pointing to something on the top sheet of paper, one from the stack he'd handed to Mileva when he first arrived in Novi Sad.

"Let me take a look," Mileva said.

She sat down on the edge of the bed and Albert thrust that paper before her eyes. He settled in beside her, leaning in to read the paper with her.

"Fascinating . . . ," Mileva murmured. "Oh, Albert, if

this is true, then . . . Oh. Oh, no. Is that a two right there or a three?"

"Let me look at that . . ." Albert took the paper from her. He stared at it for a moment, and then his face fell. "I added wrong! I thought this idea was going to change the world, but I couldn't even add . . ."

He crumpled the paper in his hand and dropped it to the floor.

"Well, let's look at what else you have," Mileva said comfortingly. "You've got a lot of papers here."

She shifted to look at the next sheet down.

This was not one that Albert had handed to Mileva. It was one that Mileva had copied from Jonah's description of the tracer pages showing what Albert had been thinking about in original time, before any time traveler had intervened. It was what Albert was supposed to be thinking about in September 1903, instead of split time.

"Imagine yourself riding a beam of light, going the same speed as light . . . ," Mileva read out loud.

"What?" Albert asked. "I didn't write that!"

"Looks like you did," Mileva said. "This is your handwriting, see?"

She held the papers closer to him, so he could have a better view. Then, with feigned playfulness, she jostled his arm.

"Must be nice to be so brilliant—you come up with

something like this and then forget you even wrote it down!" Mileva teased. "You know you forget to wear socks if I don't remind you—now you're having so many great ideas you forget one when the next one shows up. You must have written this on the train. See how the writing is a little bumpy? It's okay, you have been under a lot of strain lately. We'll just put this idea aside . . ."

She started to slide past that paper to the next one, but Albert put his hand over hers, stopping her. He yanked the paper from her hand.

"Stop! Wait!" Albert said frantically. "This is like an idea I started thinking about when I was sixteen, but then I got distracted. And yet, it's so fascinating. . . . Speed of light . . . other factors relative . . ."

He seemed to be reading all the way to the bottom of the page. Then he eagerly flipped the paper over.

The back of the paper, of course, was blank.

"Didn't I write anything else?" Albert asked, sounding a little desperate. "But, of course, it would naturally follow that . . . Mileva, don't just sit there! Give me something to write with!"

Mileva handed him a pencil. He started to write with the paper braced against his leg, but the pencil poked straight through. Albert scrambled backward to the bedside table. He shoved books and cups and the lamp to the very edge and put the paper down flat. He began writing and writing and writing.

Mileva silently moved the lamp and the books and the cups to the floor, so they wouldn't fall.

"Albert?" Mileva said.

No answer. Albert didn't even seem to have heard her.

Mileva glanced around the room, searching for Jonah. He took a step forward for the first time since watching Albert unfreeze. Mileva shook her head.

"You are so bad at being invisible," she whispered. "On top of everything else, your shoes squeak."

Jonah put his finger over his lips.

"Shh," he hissed.

"Doesn't matter. Albert's going to be distracted for hours," she whispered. "Our plan worked!"

"It did? Completely?" Jonah whispered back.

Mileva stepped closer to Jonah. She picked up the sheet of paper Albert had crumpled and dropped to the ground only moments earlier. She smoothed it out, folded it over, and handed it to Jonah.

"I think so," Mileva said. "For now. If you dispose of that. But you'll have to go back to the time hollow to know for sure." She seemed to be trying to smile, but the edges of her mouth kept slipping. She took the Elucidator out of her pocket and held it out to him as well. "Here."

Jonah stared at the wooden case of the Elucidator. Practically every other moment he'd spent in 1903—at least, the unfrozen, time-moving-forward part of 1903— he'd longed to snatch the Elucidator away from Mileva. He'd plotted for it, agonized over it, dreamed about it.

And now she was handing the Elucidator right to him, and he could only stare.

"Elucidator," Mileva said. "You can take voice commands from me or Jonah now."

"Wait—aren't you coming with me?" Jonah asked.

He'd been so focused on the first part of their plan— the need to get Albert to move past the news about Lieserl, to stop thinking about split time, and to catch up on all the thoughts he was supposed to be having in 1903 instead. Jonah had barely believed any of that was possible. So he'd barely thought about what would happen next.

He hadn't thought at all about how this moment would feel.

"Don't you at least want to come and say good-bye to Emily?" he asked. "You could zip right in and out of time—Albert would never know."

Mileva glanced quickly at Albert, who was still completely lost in the world of the papers he'd "forgotten" he wrote. It didn't look as if he would be aware of anything else for a very long time.

"It would be too . . . hard," Mileva said. She twisted

her hands. "I had thirteen years of watching Emily grow up, thirteen years of getting to know and love her. She had—what? Just a few weeks of knowing me? When she was sick and not even conscious a lot of the time, and not really herself . . ."

Jonah saw everything too clearly all of a sudden. Mileva meant that she loved Emily too much, and Emily didn't have much reason to care about her at all. What kind of good-bye would that make?

"Besides, aren't you worried that having me travel through time again would just mess things up all over again?" Mileva asked, and now there was almost a teasing tone to her voice.

The teasing didn't fool Jonah.

"After everything you've been through, after everything you've seen, how can you just . . . let it end?" Jonah asked.

Mileva put her hand over her stomach.

"End?" she said. "End? I have a new baby on the way. I have a husband who's about to have the most amazing year in science that anybody's ever had. I'll get to share that with him. I'm only twenty-seven. Some would say that my whole life lies ahead of me."

"But you know . . . you know all the bad things that are going to happen to you," Jonah whispered. "After 1905, after Albert's famous . . ."

"And I can't change any of them, right?" Mileva said,

"Isn't that what you've been telling me all along? Didn't we agree from the very start that I would sacrifice myself to make sure that Emily has a chance at a good life, and Hans Albert has a chance at a good life, and Tete has, well, at least a chance to live . . . ? Isn't that what any good mother would do?"

They had agreed on that. Jonah had known from the start that Mileva intended to go back to live out her original life, pretending at every turn that she knew nothing of time travel. That was the only way to get Albert to forget split time and focus only on the ideas he would have had in original time.

But, staring into Mileva's eyes, suddenly Jonah realized that he'd been as oblivious as Albert Einstein. He'd been so focused on the technicalities; he hadn't understood the big picture.

Mileva intended to relive all of it. The misery, the depression, the pain, the sorrow . . . what she intended was the equivalent of someone falling on a sword to save her children. But hers would be the slowest and most agonizing of deaths: more than forty years of giving up. Letting go. Avoiding practically every joy, killing almost every possibility for happiness.

Suddenly Jonah saw why Mileva had chosen to unfreeze him in the time hollow, rather than Katherine or Emily. Mileva had probably thought that Katherine or Emily would come to understand all this too soon. She'd thought that Katherine or Emily, as females, would have too much empathy for a mother's dilemma.

Mileva had been *counting* on Jonah to be as oblivious as Albert Einstein. She was counting on Jonah to be as heartless toward people in the past as JB had once been.

But Jonah wasn't like that. He couldn't be.

"No, Mileva, you can't do this," Jonah said, shaking his head. "It's not fair. There's got to be some other way."

"I'm married to arguably the most influential man of the twentieth century. *Time* magazine is going to name him the man of the century," Mileva said. "If I change anything else— who can say how much that will ruin in time? Believe me, I checked all my options. I ran through all the possibilities. I don't have any other choice."

Her voice was heavy with resignation and despair— the same kind of despair he'd already watched older versions of Mileva struggle with on the screen back in the time hollow.

"Now, go," Mileva said. "Leave me to my misery."

She shoved at his hand, pushing him away.

Jonah caught her wrist instead. He flipped her hand over and slipped his away—leaving the Elucidator in her palm.

"Keep trying to think of options," Jonah said. "Don't give up. And when you think of something, use the Elucidator to escape."

Mileva stared down at the imitation compass. She brushed a finger against the painstakingly carved surface.

"Jonah, no, it'd be too much temptation," she whispered. "In a weak moment I might give in and do something awful . . ."

"You're too strong for that," Jonah said firmly. "And— you love your kids and Albert too much. I'm not going to leave you without any options. Wouldn't it be awful if three seconds after I left, you thought of an even better solution, but you couldn't do anything about it because you didn't have an Elucidator?"

He reached out and curled her fingers inward, one by one, so she had a firm grip on the wooden case. He glanced back at Albert, still buried in his papers.

Then Jonah let go.

"Good-bye, Mileva," Jonah said. "Elucidator, send me back to the time hollow. But you stay here with Mileva. Take good care of her . . ."

His voice had already started to echo, as everything about 1903 disappeared.

FORTY-THREE

JB's going to kill me, Jonah thought, as he whirled through Outer Time.

He couldn't find it within himself to have any regrets.

I had to leave Mileva with the Elucidator, Jonah thought. *I had to. If JB doesn't understand—well, that's his problem, not mine.*

Jonah landed on the cold, bland tile of the time hollow, and immediately four people tackled him.

No, not tackled—hugged. It was just a little hard to tell the difference.

"Jonah, we were so worried about you!" Katherine shrieked.

"Is Mileva okay?" Emily asked.

"Did Outer Time look healthy again as you were traveling through?" Hadley asked.

"Did the plan work?" JB asked.

Jonah shoved Katherine's elbow out of his left ear and Hadley's beard out of his right eye.

"You're all unfrozen, aren't you?" Jonah asked. "You tell me if the plan worked!"

Hadley and JB exchanged glances over Jonah's head.

"We'll have to check in with all the other time agents, check all the relevant time coordinates," JB told Hadley.

"Right," Hadley said, already tapping instructions into his Elucidator.

It seemed as if Jonah barely had time to blink before every wall of the time hollow was covered with digital charts and graphs and long columns of numbers. It reminded Jonah of the kind of high-tech military control rooms he'd seen in movies.

Unfortunately, the movies where he'd seen those kind of control rooms were usually the ones where there'd been some kind of disaster, like aliens invading or an asteroid knocking the Earth toward the sun, putting all humanity in danger of extinction.

"Mileva and I did the only thing we could think of," Jonah said. "I mean, *she* thought of it. She's really smart. I bet if she'd been born in a different time period, people would say, 'You're as smart as Mileva Einstein!' instead of 'You're as smart as Albert Einstein!'"

"Jonah," JB said sternly, as he scanned six charts and

three graphs simultaneously. "She was born when she was born. But"—he pointed at one of the graphs—"that line right there shows the probability that the next time I return to my own native time, people *will* say 'as smart as Mileva Einstein.' About as often as they say 'as smart as Albert Einstein.'"

It was a really long line.

"Then she does manage to escape," Jonah breathed.

JB was still staring at the charts.

"Escape?" he said absentmindedly. "No, of course not. How could she? Mileva's going to be famous because people will know what she just did with you, copying the tracer pages and convincing Albert those were his current original thoughts and—" JB broke off and turned and looked directly at Jonah. "Is there any reason you think Mileva might have escaped? Escaped what? To where? And *how?*"

His gaze dropped to Jonah's hands.

Jonah decided to go into full confession mode. He held up his hands, showing exactly how empty they were.

"You . . . left . . . the Elucidator . . . behind?" JB said faintly.

"Well, it's not like I just lost it," Jonah said defensively.

"You purposely gave a time-native a second-generation, top-of-the-line, freestyle Elucidator?" JB asked.

Even as JB spoke, he was calling up a scene on the wall: Jonah's last moments in 1903. Jonah leaving the Elucidator in Mileva's hand and saying good-bye.

"She's not just any 'time-native'!" Jonah protested. "She's Mileva Einstein! She—"

He had so many arguments tangled in his head he couldn't pick which one he wanted to use first. *She just unfroze all of time. Doesn't she deserve some sort of reward?* Or, *You saw the life she was going to have to lead. Would you force her to live like that?* What he settled on was, "Don't you care?"

JB flashed Jonah a disgusted look.

"If I cared that much about every person in all of time, then how could I let anyone stay in misery?" he asked.

But he didn't seem to be paying attention to his argument, or to Jonah. He was too busy scanning the vast displays in front of him.

"She didn't use the Elucidator even once that first year," he muttered.

"I've just checked 1905, too," Hadley said behind him. "No change."

JB let out a big sigh.

"Okay, that was the big worry," he said.

"See? See? She's not going to do anything to mess things up!" Jonah crowed.

"Check the other time periods of Albert's huge

influence and revelations. What about 1915? Or 1919? Or 1939?" JB asked Hadley.

Katherine and Emily crowded near him, watching.

"Clean," Hadley reported barely a moment later.

"See, everything's going to be all right," Jonah said, with slightly more confidence than he felt.

Though he was thinking, *So everything's going to be all right—for everyone except Mileva.*

An alarm started going off on the other side of the room.

"What year is it?" JB asked resignedly. "Which year does Mileva ruin?"

Hadley dashed over to a new scene that had appeared on the wall, below flashing lights.

"Looks early twenty-first century," he said. "Not Mileva's native time period. The setting is some kind of school. Kids have cell phones, there are computers along the wall, but the teacher's still using a dry-erase marker— no, he just *dropped* his marker . . ."

"That's not Mileva's time period, then," Jonah said. "That's ours!"

"And Jonah, isn't that your science teacher?" Katherine said, peering at the wall. "What's his name? Mr. Stanley?"

Jonah rushed behind her.

"Yeah, that's the class I was in when time stopped," he

said. "You know, JB, right before Angela picked us up and took us to Chip's house . . ."

"Oh, no!" Hadley said. "Everything else Mileva resolved, and it's all going to be for nothing if Jonah and Katherine aren't back where they belong when time resumes—"

"What's the big deal?" Katherine said. "Can't you let us get back into position and then start time up again?"

Hadley and JB were shaking their heads quite violently.

"Things don't work that way when so much of time has been stopped," JB said. "We don't have that much control. You've got to get back into place as soon as you can, and we'll just have to hope—"

Jonah didn't even hear the rest of JB's sentence. Because even as he spoke, JB was wrenching the Elucidator from Hadley's grip and hitting buttons.

And before Jonah had a chance to take a breath, he and Katherine were pitching forward through time.

FORTY-FOUR

They landed back on Chip's porch, right beside Angela, right in front of Chip. Angela had her hand on Jonah's shoulder, and Katherine had her fingers against Chip's hand, and both Jonah and Katherine immediately jerked back and away from their friends.

"No! We'll fall!" Katherine screamed.

"Katherine, what are you talking about?" Angela asked. "Jonah, where'd you put the Elucidator? What were you saying about JB talking on it?"

No time at all had passed for Chip and Angela.

Does that mean everything will be all right if we just get back to school? Jonah wondered.

"No time to explain," Jonah said quickly. "You've got to get us back to school right now!"

"But what about—," Angela began. She looked at Jonah

and Katherine a little more closely. "You two have been in another time, haven't you?"

Jonah realized that Katherine's hair was longer—his probably was too—and her T-shirt had lost most of its glittery lettering. She had a hole starting in her blue jeans. Jonah looked down at his clothes: He had grass stains and mud stains across his jeans, and one sleeve of his T-shirt hung in tatters.

From being in the time hollow for decades? Jonah wondered. He reminded himself that clothes wouldn't deteriorate in a time hollow, where time stood still.

But we were in 1903 for several days, he remembered. *I guess clothes show the wear and tear pretty fast when you never change them and never wash them and go climbing trees and running away from people holding torches and . . .*

Why was Katherine stepping into Chip's house instead of running back toward the car?

"Katherine!" Jonah cried. "Come on!"

"I just have to make sure Chip's okay first!" Katherine insisted. "You didn't have another panic attack about being back in the Middle Ages, did you, Chip?"

She was leaning in toward Chip, cradling the palm of her hand against his face.

"Katherine!" Jonah cried. "Nobody wants to watch you two kiss!"

Chip took a step back, yanking away from Katherine.

"And—I've got the stomach flu," he said. "Really, that's all it is. But I don't want you to catch it."

"I am not watching anyone else puke!" Jonah insisted. He tugged on Katherine's arm. "Come on!"

He grabbed Angela's arm, too, and the three of them raced for the car.

"You *will* tell me the whole story later on," Angela said as they scrambled back in. "Wait—where's the Elucidator to make this go?"

Jonah reached over the seat and turned the key in the ignition. The engine sprang to life.

"You don't need the Elucidator for that anymore," he said. "We're back in regular time."

Angela turned toward Jonah, her eyes huge and horrified. Jonah could almost see her thinking, *Then time's started up again, and Jonah and Katherine are missing from their classrooms, and—what if that messes up time all over again?*

"I'll get you back to school immediately," Angela said.

She slammed the car into gear and squealed her tires pulling out of the driveway.

Jonah was acutely aware of all the movement around him as they sped toward school: Birds zoomed by overhead; leaves blew down from the autumn trees; cars stopped and started and changed lanes all around them.

Finally Angela pulled into the school driveway, and the three Canadian geese that had landed on the pond out front were taking off again in a flurry of wings and dropped feathers. The woman in the minivan that had been suspended over the speed bumps was driving out the exit now.

How much time had they missed? More importantly—had anyone noticed they were gone?

Angela hit the brake as they lurched toward the front entrance.

"You'll have to come in with us, to sign us in," Katherine said miserably. "We'll have to think of some good excuse—they've rigged the front doors so no one can get in the building without walking through the office first."

"Katherine, we can't go in through the front," Jonah said. "There's that security camera right there—we can't leave a record that we were outside of the school."

He saw a tall shadow just inside the front door. So *that* was where Assistant Principal Richey really lurked, watching for truants and sneaks.

"Down, Katherine!" Jonah cried, pushing her head below the level of the car window. He ducked his own head down out of sight, too.

"Jonah, you know all the other doors are locked during the day," Katherine hissed at him. "What do you want to do—break a window? Right, nobody's going to notice that."

Jonah made a quick decision.

"Drive on around to the side door," he told Angela.

"It's going to be locked, and we'll just waste even more time—," Katherine complained.

"That's where the cook and the janitor were kissing, remember?" Jonah told Katherine. "What do you bet they have the door propped open?"

Angela hit the accelerator.

The cook and the janitor were nowhere in sight when they got around to the side door. But they must have just walked back into the building, because the door was just swinging shut.

"Run!" Jonah yelled at Katherine. "Angela—"

"I know—later," Angela finished for him. "Now, go!"

Jonah dashed out of the car and dived for the door. He caught the door just a split second before it clicked into place. He stood holding it barely open for just a second while he and Katherine caught their breath.

"Just act normal," he told her. "I don't know how we can just slip back into class, but—"

The sound of the bell ringing reverberated through the building. Jonah could feel the door handle vibrating in his hand.

"Okay, that's a good thing," Jonah said. He hoped he was right. "This way, we can just blend in with everyone else changing classes."

He jerked the door all the way open and both of them slipped inside. A stampede of kids thundered through the hall in front of them.

"Jonah, this is the eighth-grade wing," Katherine whispered, her voice trembling.

Jonah almost laughed. Katherine had survived time disasters in four different centuries, but she was terrified of walking through the eighth-grade hallway?

"Yeah, well, contrary to the rumors, they do not actually eat sixth graders for lunch," Jonah said. "You'll be fine!"

"Thanks a lot," Katherine muttered, but she stepped forward into the crowd.

Jonah took a deep breath and followed her.

The sixth-, seventh-, and eighth-grade sections of Harris Middle School were laid out like spokes, each grade kept separate from the others. Jonah knew it should be a straight shot to the center of the school—the library, gym, and cafeteria—and then an easy turnoff to the seventh-grade wing. But the eighth graders who stood between him and his turnoff were huge.

Right, they don't eat sixth graders for lunch—they eat seventh graders, Jonah thought.

He took a tentative step forward—and two boys who must have been nearly six feet tall stepped out of his way.

Huh?

He heard a whisper behind him: ". . . must have been in a fight . . . don't mess with him . . ."

They think I look all tough and scary? Jonah marveled. *Because of the grass stains and the dirt and my torn sleeve?*

Or was it that he carried himself differently after helping Mileva Einstein save time, after thinking for himself and giving Mileva the Elucidator?

He stood up straighter.

Oh, yeah, nobody should mess with me, he thought.

The crowd really did seem to part before him. He made it down the eighth-grade corridor and into the seventh-grade wing in record time.

And then he heard a voice behind him.

"Jonah? Jonah Skidmore? Just the student I've been looking for."

It was Mr. Stanley. The teacher whose class Jonah had vanished from.

FORTY-FIVE

Jonah whirled around.

If Mr. Stanley asks where I disappeared to the last two minutes of class, I'll say . . . I'll say . . .

Jonah couldn't think what he could say. Why hadn't he and Katherine and Angela figured this out on the drive from Chip's house?

"Yes, Mr. Stanley?" Jonah said. Maybe he could stall for time just by acting super polite.

Close up, Mr. Stanley's skin looked even grayer and more sickly. Scarier. But Jonah had just gotten back from hanging out with a vomiting Mileva and a deathly ill toddler Lieserl—and, for that matter, a stomach-flu-ridden Chip—so he didn't recoil the way he normally would have.

"Young Jonah," Mr. Stanley said. "You rushed out from class so quickly you forgot your books. You must have been truly eager to get to lunch, eh?"

Jonah realized that Mr. Stanley was holding out Jonah's science book and his science folder. Of course. When Jonah and Katherine had dashed out of Mr. Stanley's class after time stopped, they hadn't even thought about carrying Jonah's books with them.

"I'm sorry, Mr. Stanley," Jonah said, taking the book and folder from him. "I guess I was thinking so hard about those forces of nature you were talking about that I forgot everything else."

It was such a suck-up thing to say; Jonah was sure Mr. Stanley would bust him for it. For perhaps the first time ever, Jonah looked closely at the man. He was trying to tell if Mr. Stanley saw through Jonah's act, if Mr. Stanley had noticed that Jonah had been in his seat at 11:43 and then had completely vanished a split second later.

Mr. Stanley mostly looked . . . pleased.

"Well," he said, practically puffing out his chest. "I'm always delighted to hear that my students are thinking about the knowledge I impart upon them."

Could it really be this easy? Could Jonah just flatter him a little bit more, and that would solve everything?

"And those forces of nature are fascinating," Mr. Stanley continued.

"I like that thing Einstein talked about, with the bowling ball on the trampoline," Jonah offered.

"Einstein always was so good at the word pictures," Mr.

Stanley said, and now there was an oddly wistful tone in his voice.

Mr. Stanley kept talking about Einstein's theories about gravity. Kids walking by kept shooting Jonah glances that all but spoke: *Dude, how did you get stuck listening to that old man outside of class? Isn't listening to him in class torture enough?* Anthony Brezzia and Hayden Smiley actually walked past with their hands cupped over their ears. Sneha Baskaranathan, one of the nicest girls in seventh grade, stopped behind Mr. Stanley's back and made a motion with her hands as though she were spooning food up to her mouth—obviously trying to remind Jonah, *Just tell Mr. Stanley you have to go to lunch. That's how you get away!*

But Jonah just stood there and listened. Because he'd seen something in Mr. Stanley's eyes as soon as he'd mentioned Einstein.

What if Mr. Stanley was once a young man . . . well, I guess he had to have been young, at some point, Jonah thought. *But what if, back then, he dreamed of being the next Einstein? What if he thought his own ideas were going to impress the whole world so much that people would hang on to his every word . . . ? Isn't it sad that now he only talks to kids who don't want to hear anything he has to say?*

Jonah wasn't sure how long he stood there listening to Mr. Stanley talk about bowling balls and marbles and trampolines and planets and moons and stars. But it was long enough that Jonah was certain that Mr. Stanley wasn't going to lead into, *So how did you vanish from my class like that? What happened?* Mr. Stanley had probably bent down to pick up his dropped marker at the end of class and then the bell had rung and everyone had rushed out of the room. So Jonah had gotten away with it. Even if any of the other kids had noticed Jonah missing, Jonah could just laugh it off. And Katherine was crafty about stuff like this—she'd have no problem explaining away her disappearance. So they'd gotten away with everything. Time was going on, just the way it was supposed to, and—

Jonah realized that Mr. Stanley had stopped talking about gravity and bowling balls and was digging for something in his pocket.

"Oh, here," Mr. Stanley said. "You know you weren't supposed to have this out during class. Technically I should keep it and turn it in to the office and make you fill out paperwork to get it back. But I know you weren't actually using it in class, so—here. Here's your cell phone."

He held out something small and black and sleek.

"That's—," Jonah began, all ready to add *not my cell phone.* Now that he and Mr. Stanley were so buddy-buddy, maybe he would explain, *I don't really even have a cell phone, since I have to share mine with my little sister, and she always has it, not me.* Should he tell Mr. Stanley that this was probably CC Vorlov's phone?

No, I put CC's back on her desk when I couldn't get it to work—and there's no way she would have left it behind, Jonah thought.

Then Jonah realized what the cell phone really was.

"That's . . . really nice of you," he finished weakly, taking the phone-shaped object from Mr. Stanley's hand. "I promise you, I wasn't using it in class."

"I didn't think so," Mr. Stanley said. "Because it was sitting on your chair, exactly as if it'd just fallen out of your pocket. Between you and me, I don't see any reason to punish students when they haven't actually done anything wrong." He clapped Jonah on the back. "Have a nice lunch, young man."

But Jonah didn't dash down the hallway to lunch. He ducked behind the nearest row of lockers and began poking and prodding at the "cell phone" to try to turn it on.

The screen glowed to life, holding a string of words:

Dear Jonah,

It is time to return the Elucidator to you. Thank you so much. I did actually figure out a way to use it. I—

Jonah felt a hand slam down on his shoulder. He jumped, and practically dropped the Elucidator.

Then he saw who had grabbed him: It was JB.

"Why don't we go see for ourselves exactly what Mileva did with that Elucidator?" JB asked.

FORTY-SIX

"Can't I have lunch first?" Jonah asked weakly.

"No," JB said.

Then, before Jonah had a chance to say another word, they were zooming through time.

They landed in a time hollow—was it the same one as before? Jonah had no way of knowing. He barely had a moment to look around before they had company: Hadley arrived with Emily, and Angela arrived with Katherine.

"Kind of like one big happy reunion, huh?" Jonah tried to joke. "Doesn't it seem like we just saw each other ten minutes ago? Oh, yeah—we pretty much *did*."

"JB, I wasn't done!" Katherine complained. "I'd just convinced Casey that she needed to get her eyes checked, if she didn't see me standing there in the library at the end of fifth period, and I'd confirmed that Toby was looking away at the exact moment that time stopped and started again and I seemed to disappear. And Oshka and Haley and Ocean weren't staring at me suspiciously or anything, but I still needed to make sure . . ."

Katherine was making Jonah's head hurt.

"I thought we should all watch this together," JB said through gritted teeth. "Immediately."

Jonah's heart sank. But then Emily leaned forward and whispered, "I think you did the right thing," and he felt a little bit better.

Somehow chairs appeared for them, and they all settled in facing a blank wall. JB slipped the Elucidator out of Jonah's grasp and typed in a command, and suddenly it was as if they could all look through the wall, straight into another room in another time.

It appeared to be a hospital room. An old-fashioned one, without any digital monitors glowing in the darkness.

"Just after midnight, April 18, 1955," Hadley said, peering into his own Elucidator for verification. "The night Albert Einstein dies."

Jonah shivered. Nothing had even happened yet, and already he was terrified.

"Albert had family and friends with him all day leading up to this," JB said quietly. "But he has just a nurse watching over him now—er, no, she's slipped out to use the restroom. Albert's alone."

There was just enough light in the hospital room that Jonah could make out Albert's head on the pillow of the bed. The tufts of gray hair rose and fell as Albert thrashed his head back and forth.

"Is he in pain?" Angela asked. "Or just having a bad dream?"

Before anyone could answer, a figure suddenly appeared, bending over Albert.

"Is that Mileva?" Emily asked, squinting at the scene on the wall. "But I thought, when we watched their lives play out before—didn't she die years before him?"

"Yes," JB said grimly, and Jonah slid down lower in his seat.

It was a jolt to see this version of Mileva. Jonah felt as though it'd only been a matter of minutes since he'd said good-bye to her as a lively, determined twenty-seven-year-old. But now she was ancient and stooped, her face lined, her hair as grizzled and gray as Albert's.

"Albert?" she whispered, gently touching his shoulder.

Albert startled awake, and then he gasped.

"Ghost," he moaned. "Mileva's ghost come to haunt me . . ."

The old-lady Mileva laughed, as if this amused her immensely.

"Oh, Albert, here you are the most famous scientist in the world, but you think of ghosts before you think of the scientific explanation," she said. "I'll give you a hint—your work provided the first steps toward it being possible for me to be here talking to you nearly seven years after you got the news of my death. Think about it."

Albert drew in a ragged, pained breath. Let it out. Then took another one.

"Time . . . travel," he said as he exhaled. "You . . . figured out . . . time travel just so . . . you could tell me on my deathbed . . . what a thoroughly lousy husband I was."

Mileva looked as if she might laugh again, but this time she just shook her head.

"No, Albert," she said. Her face grew serious as she stared into her ex-husband's eyes. "I am not far from death myself. Back in my own time, I am due to have a stroke in a few days—a stroke that will lead to my demise. But before my life ends, I needed to tell you: I forgive you. I forgive you for being such a lousy husband. And a lousy ex-husband. I forgive you everything."

"Well!" Jonah burst out. "Isn't this a good thing Mileva is doing? Using the Elucidator for forgiveness? Giving Albert a chance to apologize before he dies?"

JB clenched his jaw.

"She didn't come all this way just to offer forgiveness," he muttered. "She's not leaving yet, is she?" Something horrifying seemed to strike him. He pressed his hands against his face in utter dismay. "Oh, no—what if she has a stroke right there in Albert's hospital room? How is anyone ever going to find an explanation for how Albert's ex-wife, who died in 1948, could suddenly die all over again in 1955? On an entirely different continent?"

"Wait—you don't know if that happens or not?" Katherine asked. "You didn't watch this already without us?"

"No," JB said tensely.

"He thought he might need you, if things have to be fixed right away . . . ," Hadley explained, frowning behind his beard.

Jonah winced and looked back at Albert and Mileva.

Albert was still gasping, and Mileva was starting to look worried.

"Please, Johnnie, you're not supposed to die for another hour or so," Mileva said. "I was so careful about the timing of this. I thought you would welcome my forgiveness, not . . . go apoplectic."

Albert was grimacing.

"Do . . . welcome forgiveness," he murmured in an agonized voice. "It's just . . . the pain . . ."

"Of course," Mileva said. "I should have thought. Here. This will help."

She reached into her dress pocket for something—a miniature syringe, maybe? Jonah thought he saw the glint of a needle as she lowered her hand toward Albert's arm.

"No more morphine," Albert said, trying to fend her off with a shaking hand. "Morphine makes me . . . stupid. Want last moments . . . lucid."

Mileva barely hesitated.

"Oh, this isn't morphine," she said. "I don't want you to be stupid for this conversation either. I so wanted another conversation with the brilliant Johnnie I fell in love with all those years ago."

"He's gone . . . dying . . . Now I'm just a foolish old man that the youngsters in the field make fun of," Albert murmured. "My search for a unified field theory . . . just tilting at windmills, they say . . ."

Mileva brushed her hand against Albert's arm.

The change in Albert was instantaneous. He sat up straight.

"What *was* that?" he asked, his voice normal again, no longer weighed down by pain.

"Oh, never mind the technicalities," Mileva said. "You never did have much patience with chemistry. I can just tell you that it's a painkiller I picked up for you in the future . . ."

"The future!" JB exploded. "How many extra time periods did she visit? And bringing back medicines . . . that's illegal! Why didn't we detect this?"

Hadley was already hunched over his Elucidator.

"I'm not finding evidence of that," he said, frantically scanning screenfuls of information. "She must have hidden her footprints really, really well."

"Or maybe she's not telling the truth?" Emily suggested in a thin, reedy voice. "Maybe she's counting on a placebo effect—fooling him into thinking he feels better?"

As far as Jonah could tell, Albert seemed to have undergone a full recovery. He was craning his neck, flexing his arm muscles—and reaching out for Mileva as if he planned to hug her.

Mileva took a step back.

"Albert, no," she said. "I just want to talk. To tell you the secrets I had to hide from you for almost fifty years. And . . . to reveal the answers you've been trying to find for the past few decades."

JB's hand slammed into the side of his chair.

"That's it!" he cried. "She's going to ruin everything!"

"Calm down," Hadley said. "Don't you think she had a reason for waiting until an hour before his death to talk to him?"

JB glowered at Hadley, but didn't do anything else.

On the screen Albert leaned forward eagerly.

"My unified field theory? It is possible—it can work?"

Mileva tilted her head and regarded him very seriously.

"We're not newlyweds anymore," she said. "I no longer worship the ground you walk on. I'm going to tell you what's important to me first. That way, even if we run out of time, you'll hear what I want you to know."

"But—," Albert began. Then he caught himself and shrugged grudgingly. "That's fair," he admitted. "After all, you're the one who traveled through time to get to me."

Mileva nodded and sat down on the edge of the bed. She smoothed the expanse of hospital blanket that lay between her and Albert.

"First of all," she said. "Our Lieserl didn't die in 1903."

Albert gaped at her. Then he began blinking frantically—blinking back tears.

"What?" he cried. "Our Lieserl—still alive? But how—and why didn't you tell me?" He started desperately gazing all around the room. "Is she here with you? Can I finally meet her? What would she be now—fifty-three? You kept this a secret from me for more than fifty years?"

He looked positively injured at the thought of all those years of deception.

"I had to," Mileva said softly. "And—she's not fifty-three yet."

Jonah heard Katherine let out a nervous giggle beside him, but she quickly fell silent.

Mileva began telling Albert the whole story of what

had happened with Lieserl. When she got to the part about her and Jonah copying over Albert's tracer papers and convincing him that that was his current work, he wrinkled his brow in confusion.

"But—why didn't you tell everything?" he asked. "Why didn't you tell the whole world? You could have claimed credit for discovering time travel! You could have claimed credit for *my* discoveries. Why didn't you?"

"Albert, our children," Mileva murmured. "It would have endangered our children."

Albert only stared at her. She reached out and took his hand.

"And I think you've enjoyed your fame so much more than I would have," she said. She patted his hand. "And they were *your* discoveries. I couldn't steal them from you."

"You're . . . amazing," Albert murmured.

He pitched forward and drew Mileva into a hug.

This time she let him.

"Fifty-three years," he said into her hair. "Fifty-three years and you never told a soul."

"Well, it's only been forty-five for me," Mileva corrected. "Since I'm coming from 1948. Relative time and all that, remember?"

Albert laughed as he let go of her, and she sat back.

"Oh, it's good to talk to you again," he said. "Really

talk, like we used to do before you grew so sullen and silent . . ." He seemed to realize what he was saying. "Is *this* why you started acting so depressed? Because you couldn't tell anyone what you knew?"

"It gets complicated," Mileva said. "I would have been truly depressed without my secret. I mean, really, Albert, moving us to Prague with all that sooty air when you knew Tete had those lung problems, and—" She stopped herself. She waved her hands as if trying to erase everything she'd just said. "Sorry. I didn't mean to restart old fights. I really have forgiven you."

"Tete," Albert said. He rubbed the hospital sheet between his fingers. "Hans Albert was here, watching over me all day—he's such a son to be proud of. But Tete . . . I haven't communicated with Tete in years. He's had such a sad life . . . with all your secret maneuverings, why couldn't you help our Tete, too?"

A happy expression burst out over Mileva's face, and for a moment she looked young and optimistic, not old and beaten down.

"Oh, Albert, I so wanted you to ask about Tete," Mileva whispered. "I told myself I wouldn't take the risk of telling you unless you actually asked. Unless you cared!"

"Of course I care about my own son," Albert muttered. "I just never knew how to help. Mental illness is so . . . "

"Misunderstood in the twentieth century," Mileva

finished for him. "So I helped Tete the only way I knew how. I took him to the future. To a time period where they knew how to cure him."

"What?" JB exploded.

"Shh!" Jonah, Katherine, Emily, and Angela all said at once. Jonah noticed that all of them were sitting on the edge of their seats.

"No, no, Tete's still here," Albert said, screwing up his face in befuddlement. "Back in Switzerland. I still pay for his care. His—confinement." He said the last part bitterly.

"That's another young man," Mileva said. "I knew everyone had to think Tete was still in this century, still alive, so I borrowed this other man from the distant past, when madness was even more misunderstood. And . . . when those who succumbed to madness were routinely murdered. I saved this young man's life so I could send Tete to the future, to save his sanity. I made the swap when Tete was still a teenager. I only regret I couldn't save the fake Tete's sanity too, because he's such a delightful youth when he's lucid. But at least I managed to give him a better life than he would have had . . ."

Jonah missed Albert's reply because JB was screaming so loudly: "How could she have? That's two time periods she could have ruined! Why didn't we see this? How did she cover everything up so well?"

He began typing furiously on his Elucidator. Hadley was doing the same thing.

"Let's focus on the more dangerous change first—what time period could she have taken Tete to?" Hadley asked.

"This could lead to such a major paradox," JB complained, stabbing at his Elucidator as fiercely as if it were a weapon and he was at war. "People found the cure for mental illness before they figured out time travel—we're just going to have to undo this whole visit between Mileva and Albert, go back and erase Jonah giving her the Elucidator—"

"Undo? Erase? You can't do that!" Jonah complained. "Can you?"

"Aye, lad," Hadley answered. "It's true, nothing quite like that has ever been tried, and it'd be incredibly risky given the proximity to stopped time, but—"

"Can't we at least see how the rest of their conversation goes?" Emily asked.

JB and Hadley both looked at Emily. They seemed to remember all at once that these were Emily's birth parents they were watching, Emily's brother they were searching for.

"All right," JB said grudgingly. "Unless things get too dangerous."

Jonah realized that he'd missed a huge chunk of the conversation between Albert and Mileva.

"—and that's what you were missing in your unified field theory," Mileva was saying.

"I knew it would be something that simple," Albert said. He beamed at Mileva. "Thank you. Thank you. I just wanted to know that so much."

He started to reach for something on his bedside table: paper. Pen and paper.

Mileva shoved his hands away.

"Surely you understand why you can't write that down," Mileva whispered.

"But—the world would want to know," Albert said. "Other scientists . . . some of them are seeking this as earnestly as me."

"Then let other scientists find it out for themselves," Mileva said. "Albert, you've discovered so much. Why don't you leave this one to someone else?"

Albert started to answer, then lay back, groaning.

"That . . . painkiller . . . more . . . ," he whispered.

"I know, Albert, it's wearing off," Mileva said. "I'm sorry—the nurse is about to come back. I can't give you another dose. Shall I tell you how it all ends? You're going to say something in German—it really doesn't even matter what you say, because the nurse isn't going to understand."

"Maybe tell . . . dirty joke?" Albert muttered.

"If you want, Albert," Mileva whispered, leaning close. She looked over her shoulder, probably checking to make sure the nurse hadn't come back already. "But when you die, people are going to find two things on your bedside table that you'd been working on. One is a speech for Israeli Independence Day—"

"Right . . . over . . . there," Albert said, struggling to point.

"Yes, I see it, Albert," Mileva said, glancing toward the table. "I like your line, 'I speak to you today not as an American citizen and not as a Jew, but as a human being'— very nice, Albert, very consistent with your beliefs about humanity."

"Thank . . . you," Albert muttered. "I was always a better . . . defender of humanity than . . . a husband."

"We've already been over that, Albert," Mileva said. "Don't worry about it now."

"What . . . other thing . . . I'm supposed to leave?" Albert asked.

Mileva picked up a piece of paper from the table.

"A math calculation you wrote out earlier this evening," Mileva said. "People will like it that you kept looking for answers right up until you died."

"Always a seeker," Albert murmured. "Wish I could tell world . . . what I finally found."

"You can't always tell everyone everything you know," Mileva said.

She put the piece of paper back down on the nightstand,

angling it exactly the same way it'd been before. Jonah wanted to tell JB, *See? See? She's being careful to preserve time.* But he was afraid he'd miss something else.

"Shall I tell you what happened to Tete in the future?" Mileva asked, as she smoothed Albert's hair back from his face.

"Yes . . . please," Albert whispered.

He seemed barely conscious now, barely aware of Mileva's words. Strangely, she had her head turned half away from him, as though she were trying to speak to someone else as well. Jonah peered carefully at the corners of the hospital room, but there was no one there.

"I arranged Tete's transfer to the future the same way Lieserl's worked," Mileva murmured. "Through time travel he became a baby once more, so he had no memories of me or you or the twentieth century."

"At least she took that precaution," JB harrumphed.

"He was adopted by a very nice set of parents— better parents than you or me, I'm happy to say," Mileva continued. "He received a vaccine for his schizophrenia. So the thing that took over his twentieth-century life became as nothing for him, a momentary pinprick that he instantly forgot. He thrived in the future, and grew up happy, and you might say that he went into the family business—"

"Physics, you mean? Like you and me?" Albert mumbled. "Engineering, like my father and uncle and Hans Albert? Or—"

"Time," Mileva said firmly. "He became a time agent."

Now Jonah was certain that Mileva was trying to talk to someone besides just Albert. She had her head turned completely away from him, and seemed to be staring directly into the time hollow where Jonah and the others sat.

Could she know we'd be watching? Jonah wondered. *Is she trying to talk to us?*

"Nooooo," JB moaned. "Tete couldn't have become a time agent. That situation is just ripe for paradoxes. It shouldn't have been allowed. It—"

"I even met our son once, in his capacity as a time agent," Mileva was saying. "In a manner of speaking. Time was stopped then, and I didn't know who he was until later, but—"

Wait—I met Mileva during stopped time! Jonah thought. *Is she saying I was the real Tete Einstein? Mileva and Albert's second son? Am I Emily's brother?*

It wasn't possible. Nobody had developed a schizophrenia vaccine in this part of the twenty-first century. And Mileva wouldn't call him a time agent. She knew he was just a kid who'd gotten caught up in the time-travel mess. So . . .

Around him, Katherine and Emily and Angela were gasping and exclaiming. But JB and Hadley had fallen silent. They were staring at each other in a very strange way. Their faces had gone pale; Jonah realized that both of them had dropped their Elucidators.

Mileva smiled sweetly, gazing straight out at Jonah and the others.

But mostly, it seemed, at JB and Hadley.

"I'm sure everyone understands now that nothing I did can be changed," she said. "You can search for answers. You can ask how a time conundrum so intricately constructed was meant to be. But mostly I just want you to know that I did this out of love for you, Tete."

She paused. Nobody so much as took a breath.

"Or should I say, I love you, my son JB?" she asked.

EPILOGUE

Jonah stepped down from the school bus alone. Chip was still absent with the stomach bug, and Mom had picked up Katherine at school to take her to a dentist appointment. Katherine had been agonizing for days that the dentist was probably going to tell her it was time for her to get braces. To Mom and Dad she'd wailed, "I'll look hideous! I won't be able to eat!" Privately, to Jonah and Chip, she'd whined, "And what if we have to make another trip to the past? And the invisibility conks out on us again? Braces will give me away every time!"

"Katherine," Jonah had said quietly. "I'm not sure we're ever going to make another trip to the past. Everything's too confused."

And confusing, he thought now, as he kicked his way through the clumps of fallen leaves that had drifted here and there between the bus stop and his own house. For perhaps the millionth time in the past week, he mentally replayed his most recent trips through time, culminating with JB finding out that he had a secret second identity of his own.

"JB," he muttered, "you really weren't fair."

Even as Emily had stood there in the time hollow gasping, "Wait—JB—*you're* Tete Einstein? You're my *brother?*" JB had been violently shaking his head no. He'd held his hands out, as if trying to shove everyone else away.

"We can't have this," he'd cried. He'd grabbed his fallen Elucidator from the floor and begun punching in commands. "All of you—go back to your regular lives. Go back to normal. Forget all of this!"

And then Jonah had found himself back in the seventh-grade wing at Harris Middle School, right beside the lockers. And Katherine had gone back to the sixth-grade wing. He assumed that Emily and Angela had gone back to their regular lives, too, but he was afraid to contact them to find out.

With JB acting so terrified, how could that not terrify Jonah, too?

"JB," he muttered now, "you owe us some answers. If you don't come and explain things soon, I'm going to have to start searching for answers on my own!"

As threats went, this one was pretty stupid. If JB had

been monitoring Jonah's life at all, he'd know that. Of course Jonah and Katherine hadn't been able to forget anything. They couldn't go back to their regular lives. They couldn't act normal anymore—"normal" had completely changed for them.

For one thing they'd already begun searching for answers on their own.

The school bus zoomed past Jonah, driving away, and he let out a combination snort-chuckle. Just last night he and Katherine had convinced Dad to take them to the library. When they all three met back at the checkout table, Jonah and Katherine were each holding several books about Einstein and Einstein's theories.

"You're *both* doing reports about Albert Einstein for school?" Dad asked. "Wow—what are the odds of that?"

"And we didn't even know what the other person was working on!" Katherine said airily, even as she kicked Jonah under the checkout table.

Jonah knew that kick was supposed to say, *Don't tell Dad anything! Don't give anything away!*

And then Katherine started making fun of Jonah because one of the books he'd checked out was *Einstein for Dummies.*

"Oh, yeah? Well, I saw *The Complete Idiot's Guide to Understanding Einstein* on the shelf, too—want me to go back and get it for you?" Jonah asked.

But his voice came out fake and lifeless, so Dad probably did notice that there was something wrong.

And five minutes with the Einstein books had convinced Jonah that he was probably the one who needed *The Complete Idiot's Guide*. It was hard to concentrate on Einstein's examples of trains and beams of light when what Jonah really wanted to know was, *Did we ruin time forever? Did I? Was that all just fate? How much free choice did any of us have if I had to give Mileva that Elucidator for JB to grow up when he did, and become a time agent, and leave the Elucidator for Angela to give me in the first place so I could give it to Mileva?*

Forget figuring out the answers—just thinking about the questions tied Jonah's brain in knots.

"JB—help!" Jonah moaned.

He'd reached the door of his own house now. He pulled out his key and turned it in the lock, then shoved the door open. He dropped his backpack on the floor.

There! That's something I can act normal about, he thought. *I can be as messy as usual!*

He thought about how much time he'd spent watching Mileva cook and clean and scrub out cloth diapers. He thought about how all that drudgery had left her so bleached-out and sad. He thought about how hard his own mom worked.

He moved his backpack into the hall closet where it belonged.

Maybe Mom will think I'm being considerate because I know she's had to deal with Katherine whining about getting braces, Jonah told himself. *Wouldn't I have thought of that anyhow? Wasn't I sometimes a considerate kid back in my regular life, before I took my first trip through time?*

It was hard to remember what his regular life had been like, now that everything had changed.

Jonah sighed and went into the kitchen for a snack. He was standing in front of the pantry thinking about cereal choices—did he want Apple Jacks? Rice Chex? Granola?—when he heard someone clearing his throat behind him.

Jonah whirled around.

JB was sitting at the kitchen table.

Jonah clutched his hands to his chest and tried to catch his breath.

"Don't you know . . . sneaking up on people . . . is dangerous?" he gasped. "It could really mess up time if you surprise me so much that I drop dead of a heart attack!"

"Are you sure?" JB asked sardonically. "What if that's your destiny? Why would you think I have any choice in this matter—or any other?"

Jonah realized JB had been thinking about all the same questions Jonah had been thinking about.

"You did ask me to come," JB pointed out.

"Maybe the rules are different in your time period," Jonah said. "But around here it's customary to knock at the front door before entering someone's home. Not just—appear!"

"You want to run the risk that one of your neighbors might see you letting a strange man into your home? You want them to tell your parents?" JB asked.

Jonah backed up against the pantry door.

"Maybe I do want my parents to know about all this," Jonah said. "Maybe I want to tell them everything. Maybe I'm supposed to."

JB tapped a finger against the table. It was the only sound in the quiet house.

"Jonah, your parents are wonderful people," he said. "They love you and Katherine the way all kids should be loved. But they're not going to be able to give you all the answers either."

Jonah bit his lip.

"'Either'?" he repeated. "If my parents don't have all the answers 'either,' then are you saying . . . you're confused too?"

JB sighed. He shifted from tapping his finger to fiddling with the edge of the place mat on the table in front of him. Mom liked switching out the place mats by month and season, so this one was part of the November set—it had *We Give Thanks* embroidered on it.

"If you'd asked me back in the time cave, back at the beginning of all this—when it began for you, I mean—I would have said that I understood time travel perfectly," JB said. "I knew that the past was set in stone, and had to be kept that way, to prevent any paradoxes or cause-and-effect catastrophes. But I thought that the present—my present—was open and flexible and free for me to use however I wished. I thought my contemporaries and I had free will, but everyone in history was locked into . . . well, shall we call it fate?"

"You changed your mind about history," Jonah said, and his voice chose that moment to go all shrill and girly. He really wished his voice would just change and be done with it. He cleared his throat and tried again.

"You realized it was safe for us to rescue Chip and Alex from the fourteen hundreds," he said. "And you yourself refused to send all those Native American villagers back to die in 1605. And—"

"And we managed to ride out all of Second's craziness together by being flexible," JB finished for him.

"Didn't everything work out in the end with Albert and Mileva, too?" Jonah asked. His voice had gone shrill again, but he decided to ignore it. "And—for you? You're not actually wishing that you were stuck in a mental institution in the twentieth century, are you?"

JB's toying with the place mat had become so intense that he almost flipped the whole thing over. He stopped himself and laid both hands down, one on top of the other.

"Of course I'd rather be me, in my own time—what I think of as my own time, what I think of as my real self," he said. "And, yes, it does appear that Mileva covered all her bases, and fixed time completely. And somehow she managed to keep everything secret until it was too late to stop her. But . . . it shouldn't have been possible, how all that worked out! How did we get through all those layers of cause and effect in so many centuries without destroying time? Was it *all* just fate? Was everything just meant to be?"

"After Katherine and I got back from the sixteen hundreds, you told me we shouldn't feel like Second just manipulated us into everything," Jonah said. "You said we still made our own choices."

"Yeah, yeah," JB said, shrugging away this explanation. "But how did I have any choice when I *had* to be frozen in that time hollow when you went back in time with Mileva—just so I could become who I really am? So I could become the person who was frozen in that time hollow? Don't you see how circular all of this is?"

"I'm not stupid," Jonah said.

He saw that JB had begun twisting his hands together, the right hand squeezing the left, the left squeezing the right . . . His moment of letting his hands lie peacefully on top of the Thanksgiving place mat was over.

"I'm not accusing you of stupidity," JB said. "This has the smartest time experts of my era tearing their hair out."

"Just because everything fits?" Jonah asked.

"Because things that should have been random were absolutely necessary to make everything fit," JB said. "We thought it was random that you and Katherine were sucked back to 1903—just a side effect of the time chaos, and an accident of you holding the Elucidator."

"But . . . *you* sent Emily back in time," Jonah said hesitantly. He cleared his throat. "Right? That wasn't random. You did that yourself."

"Yes, but that was only because things had gotten so freaky in the time hollow," JB said. "Objects were appearing and disappearing at will—we thought Einstein was the key. Sending Emily back was a last-ditch effort, the only way I could think of to stabilize time."

"You told me you weren't going to return any more missing children to history," Jonah said stubbornly.

"Can you see why I had to change my mind?" JB asked. "And didn't get a chance to warn you?"

Reluctantly, Jonah nodded. "But things still got freakier,"

he added. "Time freezing, even in the time hollow—"

"Which everyone *used* to think was impossible," JB interrupted.

"And then Hadley appearing out of nowhere," Jonah said. "And his Elucidator appearing and disappearing—"

"The random results of time instability," JB said. "It had to be random!"

He'd stopped twisting his hands together only so he could wave them uselessly at Jonah.

Jonah was still trying to catch up. He suddenly realized why it mattered so much that JB had been frozen in the time hollow, randomly or not.

"If you hadn't been frozen, you would have stopped me from going back with Mileva," Jonah said. He meant it as a question, but the words came out more as an accusation. "You would have stopped her from learning about time travel. You would have stopped me from handing her that Elucidator."

"Of course!" JB said. "So, tell me, how did I have any choice in the matter? How did you?"

It was so weird, JB being the one with all the questions, not the answers. But Jonah thought he saw a way to try to explain.

"Katherine and I both started reading about Einstein's theories," Jonah said. "And I don't understand all of them, but maybe this whole free will versus fate thing is kind of like what Einstein thought about light. When he was starting out, everyone thought light moved in waves. Then Einstein came along and said, 'Nope, it moves in packets called quanta.'"

"Max Planck actually thought of quanta first, but so far I'm with you," JB said.

"But then later on," Jonah continued, "Einstein himself said, 'You know what, guys? Light really is kind of wave-ish, after all. So how about if we say it's both, waves and quanta all at once? Doesn't that make the most sense?'"

"You're saying our lives are like light waves/quanta?" JB asked. "We have fate and free will all at once?"

"Exactly!" Jonah said.

JB was rubbing his forehead.

"I'd have to double-check to see what scientists in this time period think about light, to really know how to answer you without ruining time," JB said. "The problem is, if you don't know if you're riding a wave or a quantum packet of light, how do you make your choices? How do you decide how to live your life? How do you know what's important?"

"Well, it seems like things work out best when time travelers try to help people," Jonah said, shrugging.

He thought about how long it'd taken him to realize

that he should give Mileva the Elucidator. Back in 1611 he'd been slow about figuring out how to help too. And in 1600 he'd been a total idiot about his priorities.

"But *which* people are you supposed to help?" JB asked, sounding as if he really wanted to know. "I'll go back to the Einstein analogy you used before, about the bowling ball on the trampoline, changing the paths of the little marbles around it. Time travelers always thought Einstein was the huge bowling ball and Mileva was just one of the inconsequential marbles orbiting around him. But it turns out she was a bowling ball in her own right."

"I hope you don't ever use that as a pickup line, trying to meet girls," Jonah said. He slipped into an imitation of some stupid, sleazy guy in a bar. Or maybe in a middle-school cafeteria. "Hey, babe, you're not just some inconsequential marble." He pretended to stick his thumbs in imaginary suspenders, then flipped both hands forward like guns. "You, babe, are a real bowling ball!"

JB laughed. He ran his hand through his hair so it stood up almost as dramatically as Albert Einstein's.

"What if it turns out that everyone's important?" JB asked. "Everybody that's ever lived, in all of history?"

"What if it does?" Jonah said. He gulped. "And, speaking of history . . . ," His voice sounded weird again, but maybe that was just because his ears were ringing. He forced himself to keep talking. "Who am I? I mean, who was I originally?"

JB froze. Then, very deliberately, he slipped his hands from above the table to beneath it. He seemed to be forcing himself to act casual.

It didn't work much better than Jonah trying to force himself to act normal.

"You want to know your other identity now?" JB asked quietly. "After weeks of avoiding every hint of it?"

Jonah nodded. "It's because of Albert Einstein," he admitted. "Your . . . dad . . . was a great man in so many ways, but he was kind of a coward, too, don't you think? When Mileva tried to tell him things he didn't know how to deal with, he just kind of tuned them out, you know? Avoided the truth? I just—" He looked down, then forced himself to look back up. "I don't want to be like that."

JB lifted his hand to his chin and rested it there.

"Interesting timing," he muttered. "Very interesting."

"So, will you tell me?" Jonah asked impatiently.

"No," JB said, shaking his head. "Not yet."

Jonah sagged against the pantry door.

"Do you know how hard it was for me to get up the courage to ask?" he said.

JB looked at him steadily.

"Yeah, I kind of do," he admitted. "And I'm proud of

you for that. But there's too much up in the air right now, too much in flux. I did take an oath to protect time, to the best of my abilities. And that's what I'm still trying to do."

JB stood up.

"Wait, where are you going?" Jonah asked. "I've still got, like, ten million questions!"

"I know," JB said. "But I don't have ten million answers."

"Am I going back in time again anytime soon?" Jonah asked. "What am I supposed to do? Will Katherine or Chip go with me? Are Emily and Angela and Hadley okay? And—"

Jonah saw that JB had picked up one of the Einstein books from the table and begun leafing through it.

"Here, this is the best I can do for you right now," JB said. "Read what Einstein had to say."

He handed the book to Jonah, and pointed to a sentence near the top of the page that quoted Einstein:

> We are in the position of a little child
> entering a huge library filled with books in
> many languages. The child dimly suspects
> a mysterious order in the arrangement of
> the books, but doesn't know what it is.
> That, it seems to me, is the attitude of even

the most intelligent human being toward
God.

"I wasn't asking anything about God," Jonah
complained.

"Yeah, you kind of were," JB said. "If there is fate, who
else would control it?"

Now JB was confusing him even more. It looked as if
JB was about to leave, so Jonah rushed over and put his
hand on JB's arm.

"Can't you tell me anything else?" Jonah begged.

JB looked at him.

"Yeah," he said. "Have the Apple Jacks."

"What?" Jonah asked.

"When I arrived, you were trying to decide which
cereal to have, weren't you?" JB asked. "Well, that's my
advice. You like Apple Jacks the best. And, believe me,
that sugary stuff doesn't taste nearly as good once you're
an adult."

Dimly, Jonah realized that this was JB's way of telling
him the same thing he'd said after Jonah returned from
the 1600s: *Have fun . . . while you still can.* Maybe it wasn't
such an ominous message. Maybe it was just the only way
anyone could enjoy any part of life, knowing there could
always be plenty of heartache and difficulty ahead.

"You'll be back soon, won't you?" Jonah asked.

"Yes," JB said. "I'm afraid so."

JB shook Jonah's hand off his arm. A second later the time traveler vanished.

Jonah felt foolish just standing there watching an empty space. Eventually he walked over to the pantry and pulled out the box of Apple Jacks. He poured the cereal in a bowl, added milk, grabbed a spoon, and sat down at the table with his snack and the Einstein book.

There was still so much he still didn't understand—so much he might never understand.

But he knew at least one thing that JB had told him was true.

The Apple Jacks really were delicious.

AUTHOR'S NOTE

Lieserl Einstein was both a missing child of history and—for decades after her 1902 birth—a very, very well-kept secret.

As described in this book, she was the first child of Albert Einstein and his first wife, Mileva Maric Einstein. Albert and Mileva met and fell in love when they were both students at the Swiss Federal Polytechnic School in Zurich. They seem to have shared a fascination with physics and a faith in Albert Einstein's genius at a time when many others looked at him and saw only a bumbler.

Albert's later accomplishments are well known, and the facts of his life have become something of a modern myth. The man whose name would become synonymous with brilliance was very slow to learn to talk as a child, but careful biographers have found no evidence that he ever flunked math, as is often alleged. He did follow an unorthodox path to scientific fame: He left high school in Germany at fifteen because he had such a problem with the strict, autocratic system. He tried but failed to qualify to skip directly to university, so he attended a more relaxed high school in Switzerland to prepare. He barely managed to graduate fourth out of five in his class at the Zurich Polytechnic, and then he constantly ran into obstacles for the next few years as he tried to get a job, earn a doctorate, and win the scientific establishment's attention. By the summer of 1903, the time of most of the action of this book, he was twenty-three, and his job as a clerk in the Swiss patent office probably seemed like proof to most people that he would never be a scientific all-star.

Mileva's early life isn't as well documented, but the details that are known mark her as extraordinary in her own right. As the daughter of a woman from a well-off family and a Serbian peasant who had done quite well for himself, Mileva seems to have been a particularly beloved child. She was born with a dislocated hip, which gave her a lifelong limp and may have made her think that marriage and children were less likely to lie in her future. With her father's strong encouragement, she focused on academics much, much more than most females of her time and place. And, at least in the beginning, she excelled at them.

After blazing a trail through various schools as the family moved around what was then the Hungarian section of Austria-Hungary, Mileva got special permission to enroll at the all-male Royal Classical High School in Zagreb, in what is now Croatia. (Her family's hometown of Novi Sad is now part of Serbia but was part of Austria-Hungary between the late 1800s and the end of World War I. However, because the Marics and their friends would have regarded themselves as Serbs, not Hungarians, that is how I refer to them in this book.) Although Mileva also had to get special permission to study physics, she ended up having the highest exam scores in her class in that subject, and in math as well.

Unlike Albert, who seemed certain that he wanted to focus on physics, Mileva wavered somewhat between academic interests. She first moved to Zurich to study medicine, then quickly switched to physics and math at the Polytechnic. She was only the fifth woman to be admitted in the school's history, and the only one in her class. However, she stayed there only a year before leaving to study at Heidelberg University in Germany instead—even though Heidelberg only let women audit classes, not actually earn degrees. Some biographers speculate that she left Zurich because she was falling in love with Albert and recognized that that was most likely a path to heartache. It's impossible to know if that's true or not, but Albert begged her to return. And, after a semester, that's exactly what she did.

Still, her stellar academic accomplishments seemed to come to an end as she grew more involved with Albert. In 1900, the year that both of them were scheduled to graduate from the Polytechnic, Mileva's dismal exam grades left her last in the class—the only student that year who didn't do better than Albert. Her grades were actually not that much worse than his, but the difference led to vastly different outcomes. With the help of a little rounding up, he passed, and earned his diploma.

Mileva failed.

Part of her problem might have been that she was still scrambling to catch up after spending time away from Zurich, following a different course of study in Heidelberg.

Some Einstein scholars speculate that Albert was also a bad influence on her—he could skip class and borrow a friend's notes and still eke out a passing grade; maybe she was trying that approach too, with less success. Or maybe the contempt he showed for some of their professors rubbed off on her, and it reflected even more in her grades than his.

Personally, I wonder if discrimination against her as a female scientist played a role as well. At a time when so few European universities even admitted females, and so many scientists were on record as claiming that females' brains just weren't capable of comprehending physics (a view that Einstein himself came awfully close to espousing later in life), it seems likely that a female would have had to work twice as hard and come across as absolutely flawless to get any credit at all.

Mileva was clearly not flawless.

She took the news of her failure hard, but vowed to study more and take the exams again the following year.

By then she was pregnant with Lieserl.

From the letters that Albert and Mileva exchanged, it appears that both of them fervently wanted to get married even before the pregnancy. But financial problems and Albert's family were working against them.

According to Albert's letters, his mother was absolutely scathing in opposing the match. Even before the two women met, when Albert told his mother in July 1900 that he wanted to marry Mileva, Albert says:

> Mama threw herself onto the bed, buried her head in the pillow, and wept like a child. After regaining her composure she immediately shifted to a desperate attack: "You are ruining your future and destroying your opportunities." "No decent family will have her." [And, presciently] "If she gets pregnant you'll really be in a mess."

Later in the same letter he describes his mother's active campaign to get him to break up with Mileva, and his stalwart resistance to it:

The only thing that is embarrassing for her
is that we want to remain together always.
Her attempts at changing my mind came
in expressions such as: "Like you, she is a
book—but you ought to have a wife." "By
the time you're 30 she'll be an old witch,"
etc. But now that she's seen that for the
time being her efforts only make me
angry, she's refrained from giving me the
"treatment" for a while.

The more Albert's family opposed the relationship,
the more Albert wrote gushing declarations of his love for
Mileva, such as:

How was I able to live alone before, my
little everything? Without you I lack self-
confidence, passion for work, and
enjoyment of life—in short, without you,
my life is no life.

And:

You are and will remain a shrine for me . . . ; I
also know that of all people, you love me the

most, and understand me the best . . . When
I see other people, I can really appreciate
how special you are!

And perhaps most interestingly:

I am so lucky to have found you, a
creature who is my equal, and who is as
strong and independent as I am! I feel
alone with everyone except you!

For all his declarations of love, Einstein believed there
was no way he could marry until he had a decent job.
His parents' own finances were in crisis, so they couldn't
have helped him even if they'd wanted to. The other
students he'd graduated with in 1900 moved quickly into
reputable academic positions, but he spent the next two
years chasing slim hopes and struggling at marginal, low-
paying jobs. He complained that a professor who should
have been giving him recommendations was actually
sabotaging all his chances—and this may well have been
true, as Albert had made no secret of his contempt for the
man's scientific views.

Faced with worries over the pregnancy and Albert's
situation, Mileva retook her exams in July 1901. She failed

a second time. Eventually she returned to her family's home in Novi Sad, and gave birth to Lieserl in January 1902. Although Albert had hoped that the child would be a boy, he responded giddily to the news of the child's arrival, writing to Mileva:

> Is she healthy, and does she cry properly?
> What are her eyes like? Which one of us
> does she more resemble? Who is giving
> her milk? Is she hungry? She must be
> completely bald. I love her so much and
> don't even know her yet! Couldn't you
> have a photograph made of her when
> you've regained your health? Is she looking
> at things yet? . . . When you feel a little
> better you'll have to draw a picture of her!

But when Mileva returned to Switzerland to be near Albert, she left the baby behind.

Albert finally found his job at the Swiss patent office in Bern with a friend's help. It wasn't the highly respected academic position that he'd longed for, but it would prove to be a better fit for his talents and interests at that point in his life. And, while still a low-level position, it paid enough that Albert believed he could finally support a wife. Then, right before his death in late 1902, Albert's father gave Albert permission to marry Mileva. Neither family came to the wedding on January 6, 1903, but a few close friends celebrated with them.

It would appear that everything was falling into place for Albert and Mileva. But they still did not bring Lieserl to live with them. There is no evidence that Albert's family or friends were ever told of the child's existence. Despite his initial enthusiasm, Albert apparently never even met her.

What plans did Albert and Mileva have for Lieserl's future? Did they intend to put her up for adoption? Was Mileva still holding on to hope (as I imagined in this book) that eventually they would be able to raise Lieserl in their own home?

Regardless of what they were planning, when they got word in August 1903 that Lieserl had scarlet fever, Mileva rushed to Novi Sad to be with her. The letters I quote from in this book are exactly what Mileva and Albert actually wrote to each other during this time, including his cryptic comments in September 1903:

> I am very sorry about what happened with
> Lieserl. Scarlet fever often leaves some
> lasting traces behind. If only everything

> passes well. How is Lieserl registered? We
> must take great care, lest difficulties arise
> for the child in the future.

Einstein experts have analyzed those few lines in depth, trying to figure out exactly what did happen to Lieserl. Some speculate that she died in 1903, as scarlet fever was frequently fatal then. One official source says roughly a thousand children lived in the Novi Sad area before the 1903 epidemic, but about 40 percent of them were dead by the end of the year.

However, Lieserl was clearly still alive at the time of Albert's letter. Other experts speculate that Lieserl was disabled somehow, blinded because of the scarlet fever or mentally challenged from birth. Still others look at Albert's question about how Lieserl was "registered" as proof that the couple was trying to get the little girl's paperwork in order so that she could be adopted.

Regardless, no birth or death certificates have been found for the girl. Except for the letters exchanged by Albert and Mileva, there's no written proof of her existence.

And she might as well have vanished from the face of the earth in 1903, for all the evidence about her that exists after that.

Meanwhile, Albert's and Mileva's lives went on. Their

second child, a son this time—Hans Albert—was born on May 14, 1904. Their other son, Eduard, who was nicknamed Tete, was born on July 28, 1910. Albert had one of the greatest years any scientist had ever had with his "miracle year" of 1905: In just a matter of months, he published four scientific papers, which held ideas that would revolutionize physics forever. The last of those papers included the now-famous $E = mc^2$ formula, connecting the concepts of energy and mass.

The acclaim for Albert was not instantaneous, but within a few years he was fielding his choice of academic job offers and invitations to notable conferences and requests from famous scientists to meet and discuss his ideas.

Albert thrived on all the attention. Mileva faded further and further into the shadows, writing to one of her closest friends in December 1912:

> Albert has become a famous physicist who is highly esteemed by the professionals enthusing about him. He is tirelessly working on his problems; one can say that he lives only for them. I must confess with a bit of shame that we are unimportant to him and take second place.

Mileva had numerous health problems, but descriptions of her behavior during this time period seem to indicate that she also struggled with severe bouts of depression. One scholar who met her during a particularly difficult point in her life—when Albert briefly moved the family to Prague—speculated that she might have suffered from schizophrenia as well.

Albert, caught up in his own ideas, was anything but a sympathetic husband. As his fame increased, his relationship with Mileva unraveled to the point that in 1914 he laid down a severe list of rules that he ordered her to follow if she intended to stay married to him. These included demands that she would "stop talking to me if I request it" and "leave my bedroom or study immediately without protest if I request it" and that she would forgo "all personal relations with me insofar as they are not completely necessary for social reasons."

Albert also ordered her not to "belittle" him in front of their children.

Amazingly, Mileva at first accepted even his most severe terms, before apparently realizing that the relationship was damaged beyond repair. The two agreed to separate. Albert got caught up in a high-profile life in Berlin (and a relationship with the woman who would become his second wife, his cousin Elsa Einstein). Mileva took the children back to Zurich, and would live there the rest of her life. The couple eventually divorced in 1919.

In spite of the relationship turmoil—or, perhaps to a certain extent, because of it—Albert had another burst of amazing scientific creativity around this time, unveiling his general theory of relativity in 1915. And photographs taken during a solar eclipse in 1919 confirmed Albert's theories about light bending due to gravity. With these developments, Albert won the attention of not just the scientific world but the general public as well. The media loved him—he gave great quotes, and didn't mind being photographed doing things like sticking out his tongue. He seemed to be a good sport about everything, even when reporters admitted that they didn't understand his ideas at all. No matter, they still adored Albert, who became everyone's idea of the lovable absentminded genius.

Everyone's, that is, except the Nazis, who were gaining power in his native Germany in the early 1930s. They resented a Jewish man holding such an esteemed position in the German scientific world. Facing death threats and listed as a major target, Einstein fled, eventually moving to the United States to take a position at Princeton University.

Einstein worked on his scientific ideas the rest of his life, seeking a unified field theory that would bring together all the laws of physics and connect all the forces of the universe. As depicted in this book, he was still trying to figure out that theory the night he died. But he became known almost as much for his work outside science. During World War I, his was one of the rare, lonely voices among German scientists pointing out the insanity of war. Despite his near-lifelong pacifism, during World War II he came to believe that the evils of Nazism had to be countered, and he played an important role in warning the United States that Germany might be developing nuclear weapons. However, he lamented his part in laying the groundwork for the atomic bombs the United States dropped on Hiroshima and Nagasaki. After the war, his was an important voice calling on scientists to work together to prevent any further use of such devastating weapons. He also became a strong and outspoken supporter of the new nation of Israel.

By the time of his death in 1955, Einstein was viewed as something of a secular saint, a holy man of science. His oldest son, Hans Albert, an engineer who'd moved to California, had rushed to be by his side when he got the news that his father was dying. But at that point Einstein hadn't seen his troubled younger son in more than twenty years, and hadn't even sent him a letter since 1944.

After Einstein's death, his papers were closely guarded and maintained by his longtime loyal secretary, Helen

Dukas. Some of the information that paints him as something less than a completely saintly figure has been released only in more recent years, after Dukas died as well.

Some of the biggest revelations about his personal life came in 1986 when Hans Albert's daughter, Evelyn, found a stash of letters that first Mileva and then Hans Albert's wife had kept. These were letters that Albert and Mileva had exchanged beginning in 1897. A collection of these letters from the couple's courtship and first several months of marriage has since been published by Princeton University Press under the title *Albert Einstein, Mileva Maric: The Love Letters.*

The letters set off a controversy in part because of Albert's references to "our work" and "our theory" and "our paper" in his letters to Mileva. Their letters are full of physics discussions, back and forth. Did that mean that Mileva actually deserved joint credit for some of Albert's brilliant work? Albert's output in 1905 had always seemed incredible given that he was working six days a week at the patent office during that time. Was the explanation that he'd actually done only part of the work himself?

Those who argue that Mileva deserves more credit point to the fact that, in their divorce settlement, Albert promised to give her all the money he would earn from any future Nobel Prize. Was that his way of acknowledging her role? Or was it just the easiest way for him to arrange to provide for her and their sons?

Tellingly, there is no evidence that Mileva ever sought credit for any of Albert's work, even at the most bitter moments of their relationship. But it's a fascinating issue to read about. Many of the pro-Mileva arguments can be found in a 2003 PBS documentary and an accompanying website, www.pbs.org/opb/einsteinswife. The debate and arguments against giving Mileva more credit can be found in the PBS ombudsman's letter linked from that site.

Given the evidence, I felt it was reasonable for me to depict Mileva as being very intelligent, very familiar with Albert's work, very well versed in physics herself—and very good at double-checking his math.

The other bombshell that came with the release of the Albert-Mileva letters was the revelation of Lieserl's existence. This set off a flurry of interest among researchers. A 1999 book, *Einstein's Daughter*, details an extensive search by author Michele Zackheim between 1987 and the late 1990s, and it provides interesting background information, anecdotal evidence, and her own speculations. But Zackheim could never find any concrete proof of what actually happened to Lieserl.

It appears that some potential sources of information

about Lieserl were intentionally destroyed, including other letters. Of course, Mileva easily could have destroyed every single one of the letters in her possession that mentioned the girl. But she didn't. Did she perhaps hope that one day the whole world would know about her daughter? Was that her small way of rebelling against the secrecy that protected her famous ex-husband but threatened to erase all signs that their daughter had ever lived?

Even if Lieserl died as a toddler in 1903, it's possible to argue that she had an important impact on history. Albert Einstein followed a pattern throughout his life of dealing with personal problems by throwing himself intently into his work. Could the challenges of dealing with Lieserl's birth and illness—and perhaps grief over her death—have been one of the spurs for Albert's incredible burst of creativity and productivity leading up to 1905?

And if Lieserl lived past 1903, who knows what other impact she secretly might have had on history?

ABOUT THE AUTHOR

MARGARET PETERSON HADDIX is the author of many critically and popularly acclaimed teen and middle-grade novels, including The Missing series, the Shadow Children series, *Claim to Fame*, *Palace of Mirrors*, and *Uprising*. A graduate of Miami University (of Ohio), she worked for several years as a reporter for the *Indianapolis News*. She also taught at Danville (Illinois) Area Community College. She lives with her family in Columbus, Ohio. Visit her at haddixbooks.com.